THE GHOSTS WE KNOW

THE **GHOSTS** WE **KNOW**

Published by Lonely Whale Press
Astoria, Oregon

This is a work of fiction. All names, characters, places and incidents either are products of the author's imagination or are used fictitiously. No reference to any real person is intended or should be inferred.

Cover and Interior Design by We Got You Covered Book Design

ISBN: 978-1-73733452-2-0

THE
GHOSTS
WE
KNOW

A NOVEL

WILLIAM DEAN

CONTENTS

IN MEMORY OF MY FATHER

The mother in her bottomless grief sat alone.

Harry couldn't bear it. He moved beside her, accepted her tear-streaked face pressed into his shoulder, felt her sobs rolling through his body like a terrible thunder, as the pastor attempted the impossible.

Consoling the inconsolable.

"There are scant prayers, few words of wisdom, to utter on such an occasion as this," the minister told mourners filling the maple pews at his small Methodist church. "When a child is taken from us. A boy filled with bright dreams, with such promise."

Harry Bolden was just the next-door neighbor to the 38-year-old woman he was comforting, but that was enough. He had watched Sam Mendez grow up, tossed a football and a Frisbee with him too many times to count. They shared stories for hours at a time on their sun-warmed porches, sipping lemonade together, as if the boy were a second grandson.

Sam had been enthralled by the war medals and photographs of American airmen in uniform that Harry, or, more accurately, his wife, had framed and hung on the wall, the one along the staircase. Those were the stories the curious boy wanted to hear — the ones bringing life to the black-and-white photos of heroic men kneeling before their plane and the most eye-catching of the medals dangling from blue ribbons, the Distinguished Flying Cross and Purple Heart.

Harry obliged, omitting the more gruesome details that still haunted him more than a half-century later.

Sam was well-mannered and always welcome in the Bolden house, even after Mrs. Bolden passed. But the visits suddenly stopped when the boy turned 14.

Harry figured Sam was just going through adolescence and became more interested in girls than an aging veteran afflicted with Parkinson's. That made him sad, because he was lonely and missed the boy's company.

When he learned that Sam had taken his own life, Harry couldn't believe it. The boy was always so upbeat, so excited about the future. He wanted to be a football player and then maybe an astronaut. His room was decorated with posters of space shuttles and quarterbacks. He knew all the NASA missions, past and future, by heart. He could recite all of Joe Montana's greatest clutch moments with equal fervor.

What could possibly cause someone like that – his innocent young friend – to commit suicide?

———

Maria Mendez didn't know the answer, which only added to her sorrow.

The single mom had noticed that her son's grades had suddenly slipped, that he had nothing to say at the dinner table, that he spent most of his time silently watching TV or in his bedroom, the door closed.

Convinced he was being bullied, she marched into the administrative offices at Two Rivers Middle School and demanded to know what was going on.

The vice principal investigated, talking privately to Sam's teachers and observing him from a distance in the cafeteria and on the playground. After two weeks, not a single clue had emerged that could explain the boy's freefall.

Frustrated that she couldn't get anything out of her son, with whom she had forged the closest of bonds on the battlefield of an acrimonious divorce, Maria hired a counselor with experience in child abuse.

The counselor came to the house and managed to get a few minutes alone with Sam in his room.

"Sam, why won't you talk to your mother?" the woman in the sky-blue suit and ruffled white blouse asked softly. She made the question sound almost nurturing – not at all like the surgical incision that it was.

The boy shrugged. He was sitting on his bed, hands pinning his knees to his chest.

"Are you mad at her?"

He shook his head.

"Did she do something wrong?"

Another shake.

"Is it something that happened at school?"

"No, please stop."

"Is somebody hurting you, Sam?"

The boy's eyes widened. There was a flicker of pain and then anger.

"Get out! Get out!" he screamed. *"Leave me alone!!"*

After that episode, Maria decided not to try counseling again. But she became even more convinced that someone was bullying her son.

The following morning, she walked next door with a bag of fresh bagels. There were few things that Harry, the former Brooklynite, coveted in the morning more than that. He even accepted the Pacific Northwest version of a bagel – smaller, somewhat bland, with a softer crust.

As he poured some dark-roast coffee and toasted sesame bagels, Maria recapped her efforts to get to the root of her son's malaise. It was getting worse, she said, sounding scared. Sam had been one of the school's top students. Now he was barely passing his classes, even science. He stopped showing up at football practice.

Instead of reading books about deep space and fantasizing about walking on Mars, he had taken to writing dark poems accompanied by disturbing drawings of winged beasts with fangs and razor-sharp claws.

"What should I do?" she asked.

"I thought it was just a teenage thing, but after what you just told me, I'm sure you're right. It's more serious than that."

"Will you talk to him? He's close to you. You're like a father to him."

"Sure," Harry said, bringing two plates to the table – a half bagel each, open face, with schmear, lox and thin slices of red onion and tomato. "I'll come over this afternoon when he's home from school."

"I'll be at the office until 6, but just knock and Sam will let you in. Tell him, oh, I don't know, that you're checking something for me."

Maria worked as an attorney at the county public defender's office. Six years earlier, she had split from her philandering husband, a computer salesman who did his cheating at trade shows. She hadn't dated much since, focusing instead on rebuilding her shattered self-esteem while nurturing both Sam and a promising legal career. Her son came first.

After their gloomy breakfast conversation, Maria told her neighbor she had to go to work. At the door, she turned around. Looking deep into Harry's blue eyes, she said, "You're my best hope."

"I'll see what I can find out. Lord knows, he owes me a story."

When his alarm sounded later that afternoon signaling the end of his daily power nap, Harry ambled down the stairs to the living room, wincing a bit from the strain on his aching knees. He waited by the front window until he heard footsteps next door and caught a glimpse of Sam walking up his front steps.

Minutes later, Harry rapped on the door. He had a football in his hands.

Sam opened it a crack, saw who it was and pulled it wide. Surprising Harry, the boy rushed over and gave him a hug.

When the young teen pulled back there were tears in his eyes. Harry could have asked his questions then, right on the porch. But he told himself to move slowly on the thin ice surrounding the troubled teen.

Bouncing the ball in his right hand, he grinned.

"Thought you might be interested in a little catch today. Want to see how your spiral is coming along."

Sam hesitated. His brow briefly furrowed, as if he were trying to fight past his depression. Then his slender body sagged.

"Can't. Homework."

"Ah, that's too bad. Sure it can't wait? A few minutes? We can toss it in the street."

"Sorry, no time."

Sam stepped back inside and was about to close the door when Harry slid past him sideways.

"Your mom asked me to check on your bathroom pipes. Mind if I take a quick look?"

"Um, sure … but I'll be in my room."

"Right, homework."

They walked up the stairs, Harry trailing. The old man watched with sadness as Sam went into his room and immediately shut the door. Even though he often did small repairs for Maria, Harry ran some water in the bathroom to make his ploy seem more plausible.

After a few minutes, he knocked on Sam's door and walked in without waiting for an invitation. The boy was lying on his bed, staring at the ceiling. His eyes were puffy and red.

"Tell your mom the pipes seem fine."

Harry sat on the edge of the single bed with its moon-and-stars comforter. He was known more for blunt candor than subtlety, but he decided to give the latter his best shot.

"Nice sneakers," he said, admiring Sam's immaculate white Air Jordans with contrasting black laces. "Bet you can dunk with those suckers."

Sam, who would normally laugh at such a remark, cringed.

"I don't want to talk. I need to be alone. I'm sorry."

"I miss my buddy. You haven't been over in a while."

"I know."

"You okay?"

"Yeah."

"You know, there's nothing we can't talk about, man to man."

"I know."

"I mean, if it's drugs …"

"It's not."

"So, is there something bothering you?"

"I … don't want to talk about it."

Harry looked at Sam intently, then lowered his voice as if to prevent anyone lurking in the shadows from overhearing.

"I won't let anybody mess with you, pal. I've got your back, understand?"

A tear rolled down Sam's cheek and he looked away.

"Please leave."

Harry stood and gently tousled the boy's bushy brown hair. *His mother is right. There's something bad going on.*

"Come see me when you're ready. I'm right next door."

But Sam never did.

———

When the service ended, Harry walked Maria out, following the shiny mahogany casket that held her son's body.

A couple of uncles and aunts, some nieces and nephews and cousins, and a few dozen shocked members of the community were in attendance, but her closest family wasn't there.

Her parents lived in Costa Rica on the fringe of a rainforest and wouldn't arrive for several days, and her younger sister was in a remote part of Ghana working for the Peace Corps and hadn't yet responded to Maria's tearful calls. So, it fell on Harry to host the wake.

The non-practicing Jew did the best he could. He hired a caterer with experience in such things and had his home filled with food and booze and white lilies. There was even a platter filled with chopped liver and sliced bread, which he'd seen when sitting shiva a few times in New York City. He was covering all bases.

Harry debated whether to include the large, framed 7th grade portrait of Sam that had rested in front of the coffin in the church. He wound up placing it on a chair in the living room so that guests would see it when they arrived but could escape the boy's eerily happy gaze when it came time to eat and drink.

"Thank you, Harry – for everything," Maria said, squeezing her neighbor's arm. They had been the first to arrive and were standing in the kitchen.

"Glad to help."

"Sam appeared to me last night. I could feel his presence in my bedroom, and I looked up and he was sitting across from me, in a sort of shimmering light. He looked at me and smiled and said, 'It's not your fault, Mom.' His lips didn't move, but his words entered my brain somehow. Does that sound crazy? Am I losing my mind?"

Harry smiled. A similar thing happened to him when his wife died. He could still remember the relief and comfort he felt.

"On the eve of her funeral, Bonnie told me she loved me and to be strong. No, it's not crazy."

"Will he … see me again?"

"Maybe, if you need him to. He's watching from heaven. The last thing he wants is for you to suffer."

People dressed in black were starting to enter the house, momentarily silenced by the power of Sam's portrait.

Maria drew closer to Harry. There was a strange look on her face, a mix of despair and determination.

"There's more to Sam's death than you know," she whispered.

PART ONE
HARRY, OF SUNNY SLOPE

CHAPTER
ONE

"Five, six, seven …

"Eight, nine …

"Ten, eleven … *ah, crap!*"

Harry lost his grip on the hallway chin-up bar and dropped to the ground noisily, causing Honey to spring to her feet in alarm. He gave the 10-year-old golden retriever a pat on the head and shook his right arm in hopes of setting the muscles right.

"We'll do more tomorrow. Not bad for an old man, though. Right?"

Honey barked in agreement and followed Harry out of the seldom-used guest bedroom that he'd converted into a modest home gym, complete with an exercise mat, medicine ball, dumbbells and no-frills exercise bike.

Every day for an hour, whether he felt up to it or not, Harry worked up a sweat, following a fitness routine shared only with his doctor and canine companion. Today, there were 100 reps on the 15-pounders and five miles on the bike, followed by 25 sit-ups and 15 pull-ups that turned out to be 11.

Harry was never a Marine, but he resembled one with his broad Chuck Norris chest, powerful Popeye arms, square jaw and close-cropped hair, once black but now almost entirely gray. He had become craggy, but the lines in his face made him appear rugged – not at all like a man who could be a few years away from assisted living. Or worse.

He lived alone in a two-story house that for many years he had shared with his wife and son. There were far too many stairs for a 74-year-old man – the ones leading to the upstairs bedrooms and the ones dropping into the basement – but he couldn't abandon the memories embedded in the 1925 Craftsman, as if grafted to the very structure over time. He couldn't leave. At least not yet.

Harry trudged down the dozen stairs to the kitchen and poured himself a pre-shower glass of whole milk. He eyed the calendar on the wall, opened to May, and grunted.

That afternoon he had an appointment with his Parkinson's specialist, the same doctor his wife had prodded him to see nearly a decade ago.

Back then, after a couple of hours of tests, the chilling diagnosis – the one that would alter his life in so many ways, like a locomotive changing tracks – had been handed down.

That was tough to take. Accepting his grim new fate was harder.

———

Harry had been a captain at the Two Rivers Police Department and part of his job was standing in front of the young officers to assist with the daily briefing.

When the tremors first began, he was able to conceal them by holding the offending hand or subtly changing the position of his body. But they gradually became more noticeable and Harry would catch people staring with a touch of pity in their eyes. That was something he absolutely couldn't endure.

He became obsessed with fitness, running half-marathons and swimming for hours at the aquatic center on weekends. He cut back on alcohol and added vitamins and healthier foods, but the only thing that really controlled the shaking were the drugs.

They worked well at first, hiding his symptoms, but they also clouded his brain at times, making it difficult to make the split-second decisions expected of a top police official, sometimes with lives in the balance.

Harry eventually put in for retirement. He was 66, a normal age for such a life change, but he couldn't help but feel defeated by the incurable malady worming its way into his brain.

Other smaller sacrifices soon followed: The switch from laces to loafers, the gradual purging of button-down shirts and belted slacks in favor of pullovers and sweatpants.

The fancy electric razor disguised as a Christmas gift was really just another concession. So were the clip-on ties and the assorted products with Velcro fasteners that began flooding the Bolden home.

Bonnie urged her routine-obsessed husband to get counseling to help with his daunting transition but she knew he wouldn't go willingly. At least she had provided something of a road map for him to follow: retiring from her job as a registered nurse at the local hospital two years ahead of him and thrusting herself into hobbies, a book club and all things grandson-related.

When Harry stopped being a cop, she convinced him it was the perfect time to travel. It was their golden window of opportunity —

while he was in control of his disease and not the other way around.

They wrote down the exotic places they each wanted to visit on strips of colored paper – red for Harry, blue for Bonnie. She folded the strips and put them in a bowl. Then they each picked one of their spouse's most desired destinations.

The first time, Harry chose New Zealand. Bonnie picked Greece. Delighted, they went to the public library and checked out travel guides to both places. The fun of planning the trips had begun.

They had completed three wonderful years of wandering, filling photo albums and scrapbooks, when Bonnie suddenly fell ill.

The pancreatic cancer came out of nowhere, shocking Harry and the family. There was a year of aggressive treatment, including radiation, but it failed to stop the spread, and soon doctors were telling the patient that she should get her affairs in order. There was nothing they could do.

They released her so she could die at home as comfortably as possible, and Harry did his best to make it so. He cooked for his wife every day, kept the house clean and even managed to do the laundry without too many casualties.

Just before she passed, she held his hand and gave him one last brave smile.

"I love you," she said. "Remember to be kind. Always kind."

"I will," he replied in a hoarse whisper.

The next night, after shedding an abundance of tears, Harry held his old war pistol in his hands, wondering darkly if he should follow his love to heaven now rather than wait his turn. He put the barrel of the black Colt .45 to his temple.

His index finger curled around the trigger.

Then he cried, head bowed. He didn't know if what had happened was cowardice or a sign of strength. He called his son Charlie who lived a short drive away by the river and talked for an hour, the gun still in his hands.

They spoke about a lot of things but mostly it was about living, not dying. And in that way, father and son helped each other face one of the worst tragedies imaginable.

After hanging up, Harry returned the gun to its wooden case and carried it up to the musty attic, where he buried it deep in the cedar-lined chest that held his olive drab war uniform and other artifacts from his past.

A few days later, Charlie Bolden gave a halting eulogy, interrupted by the spasms of his sobs, until his wife Liz stepped up to the podium and stood beside him, wrapping an arm around his waist. Soothed, he managed to press on.

Harry sat in the front row with Buster, who was familiar with his grandfather's shaking and held his vibrating right hand.

After that, loneliness entered Harry's life like a thief, ransacking his soul.

Bonnie was no longer there to offer comfort, to tell him in a loving way when his thoughts became twisted that it was only the powerful drugs kicking in and that he'd soon be fine.

The flashbacks featuring her were to be expected, he supposed. Some of them resembled Super 8 family films, full of smiles and playful posing. Because Bonnie had been nothing less than a perfect patient despite her agony, even memories of her final days were calming.

What he hadn't counted on were the flurry of nightmares, some reaching deep into his past. They were so vivid and often so disturbing that he'd wake up in a cold sweat and find himself, for a few minutes, unable to distinguish what he'd just experienced from reality.

Before dawn one morning, he jumped to his feet, certain that he was in his flight jumpsuit and needed to run across the tarmac to his hulking B-29, its silver engines roaring.

He made it to the mailbox by the white picket fence before cold Oregon rain lashed his face. He turned to see Honey pulling on his robe with her teeth.

"Atta girl," he said.

———

Harry entered the Portland medical office for the 15th time two weeks after Sam's funeral. He knew the drill.

Every damn, humiliating bit of it.

There would be a battery of cognitive tests followed by a series of physical tasks, similar to what he used to put suspected drunken drivers through on the side of the road.

Harry passed them all, he thought, but he looked up and saw Adam Goldstein frowning.

"Your disease is progressing, Harry," the doctor said as he returned to his desk to jot some notes in the file. The patient filled the seat on the other side, not bothering to try to read what Goldstein was writing.

After a few minutes, Goldstein, head dipped, looked at his patient over his reading glasses.

"I know this isn't what you want to hear, but I also know you want me to be upfront with you, so here it is: I am seeing some deterioration in your cognitive abilities, particularly in memory functions. And in terms of motor skills, you are beginning to sway and shuffle your feet when you walk."

"That's part of being older," Harry grumbled.

"That's true, but you are 74, not 84. And while you are fit for your age, you can't hide the symptoms of Parkinson's. Haven't you noticed an increasing weakness on your right side?"

The slip from the chin-up bar popped into his head like a warning light, but he pushed it aside. "Not really, Doc."

"I'm going to increase your dopamine dosage and place you on the Stage 2 scale for now, Harry. I also want to recommend that you cut back your fitness regimen to avoid over-stressing the muscles in your right arm and leg."

Stage 2 meant moderate symptoms, Harry knew. Stage 4 was the end of the line: Full body shaking, unable to move on your own, unable to think clearly.

A fate worse than death.

Goldstein scribbled a prescription and handed the slip to Harry.

"Don't be a hero. Get this filled. I'll be calling in a few days to see how you're doing."

"Okay, Doc. What did I get wrong on the memory stuff?"

"Don't worry about that."

"No, seriously. What did I screw up?"

The doctor sighed.

"When I asked you what year it was, you said '1945.' "

CHAPTER
TWO

The Sunny Slope neighborhood where Harry lived was built around a small park featuring a playground ringed by wood-and-steel benches and a quarter-acre square of mowed bluegrass well-suited for sunbathing, flying kites or tossing balls around. Sometimes, on the most pleasant sunny days, it all happened at once in a merry free-for-all.

The ridgetop subdivision was one of the town's first, platted in the early 1920s, with handsome homes with broad, friendly porches ringing the park in a series of circles.

Most of the pastel houses were blessed with excellent views of Two Rivers' small but vibrant downtown. There were artists and their galleries and shops, a marina equally divided between commercial fishing boats and pleasure vessels, and a bustling boardwalk peppered with sea lion vista points. Beyond that there was a confluence of rivers that formed a lovely expanse of drifting blue. A parting gift to town folk before spilling into the Pacific.

Harry grabbed his weathered chess board and a fraying Florsheim shoebox filled with plastic playing pieces and headed across the street to the park, Honey at his heels.

He would prove that his mental acuity was just fine.

The playground, while open to the public and unfenced, was mostly used by neighbors and their guests. It was modernized from time to time with a mix of town funds and homeowners' association dues. Newly-retired Harry managed to convince the overseers to add a permanent chess table and a couple of concrete stools in the most recent upgrade about seven years earlier.

A chess board design was etched into the square top of the table, but it had faded and was always dusted with pine needles or dotted with bird droppings so Harry had taken to covering it with his 1950s-vintage folding game board. It was the cheap kind, made of papered-over cardboard with red and black squares.

As Honey surveyed the crowded playground, her feathery tail swishing like a fan, he set up the black and white pieces that he had used to teach his son the game.

Nobody had ever tried to buy Harry a new set. It would only gather dust, they knew. The TV had to break down before Harry would replace it. Same with the family car, stove, fridge, his favorite jeans, and just about everything else. "Why waste money?" he'd say. "It's perfectly fine."

The chess set fit squarely in that category. A black bishop had a crack that required a Scotch tape bundage and the white king's crown was chipped, but the set was otherwise complete. And therefore perfect.

Looking past the children swooshing down the slide and soaring bravely on the swings, and the dozen or so more chasing each other in shrieking circles, he spotted a man of similar age sitting serenely on a bench.

The man was wearing a tan, button-down sweater with brown leather patches on the elbows, smoking a pipe while reading a magazine. He had a full head of silver hair that was brushed back and slicked into place and a thin mustache that gave him a cultured look.

Harry had seen the man at the playground a number of times, but he never seemed to have any children with him and, as a result, seldom stayed longer than an hour. That made him an unlikely chess player, but Harry was feeling an urgent need to play. He resolved to make this stranger his first victim.

Springing to his feet, though, wasn't the best idea. His leg muscles twitched, causing him to bump the table hard. The pieces on the board hardly moved. The table was cemented to the ground and impervious to jostling, which was a very good thing in such a busy place.

Rebounding swiftly from the minor embarrassment, he kneaded his right leg for a few seconds then strode over to the man with the pipe.

"Hello, I'm Harry. Up for a game of chess?"

"I am Friedrich, but you may call me Fred. A pleasure to meet you. Are you a skilled player?"

No one had ever asked Harry that before. He usually lured them in and methodically proceeded to checkmate, always thinking at least three moves ahead. But that was before his disturbing checkup.

Did I really say 1945?

"Maybe once. Now, I don't know."

"Ah, an honest man. You want to win, but you aren't so certain of the outcome and you desire a test."

Reading Harry's mind, Fred added with a smile, "And my accent, you are wondering. It is German. Bavarian, more precisely."

"I wasn't wondering," Harry said, but he really was.

"Well, now you know. I would be delighted to play chess with you."

They walked to the table and Fred grinned when he saw Harry's worn board and pieces.

"Your outdoor set, I presume?"

"My one and only."

"Ah, I have read that the great Bobby Fischer preferred dime-store chess sets. I should be wary, yes?"

They sat on the stools and Fred struck a match to re-light his pipe. He reached into his sweater and pulled out a silver pocket watch, which he placed on the table.

"Standard rules? Ninety minutes each?"

"Sure," Harry answered, a bit surprised by the formality. "I don't bring a clock because I move kinda fast."

"You reveal too much, sir," Fred said, grinning. "Now when you take your time I shall know you are in mortal danger."

Harry shrugged. He was starting to dislike this stuffy old Kraut. Even the smell of his flavored tobacco, a blend approximating buttery baklava, was irritating. But that was good. He'd have no remorse when he crushed him in five bold moves. Maybe four.

He advanced one of his pawns and Fred, nodding, did the same. The battle was on.

"Do you live here, Fred?" Harry asked.

"Not in this lovely community. Closer to downtown, in an apartment. I take a walk every day and often I end up here."

Just then a train of children raced past, screaming in delight in their shrill way.

"But there must be quieter places to read."

"Indeed, there are many. But, you see, I am not really here to read. I am here to experience the purest of joys." He turned to smile at the children. "I assume you are as well."

Harry took a bishop, prompting his opponent to raise an eyebrow. But moments later Fred slashed through Harry's ranks and vanquished the rook guarding his queen.

"The way we play, there is no need for a clock," Fred said, closing the timepiece.

"I told you."

"What brings you to this park besides the need to prove yourself worthy of the Game of Kings?"

"I live across the street, and I guess I like the joy, too."

As if to illustrate the point, a boy suddenly raced up from behind and surprised Harry with a bear hug.

"Sorry, Pops," Charlie said, puffing a bit from dashing after his son. "Buster has something to show you."

The boy dug into his father's shopping bag and pulled out a box sealed in clear plastic. He handed it to Harry, who immediately recognized a full-color illustration of his old warplane, the Superfortress bomber that had been built by the hundreds up the coast in a Boeing factory.

Harry could see it was a model of the Enola Gay, the B-29 that dropped the A-bomb on Hiroshima. His plane was the Dancing Damsel and not famous at all, but he didn't tell his grandson that.

"That's the one all right. Isn't she a beauty?"

"Sure is. The order finally came in at the hobby shop. Can we start building it today?"

"Absolutely. I know how much you love models. But first I have to win this game."

The gentleman across the table rose to his feet and smiled, a twinkle in his eyes.

"Nonsense. I must resume my walk before it gets too late. I shall surrender and live to fight again another day."

The septuagenarians shook hands. Harry watched as Fred wedged the rolled-up magazine under an arm and bound off in the direction of downtown, puffs of white smoke rising above his head.

Harry headed home with his son and 13-year-old grandson, Honey leading the way. He knew Charlie would ask about the doctor's appointment and that it was the true reason he was visiting. But that was okay. He deserved to know.

The aging veteran, though, would keep that little memory glitch to himself.

CHAPTER
THREE

Harry held the plastic plane in his hands, spinning it in front of his eyes.

It really was an excellent model. So accurate in every detail, down to the decals identifying the bomber and its squadron.

When he and Buster built it, they decided to keep the landing gear down, so it could stand proudly on its own, poised for the next mission.

He blew like a Norse god until the propellers turned.

The veteran remembered when he saw the high-flying plane for the first time, and though he was an impressionable young man at the time, just 18 years old, every member of his flight crew did the same thing. Their eyes bulged in amazement, then they whistled.

How futuristic the Superfortress looked with its silver paint and sleek, slender body that seemed stretched beyond reason. *And those wings!* Strong enough to hold four massive engines and 141 feet tip to tip.

What the teenager from Brooklyn saw on the tarmac that day was both beautiful and brutal. A killing machine like no other.

Surely the war would be over soon, he thought then.

———

"Keep a sharp eye back there. We'll be over the target in a few minutes."

"Roger that."

The pilot's warning wasn't necessary. The men in the bubbles – the Plexiglas domes protruding like blisters from the sides of the plane – had been on alert for the past hour.

They'd been scanning the horizon for enemy fighters as the Damsel roared over the ocean. This was their 16th mission out of Saipan and their third shot at target No. 474 – an aircraft engine plant in Nagoya, Japan.

Nagoya was risky business, they knew.

The city was about 30 miles inland at the end of a deep bay protected by anti-aircraft batteries on both sides, earning it the nickname Flak Alley. There were also swarms of Japanese fighters to contend with. Some would try to shoot the bombers down. Others would try to ram them in a suicidal frenzy.

It was the spring of '45. The war in the Pacific had turned. The Japanese were retreating to their homeland. The emperor and his generals intended to make a final, bloody stand.

Prior missions over Japan hadn't gone well. At least a half-dozen B-29s assigned to the 73rd Bombardment Wing had been gunned down. But now the Damsel, part of a formation of 18 other "Superforts," was patched up and in the clouds, making the thousand-mile trip again.

They were part of the first wave.

"Four miles," said the captain, a lanky Iowa farmer's son named Monroe. He tightened his grip on the throttle.

"Roger," Harry said from his seat in the left-side machine gun bubble.

Across the fuselage, Eddie, the right gunner, called out, "Hey, Brooklyn, third time's the charm?"

"God, I hope so," he replied.

Eddie was a high school math teacher from upstate New York. He and Harry were best friends – an Irishman and a Jew. Long into the night, they drank Scotch and played chess. The wager was a quarter a game and Harry was currently up $10, according to the scorecard tucked under his mattress.

Harry had just turned 19 and was still the youngest member of the crew by several years. He looked like a tough kid from the inner city with his dark curly hair and practiced snarl. But he'd find a hidden place to vomit before each mission, and sometimes afterward. It was a vulnerability he found humiliating. He didn't want his crew thinking he couldn't handle the unrelenting stress of war, or worse, that he was some kind of coward.

"Two miles," Monroe said in his graveyard baritone. "Flak jackets and helmets, everyone."

These were the minutes that seemed to last hours as the target crept into view and the 11-member crew braced for the inevitable barrage from 25,000 feet below.

The B-29 was built for exactly this: a precision-bombing run in broad daylight. U.S. commanders were bringing hundreds of Superforts to bases in China, the Marianas and other recently liberated islands, loading them with 2,000 tons of TNT apiece and unleashing them on every known Japanese factory, port, base and railyard.

The next step, the crews knew, would be to bomb cities and shorelines, softening them up for a D-Day-like invasion. There was also a lot of talk about using napalm. Or unleashing the top-secret "super bomb" being tested in the Nevada desert, according to the latest rumors circulating at the base.

Germany had just been defeated. One way or another, the war in the Pacific would be over soon. That was what everyone believed at least.

"Bombardier to pilot."

"Yes?"

"Level, please."

Smitty, the bombardier, was making his final calculations, using his state-of-the-art Norden sight to figure out when to drop the bombs, while factoring in the altitude and 150 mph winds, courtesy of the jet stream. The big bird had to be level for the bombs to hit their target.

"All right," Monroe said, squeezing the controls. "Straight and level."

"I see the factory," Smitty yelled from his berth in the plane's see-through nose below the pilots.

Seconds later, the sky exploded. Black balls erupted around them. The flak from anti-aircraft guns hammered the aluminum skin of the plane. It sounded like someone was outside, pounding the fuselage with a club.

"Bombs away!" Smitty said.

Harry, glancing to his right, could see a stream of black bombs dropping through the clouds.

"Rear bomb bay clear!" he reported

"Front bomb bay clear!" Eddie echoed.

Moments later, Smitty exulted, "Target hit! Bullseye!"

Before anyone could react, an artillery shell fired from a warship hit the fuselage, rocking the plane.

The blast sent Harry tumbling in pain, but he managed to pull himself up and return to his bubble.

A few bursts later, the flak finally stopped. They had to get their crippled plane back to the base over hundreds of miles of ocean.

Home was Isley Field on Saipan, but the pilots had already ruled out trying to make it that far. The bomber was too damaged and they had no escort. If they came up short, rescue wasn't likely. They'd all be headed to watery graves.

Monroe decided to shoot for a closer refuge: Iwo Jima. The little island formed around an active volcano had only recently been conquered by Marines, who took heavy casualties from dug-in Japanese regulars willing to fight to the death.

Despite still taking occasional mortar rounds from enemy holdouts hidden inside Mount Turabashi, Seabees had built a huge runway that took up nearly half of the island. It was now an emergency landing field for B-29 crews.

Squinting into the horizon, Harry did a double take. "Enemy planes closing in from 7 o'clock!" he roared into the intercom.

"How many?"

The young airman gulped. "Three, maybe four."

The silence that followed was unbearable. Every second that passed amped up the crews' nerves.

Harry gripped his .50-caliber machine gun tight.

"Here they come!"

The first two Zeros swooped in to attack the nose of the plane. They were greeted with machine gun fire from the B-29's front turrets, forcing them to peel off. Two other fighters made a pretty roll and came at the side of the plane – right at Harry.

He could see the red "meatballs" on the wings.

Harry took aim.

Hold.

The pilot was visible now. He had a scarf around his neck. And he was …. smiling?

Hold.

Harry tracked the fighter for a few more seconds then pulled the trigger, sending out a long burst. A streak of smoke poured from the cowling of the fighter, now less than 20 yards away. It dropped below the bomber, spinning toward the ocean.

"Got him!" Harry yelled.

No one cheered. There wasn't time. The enemy pilots were regrouping.

Monroe coaxed more speed out of his damaged plane, knowing the limited range of the fighters would work in his favor – if they could just fend off one more attack.

The good news didn't last long.

The co-pilot pointed at the right wing. "Jesus! No. 4 engine is on fire."

Black smoke began streaming from the crippled engine. The big plane dropped to a few hundred feet, roaring over the ocean.

Then a strange but beautiful thing happened. The Zeros suddenly turned away, convinced the American bomber was doomed.

By the time Iwo Jima came into view, a second engine had failed. Monroe, relieved the landing gear still worked, set the smoking bird down with a couple of hops.

Ambulances greeted the weary but thankful crew. A medic pointed in amazement at the jagged hole in the side of the plane.

"Holy cow, how'd you land this thing?" he asked.

Monroe shrugged. Drenched in sweat, he walked up to Harry, who was looking for a private spot to retch.

"Hey, Brooklyn, you're bleeding," the pilot said, pointing at the airman's chest. "Medic!"

Despite his flak jacket, a piece of shrapnel had pierced Harry's chest. As a doctor stitched him up, he told him how lucky he was. He'd be ready to fly again in a few days.

That didn't seem very lucky, Harry thought. Not at all.

———

The silver-haired veteran stirred from his trance with a ringing in his head.

Seconds later, he realized it was the front doorbell. Harry put down the B-29 model he had been clutching and walked over to open the door.

"Hello, Harry. Can I talk to you for a minute?"

Maria was standing on the welcome mat, looking worried.

"Come in."

"You okay? You seem a little … distracted."

"I'm good, I'm good," he said, gesturing for her to take a seat.

The living room was filled with a marble-topped coffee table, long white sofa and a pair of restored antique chairs. The sofa faced a fireplace surrounded by round river rocks in gray and brown that begged to be touched, topped by a painting framed in gold – a fantasy-like forest scene with a bashful fairy partially hidden behind a tree. It had been Bonnie's favorite room, where she had tea with her friends.

"What's up?"

Maria, on the edge of a chair, gave Harry a pleading look – probably the same one she presented to judges and juries while seeking mercy on behalf of her clients.

"I need your help – not so much as my friend, but as a trained skeptic. A former cop."

"I'll do whatever I can, you know that."

"I do, and for that I can't thank you enough. The thing is, a woman I'd never seen before approached me last night at the grocery store with some disturbing news. And I want you to help me sort it out."

"What kind of news?"

"I'm going to let her explain. We only talked for a minute or two. She seemed a bit paranoid. She's meeting me at the playground in an hour. I'd like it if you could come. Sorry, but I dropped your name."

"Why the playground?"

"I don't know, it was her choice. Maybe she thought a public place was safer."

Harry wondered what he was getting himself into. Internal alarms were sounding. "What do you want me to do?"

"Just listen and tell me later what you think."

"Okay, Maria, but what does this have to do with Sam?"

Maria's eyes narrowed.

"He's not the only one," she said.

CHAPTER
FOUR

The park was bustling as usual on a sunny Sunday morning, full of dog-walkers, parents and children. In the distance, a rainbow kite soared. Below, plastic saucers whirled.

Harry looked across the playground and saw Fred sitting by himself near the swing set, serenely smoking his pipe, newspaper on his lap.

Maria and Harry sat on a bench near his chess table and waited for their visitor. He wished he was playing a game with his stuffy German challenger – anything but this bleak task.

"Here she comes," Maria whispered as a woman approached.

She was wearing dark sunglasses and a scarf over her hair that made her resemble either a spy or a domestic violence victim.

"This is my friend Harry. I'm sorry, but I didn't catch your name."

"I'd rather not tell you," the woman said, claiming Harry's favorite stool. "Not yet anyway."

"That's fine," Maria said, exchanging glances with Harry. "You said you have something urgent to tell me?"

The woman nodded. "I was at Sam's funeral. My heart went out to you. No mother should have to bear it. The loss of a child."

There was a brief silence and then she continued.

"But whatever dark cloud came over your son is now hovering over mine. He is 14 and was doing well in school, just like Sam. Then all of sudden, his favorite teacher called to tell me that he's failing."

"I'm so sorry," Maria said.

"He is so depressed I hardly recognize him," the mother lamented. "He won't talk to me – not like he used to. Now, there's this space between us. I'm at wit's end, so I did some snooping. I had to. On his computer, I found something … something awful."

"What was it?" Harry asked, unable to stay silent.

"He was researching how to make a hangman's noose."

Maria gasped, loud enough to draw stares from people nearby.

"I think whatever happened to Sam is happening to my boy. I'm afraid … he's going to try to kill himself."

The woman shuddered and began to cry. Maria stood and draped her arms around her until the sobs stopped.

Harry leaned in. "When you searched his room did you find anything else out of the ordinary?"

Wiping away tears, the mother thought for a few moments. Then she nodded.

"There were a couple of new video games – the violent kind that I'd never buy for him or let him play. They were hidden in his closet."

"That's interesting," Harry said without elaborating.

"There's one more thing. About a week ago, I heard a sound in the backyard in the middle of the night and could see my son climbing into his bedroom window. I thought I saw someone in the dark staring at me. A man.

"When I confronted my boy about it the next morning, he denied everything – said he never left his room. It made me feel like I was going crazy, that it was a nightmare or something. But it's not. It was real. I think somebody's out there. And he's preying on our children."

"For what reason?" Harry asked.

The mother shook her head.

"I don't know. I'm telling you two so you can try to find out before it's too late."

The retired cop didn't know what to make of the story. Shadowy figures in the night, someone abusing children? If it hadn't been for the stark reality of Sam's suicide, he would have dismissed it as nonsense.

He saw that the woman was wearing a wedding ring – a plain gold band.

"What does your husband think about this?" he asked.

She grimaced. "He doesn't know. He's deployed, on a ship somewhere in the Persian Gulf. We talk once or twice a week, but I don't want to stress him out until I have something more … more concrete."

"How about going to the police? Or hiring a private detective?" Harry asked.

"And put my son and myself at risk? What if he's out there, watching me now?"

Maria took the frightened woman's hand.

"Thank you for sharing this. I know how hard it must be, but you did the right thing."

The woman suddenly stood and anxiously scanned the park. "I'm sorry, I have to go."

Harry and Maria watched with heavy hearts as the mother hustled through the park.

The neighbors sat in silence for a while, surrounded by children at play. Then Maria asked, "What do you think?"

"If she was less paranoid, I'd offer to tail her son for a few nights, see where he goes."

"I have another idea. It just occurred to me."

"Oh yeah?"

"I think we should take it to the school board."

"The monthly meeting is coming up."

"Exactly. I'll bring it up during the 'new business' part of the agenda. Just put it out there: Somebody may be harming our children."

"I don't know, Maria. This woman wouldn't even give us her name. You can't count on her help."

"No, but that's okay. We're really just sending up a flare. It's worth a shot, I think. The meeting is next week at the high school. There will be dozens of parents there. It may be the best way to get the word out."

"They may think you're nuts. They'll start talking behind your back."

"I don't care. Let them. I've got nothing to lose."

Harry reached out and touched her shoulder tenderly. "It'll get better, trust me."

Maria turned to face her neighbor. Her face had changed like a weather front, becoming more intense and desperate.

"Can you help me find out what's going on?" she asked. "Start digging?"

Harry hesitated. Instincts honed over many years of police work told him not to penetrate the darkness of a boy's suicide. Who knew where such a trail might lead?

But then he looked in Maria's eyes, saw her helplessness and pain.

"If you want me to," he said finally.

"Thank you!" she said, brightening. "I can't do it by myself. Besides, my parents have been staying with me and they mean well, but they expect me to entertain them."

"I'll see what I can find out. You, me, the whole community, need answers."

Maria, turning serious, nodded. "You never asked me how Sam died."

"I didn't want to intrude."

"That's nice, but if you're going to get involved, you need to know."

"Yeah, suppose so." He felt a sudden apprehension.

"I found him hanging by a rope in the basement. He had made a crude noose, tied it to a cedar beam, then stepped off a bucket."

Maria paused, looking away. "There was a note nearby that said, 'I love you Mom. I hate what I've become.' I found his basketball shoes in the trash can outside. He had set them on fire."

She stared at Harry, who had grown pale, remembering his last chat with Sam. And those fancy high-tops.

"Why would he do that?" Maria asked. *"Burn his shoes?"*

Harry shook his head. He had no clue. "Did you buy him those sneakers?"

"No, he told me you'd given him money for mowing your lawn and cleaning windows."

The old man stared at the grieving woman, wondering if he should say anything. He didn't want to upset her any further. But after a long pause, the former cop opted for candor.

"Maria, I didn't give Sam any money, and I wouldn't have him do any odd jobs without telling you first. Those are expensive shoes. My grandson wants a pair in the worst way, but his parents won't spend that much."

"What are you saying?"

"I'm saying we need to find who gave Sam those damn shoes."

CHAPTER
FIVE

Harry woke to find Honey in his bed, blonde paws stretched across his faulty right leg.

Judging by the twisted sheets, he knew he'd been shaking in his sleep – violently enough to cause his dog to thrust herself against the trembling limbs like a heroic soldier diving on a live grenade.

"Thanks, Fluff," he muttered, giving her a head scratch.

He got out of bed, stepped into his slippers and pulled on his blue-and-green plaid polyester robe, cinching the belt. As usual, he paused by his dresser to touch the framed picture of his late wife resting on top. In his mind, he could hear her say "Good morning, darling."

Downstairs, Harry made his extra-strength coffee and poured himself a cup with a splash of milk. He noticed the prescription for stronger Parkinson's meds lying on the kitchen counter and sighed. He could only put it off for so long.

Getting older seemed to consist of a constant series of numbing discoveries: The first gray hairs, the first wrinkles, the muscle aches that never go away, the sprains that come out of nowhere, the forgetfulness. Harry kept some of that at bay with his exercise program and vitamins, but now his disease was asserting itself. There was always a price to pay with Parkinson's and the bill was coming due.

The tradeoffs were what concerned Harry the most. He needed the drugs to control his tremors, but what if they made it harder to think clearly? What if they caused him to hallucinate? Worse still, what if they became the reason he couldn't stay in his beloved home?

Honey barked and Harry realized he had been standing by the breakfast table with a special treat in his hand – a small rawhide bone.

Offering it, she grabbed it with her teeth and dropped to the floor.

"Enjoy, my furry friend," he said, smiling. "A reward for valor in combat."

A couple of hours later, Harry was dressed and clean-shaven. He'd managed to get through half his fitness regimen, which he deemed satisfactory.

Armed with his shoebox and game board, he headed across the street to his favorite spot, leaving Honey at home to rest after her long night.

He was hoping the serious German fellow would be at the park and up for a game, but it was a bit early. The bench by the swings was empty.

Harry looked around and didn't see any fellow seniors, but that didn't matter. He'd played people of all ages since he retired, even patiently teaching youngsters the game. But he did keep to himself certain tricks he'd accumulated over the years. Those were his and his alone, to be unleashed like dragons in hard-fought games when the time was right.

Harry sat on his stool, felt his butt adjust to the hardness. He didn't worry about finding someone to play. The chess table, once set up, was like a beacon.

He was placing the last pieces on the board when a shadow suddenly fell across it. He looked up and saw Fred smiling down on him.

"Preparing for battle, I see. Might I play, or do you have someone else in mind?"

"I dunno, you have a habit of running off in the middle of a game."

Fred laughed, and for the first time Harry saw the mirth in his eyes, green with a hint of gold.

"As I recall, you were rescued by a young man as I was advancing on your queen. Your grandson, I presume?"

"Yeah, that's Buster. He's 13. Great kid."

"I envy you," Fred said, taking the stool opposite Harry. "Alas, I have no grandchildren."

"Any grown children?"

"None, I'm afraid. I am a widower and I live alone."

"Me, too. Your move."

"It's not so bad, is it – being alone?" Fred said, marching a pawn forward from his front rank. "Life is what you make of it, yes?"

Harry nodded. "The way I see it, the trick is to squeeze all the juice out of the good days that you can. That way the bad days don't seem so bad."

"Ah, yes. Squeeze the juice. Turn lemons into lemonade."

"That's something different, but you get the idea."

An hour later, slaughtered pieces littered the side of the table. Harry was losing, but the war was far from over. He had a counter-attack coming in two, maybe three turns, if the man across the table fell into his trap.

During the match, curious children would sometimes stand by the table and watch, occasionally offering the men baby carrots or

Fig Newtons from the small Ziploc bags they always seemed to be carrying. Neither man shooed them away. The fresh faces with rosy cheeks and ready smiles were their secret energy source.

The game, both men knew, was far more about companionship than competition. Gradually, they learned interesting things about each other – what they had in common and what they absolutely did not.

Harry and Fred were the same age, the American just a few months older. They both had served in combat during World War II, but on opposite sides. It quickly became evident that the passage of time hadn't erased either man's psychological scars, or the pain behind them. They were just harder to see.

They had another thing in common. Each had lost his wife in tragic ways – Harry's to disease, Fred's in a car crash that he politely declined to discuss.

The never-ending toll from a savage war. Heartbreak that refused to heal. How could they overcome such vast ruins to forge a friendship?

For now, there was chess and a mutual thirst for company, to salve the sting of loneliness, if only for an hour or two.

Harry moved his remaining rook deep into Fred's territory. A final offensive.

"Check," he said, but it wasn't much of a threat.

Fred deftly slid his king out of danger behind a protective wall of pieces. Several moves later, Harry's queen would fall and the battle would be over.

The rivals shook hands and began returning the pieces to the shoebox, its cracked corners mended with masking tape that had yellowed and curled with age.

The slender German stood and sent pipe smoke rising into the pale blue sky. Harry appreciated that his conqueror didn't gloat. Instead, he offered a compliment.

"I enjoyed our match very much. You have passed your test, my friend."

"Thanks, I guess."

"Don't be glum, I will be here tomorrow. If you desire a rematch, I will be happy to oblige."

Harry couldn't tell if Fred was mocking him or being a gentleman.

The sun was beginning to set, painting the horizon a fiery orange. Fred gave his acquaintance a nod and headed briskly down the hill.

Harry, watching, shook his head.

Who is this guy?

CHAPTER
SIX

Maria and Harry entered the gym at Two Rivers High School and found an empty space in the bleachers.

The five-member school board was seated behind a folding table on the gleaming floor. There was a podium with a microphone between the table and the modest crowd of about 50 people.

"Here we go," Maria whispered to her neighbor.

"Still want to do this?" Harry asked.

"Oh yeah. Absolutely."

"For Sam?"

"For Sam and any others."

It was the board's practice to open the floor to anyone who wished to speak before their attention turned to the items on their agenda. There were no restrictions on topics and no time limits, although long-winded speakers were often given not-so-subtle hints to wrap things up.

Maria waited patiently for several parents to voice their concerns about littering near the middle school and the "gang-style" graffiti found on a retaining wall near the district administration building.

A brief debate then ensued, with trustees ultimately agreeing to consult with the police department on the matter.

"Anyone else wish to address the board?" Bella Rose, the board president, inquired after a brief lull.

Rose was the owner of the local independent bookstore, Books in Bloom. She was 55, with a ready smile, long brown hair knotted in a bun and reading glasses balanced on the tip of her nose.

Maria, too experienced a lawyer to fear a microphone or an audience, stepped up to the lectern.

"I am Maria Mendez. I believe some of you know me," she began. "Thank you for your flowers and cards and tender words."

"We are so sorry for your loss," Rose said in a mournful way. The other board members nodded solemnly.

"I am here tonight," Maria continued, "not because of what happened, but because of what *may happen*. I am worried that whatever it was that led to my son's death may now be affecting other boys his age. I am worried that they may be at risk."

"Please explain," a man on the school board said.

Maria nodded.

"I'll do my best. I know that a number of you attended my son's funeral, but one thing you don't know is that before Sam took his life he wrote a note addressed to me that said, 'I hate what I've become.' He set fire to his brand-new basketball shoes – shoes that someone other than me had given him. I don't know why he did that. I may never know. But the other day I learned something that made me fear for Two Rivers and Sunny Slope.

"A mother of a 14-year-old boy told me her son, too, is suddenly struggling in school. She found expensive video games in his room that she didn't know anything about. And she's worried he may take his own life."

There were murmurs of alarm in the crowd, prompting Rose to ask, "Is that mother planning to address the board?"

"No," Maria said. "Not yet. She's frightened, so I'm speaking for her."

A pudgy man behind the table, a retired teacher named Herbert Brooks, spoke up.

"Our hearts go out to you, Ms. Mendez, but what do you expect the board to do? We can't act on such vague information."

"I expect the board to protect our children," Maria replied sharply, dark eyes flashing. "I expect the board to investigate."

"Investigate *what* exactly?" Brooks said, shrugging.

"Why some of your best students are suddenly failing their classes. Why they are looking up how to make a noose."

There were audible gasps. Rose, looking stricken, tapped her gavel.

"I think that's enough, Ms. Mendez," she said. "Nobody wants any of our students to fail … or to harm themselves in any way. Two Rivers is one of the finest public school districts in the Northwest. I'm sure Mr. Sinclair will look into what you said."

Robert Sinclair, the district superintendent who was seated next to the board members' table on a folding chair, nodded his agreement.

"Please do," Maria snapped, angered by the fake smile on Sinclair's face. "Before it's too late."

Harry saw pity in many of the faces around him as Maria walked away. He caught up to her outside the gym.

"They'll be talking behind my back now, just like you said," she said.

"What you did was brave, Maria."

"Or stupid."

"Parents have been put on notice, like you wanted. If their son or daughter is suddenly depressed and struggling in school, they'll think about what you said. Give it time."

Maria stopped at her car and shook her head.

"We don't have time, Harry."

———

Harry had been meeting Fred at the park for a few weeks, and they no longer exclusively played chess.

Sometimes, they shared a bench and simply watched the children play. They told well-rehearsed stories from their past, and Harry came to enjoy Fred's dry wit and talent for spinning amusing tales. To anyone passing by, they'd look like dear friends, a couple of old men sharing a laugh.

Their budding relationship took a leap forward one afternoon when Fred surprised Harry with an invitation.

"Tomorrow, I am making a special dinner that deserves to be shared. I would be honored if you would join me," he said.

Harry hesitated long enough for Fred to add, "I will not be offended if you have other obligations. I apologize for the short notice."

Harry chuckled. "It's not that. I'm just so used to checking with Bonnie on things like this – social stuff. Even after four years. Sure, I'll come over."

"*Wunderbar*," Fred said, scribbling the address on a piece of the newspaper he always seemed to be carrying.

"I shall see you at 7. Bring nothing."

———

Fred lived in a beautifully restored three-story building on the first slope off downtown, that had been painted forest green with gold trim and raspberry accents. A bronze plaque by the entrance proudly hailed the structure's historic significance and its birth year: 1921.

When Harry entered the lobby, he was greeted with the pungent scent of sauerkraut and knew immediately it had to be coming from Fred's top-floor apartment.

He looked around for an elevator and, finding none, walked up two flights of wooden stairs. At the door to No. 5, he knocked twice and saw it quickly swing open. Fred was wearing a white apron with blue vertical stripes, a large metal whisk in his hand.

"*Hallo*," he said, beaming. "Please come in."

The host ushered his guest into a large room furnished with a smattering of antiques, fully laden bookcases and a polished upright piano. The view of the deep-blue river from the windows, over the rooftops of downtown buildings, was breathtaking.

Unlike in Sunny Slope further up the hill, Harry could hear the barks of frolicking sea lions and the blast of a horn as a freighter cruised past, filled with cargo containers. The experience of living by the water felt more vibrant, more alive, than in his cozy subdivision.

He took a seat on a Queen Anne sofa, upholstered in blue and gold with an elegant, curving back.

"May I offer you a Spaten?"

Fred saw the puzzled look on Harry's face. "It's a German lager. Pairs nicely with schweinebraten. Or I could offer you a glass of wine."

"Beer sounds great, thanks."

Fred nodded like a waiter and returned a couple of minutes later with a chilled glass mug filled with a pale brew, an inch-thick layer of foam on top.

As the aromas from the kitchen reached him, Harry felt his stomach rumble in anticipation. "Whatever you're cooking, it smells good."

The chef called out from behind a wall. "Schweinebraten. It's a Bavarian pork roast with gravy, best served with potato dumplings and sauerkraut – my grandmother's recipe."

Harry knew he'd detected fresh sauerkraut. He'd spent too many years in close proximity to Brooklyn delis not to recognize that particular scent.

A short time later, they were seated across from one another at the dining room table, set for a formal occasion with a floral centerpiece and a long white candle in a crystal holder.

Fred had brought out the food, artistically arranged on china plates. Some kind of German folk music featuring a heavy dose of accordion was playing in the background.

Bonnie would like this, Harry thought. As for himself, it seemed awfully fussy.

Fred lit the candle, closed his eyes and whispered a few words in German that he did not translate.

"This is the day I honor my Hildy by cooking her favorite meal," he told Harry. "Thank you for sharing this moment with me. She would be pleased that I am not alone and still desperately mourning, although, to be perfectly honest, I am, and will continue to be, until my last breaths."

"Hildy was your wife?"

"Yes, my great love." He raised his mug. "To Hildy!"

They drank to seal the toast and then Fred urged his guest to eat. "Please, before it gets cold."

Harry took a bite of the tender, slow-cooked pork in its savory sauce and then another.

"Delicious," he declared. "How long did this take to cook?"

"About five hours for the roast. Sauerkraut, of course, takes longer."

"How much longer?"

Fred continued with a science professor's flourish. "Well, you must ferment the cabbage for several days after adding the spices. I use what you Americans call a Mason jar. Then it goes in the refrigerator for another week or so to complete the process."

"Another *week*?" Harry nearly spit out a dumpling. His dinner prep averaged less than 20 minutes – about the time it took to boil some spaghetti and throw on jarred sauce. And that was when he was feeling ambitious. More often, dinner was a frozen pizza or a bucket of takeout chicken accompanied by salad poured from a bag.

Within minutes, Harry had cleaned his plate so well he could see himself in the shine. Fred, pleased by his guest's apparent approval, brought out more of the pork and trimmings.

"I want to tell you how much I enjoy our time at the park," Fred said as the man across the table began eagerly re-filling his plate.

"Because you win most of the time," Harry cracked. He took another scoop of sauerkraut, which he wouldn't normally do. In his mind, it was more of a garnish than a side dish, but he now looked at the pickled white cabbage with new appreciation. *A week!*

"I actually was thinking about our conversation. It comes easily with you."

"Maybe it's because we're the same age."

"Or kindred spirits, perhaps. Harry, if you don't mind me asking, what was your occupation?"

"I was a cop for 35 years – NYPD, Miami. Ended my career here, in the slow lane. Retired eight years ago. What about yourself?

Gourmet chef?"

Fred gave a merry laugh that made his sea-green eyes twinkle. "I don't usually dine like this. As I said, this is for Hildy – to mark our anniversary, not her passing. No, I was a music teacher for many years. After the war, I attended the conservatory in Berlin, then I joined the orchestra in Munich. I had ambitions of becoming a serious pianist and composer. I had concerts and a recording session booked, but then … reality interfered, you could say."

"What reality was that?"

Fred took a deep breath.

"I was picking wild mushrooms one day, a very German thing to do, and I slipped on some wet moss and fell 20 feet down a cliff. I landed hard on some rocks and broke every finger in my right hand."

He held the hand by the flame of the candle and Harry could see a series of faint scars.

"And you couldn't play piano anymore?"

"No, after the surgeries, I could. It just wasn't the same. I searched and searched but couldn't find the spark again – the magical spark you need to be more than good at something, to be great, to be the best. I think it passed from me to somebody else. Inspiration doesn't like to be kept waiting, you see."

"That must have been tough."

"It was, but it also taught me some valuable lessons about humility and the true meaning of success. But that's a conversation for another time, yes?"

He studied Harry's face as if trying to read his mind. "What has your disease taught you, my friend?"

Harry's eyes widened. He thought he'd hidden his tremors from his chess rival.

"How did you know?"

"Most people wouldn't. You hide your symptoms well and you are strong. But when you get tired, you begin to hold your right hand with your left, your right foot taps a little, and you start to slur a few words."

"You noticed all that? Maybe you should have been a detective."

Fred shook his head. "I am not trying to embarrass you, Harry. Far from it. I am liberating you from having to hide your condition when we are together."

"I guess now we have to be friends," Harry said with a lopsided grin.

"That calls for a drink." Fred popped up and pulled open a stained-glass door in the china cabinet. He placed a half-filled crystal decanter and a pair of tulip-shaped glasses on the table.

"Single-malt Scotch. Definitely not German." He poured the amber whisky into the glasses and handed one to Harry.

"To new friends and happy times," Fred said.

"New friends," Harry repeated.

CHAPTER
SEVEN

Shortly after dawn, Harry was out walking Honey on her bright red leash. The plan, incorporated into his fitness regimen, was to complete four loops around the park.

Most houses were still dark. The streets were quiet.

In the distance he saw someone heading his way, moving fast, and he squinted to get a better look.

Probably a jogger.

But as the person drew closer he could see it was a woman in a flapping white nightgown.

He stopped and Honey, alarmed, assumed a protective stance beside her master. The woman was coming right at him, practically running in her slippers. They made a *shlop-shlop* sound on the pavement.

She stopped directly in front of Harry. Then she slapped him in the face hard enough to knock him back a step.

It was the panic-stricken mother who'd met him at the park. Her dark brown hair was wild. Her lips were pursed in anger. There was a crazed, sleep-deprived look in her eyes.

"My son has disappeared," she seethed. "Because of you."

"We went to the school board last week," Harry said, rubbing his cheek. "We informed the community. We tried to help."

"You shouldn't have done that. He was watching. And now my son is gone."

She turned and strode away just as fiercely as before.

"I can help you look for him!" Harry shouted, but she didn't hear.

News of the disappearance of 14-year-old Nate Caruthers surged through the tight-knit community like a tsunami.

Just a week earlier, a grieving mother had appeared before the school board. Now it seemed her dire warning wasn't a figment of her fears as most people had assumed.

For days, police scoured the area looking for Nate with the help of scores of volunteers and trained dogs. Divers were brought in to drag the rivers. A helicopter with a powerful searchlight became a constant presence overhead.

But no trace of the former honor student could be found.

The investigation would determine that he arrived at school as usual just before 7:30 a.m. on a Thursday, attended all of his classes and got on the afternoon bus like the other kids. The driver remembered seeing Nate get off a couple of blocks from his Sunny Slope house. Nothing appeared out of the ordinary.

He just never made it home.

Carla Caruthers had waited until 10 p.m. before calling 911. Knowing how depressed and suicidal her son had been, she begged the dispatcher to start a search immediately. The woman on the phone sent an officer to the Caruthers home to take a statement and collect a photo of the boy.

Nate was probably just acting out or at a friend's house, the officer told the fretful mother. It was department policy to wait at least 24 hours before investigating.

Caruthers had been out searching frantically on her own for many hours by the time police sprang into action. They sent a description of Nate and his picture out far and wide to no avail.

The mayor and police chief held a joint televised press conference, urging the public to help find the boy. The mother did tearful TV interviews begging for the safe return of her only child. A hotline was set up. Tips started pouring in but led nowhere.

Detectives scoured every inch of the Caruthers home looking for clues, from the basement to the attic, and turned up nothing other than evidence of Nate's sudden interest in suicide, as reflected in gruesome notebook drawings and disturbing computer searches.

Harry and Maria joined the volunteers in the woods and hills ringing the community, shouting the boy's name every few minutes. But there was never an answer.

"The mother blames me for this," Harry told Maria after another day of fruitless searching. They were sitting on his porch, sipping ice water and resting their tired feet.

"She was just lashing out. Don't take it personally."

"She's convinced that whoever is responsible for this had been watching her, and that when she came to us for help, he became incensed."

"Yeah, I heard some of that at our meeting. But she could also be delusional – scared out of her mind."

"She's scared all right. I would be, too, if Buster suddenly was gone without a trace."

"Everybody's scared right now. They're holding a special meeting of the school board in a couple days to address it. I thought I'd go.

Want to tag along?"

"Somebody needs to protect you if the villagers bring pitchforks and torches. You are the messenger, after all."

"Can I borrow one of your old Kevlar vests?"

"Don't have any, but speaking of torches, it's about time I put one under the ass of the detective assigned to this case."

Maria grinned. "I'd pay to be in the room for that. Captain Harry Bolden rides again."

"I like the sound of that," he said, taking a sip. "Maybe I'll put it on my tombstone. Past tense, of course."

CHAPTER
EIGHT

Harry's son and his wife lived in a luxurious contemporary home with five bedrooms and three baths that Harry called "the mansion."

While Harry preferred older homes with their wavy glass, hand-crafted cabinets and real, creaky wood floors, he appreciated the modern conveniences in the big riverfront house: The temperature-controlled wine closet. The granite-topped center island in the kitchen with the built-in gas range. The Finnish sauna in the basement. The home theater with motorized curtains and overstuffed lounge chairs.

The real estate attorney and his bookkeeper wife had planned for a big family, but after Buster and two miscarriages, the couple had given up trying to have more children. They were now setting their sights on Harry.

For the past year and a half, Charlie, an only child, had been pushing his father to put his aging home up for sale and move into their guest cottage, fully furnished and just steps away. There were no staircases to strain an old man's back and knees, and all the privacy he could want.

For most ailing seniors, it would be a tempting offer. But Harry still felt the warmth of his wife's presence every day in his old bungalow. He'd never willingly sacrifice something so precious.

Charlie had invited his dad over to watch a Mariners game on TV but their team was getting blown out and there was plenty of time to chat. Buster was at the breakfast table in the other room, hunched over his latest model – a sand-colored Israeli tank with a movable turret.

"I heard you've been pretty involved in this missing-child thing," Charlie said, handing Harry another Corona.

Harry shoved the lime wedge into the bottle and took a gulp.

"Yeah, me and Maria from next door. We had to do something."

Charlie nodded. "Liz was out tacking up fliers. The community really came together. The Boy Scouts, Elks Lodge, VFW, church groups – they were all out looking."

"It's like finding a needle in …, well, you know."

"I hear your old boss is about to call the search off. It's been five weeks."

Harry frowned. The Two Rivers police chief wasn't known for being particularly thorough – or patient. "Way too soon for that. These things take time."

"What does your famous gut tell you?"

"That maybe we've been looking in the wrong places."

"What do you mean?"

"Seems like everyone is assuming this kid went off someplace and killed himself."

"The paper said he was depressed. There's speculation that he and Sam made some kind of suicide pact."

Harry snorted. "That's speculation all right. Reckless nonsense, based on nothing. I hope Maria didn't see that."

"What are you thinking really happened?"

"I'm thinking that this isn't a disappearance or even a suicide. It's a homicide."

Charlie's wife walked into the room in time to hear those words. A look of alarm spread across her face.

"A homicide?" Liz said. "Are you saying that poor boy was murdered?"

Trying to calm his wife, Charlie quickly interjected, "I don't think Pops is say—"

"Yes," Harry said emphatically. "And I think the killer lives in Sunny Slope."

"Okay, Pops. That's enough. You're scaring Liz." He lowered his voice. "Buster's in the next room, for goodness sake."

"Right you are. My apologies. I'll keep my mouth shut."

Liz stared at Charlie. "We need to go to the school board meeting tomorrow night, find out more about what's going on," she said, before walking away.

Charlie gave his father a disapproving look.

"See what you've done? Now Liz is in a panic."

———

The Two Rivers Police Department occupied a no-frills, one-story building – brick painted a dull brown topped with a flat metal roof of the same color. The squat structure was conveniently located off the two-lane state highway on the west side of town.

Harry hadn't stepped inside since his retirement because he didn't want people to see the progress of his disease. But he had to talk to the man assigned to the Caruthers case, share what little information he had, maybe get a little back for Maria.

He approached the glass front doors, saw the taped sign warning visitors not to bring in firearms or illicit drugs, and entered anxiously.

Marjorie, the plump woman behind the front desk, jumped to her feet. A big smile creased her face.

"Captain Bolden!"

Moments later, officers emerged from various offices like curious prairie dogs. They rushed up to Harry and began slapping his back. It was a heartwarming show of affection but exactly what he had feared. He could see them looking him up and down, assessing the severity of his tremors. Or at least that's how it felt.

Thankfully, the crowd parted as the bald, barrel-chested chief strode toward Harry.

"Okay, back to work," Barry Huggins said gruffly, staring down the cops until they peeled off. Then he laughed in a merry way, taking in his former right-hand man.

"Jesus Christ, how long has it been?"

"Eight years."

"Wow, time sure flies."

"Sure does."

"Sorry about Bonnie. That must have been rough."

"Thanks, chief. It was. Appreciate the card … and your call."

"I wished I could have done more. What brings you here? If I knew you were coming, I'd have rolled out the red carpet. You know, like we do once every election cycle when the governor visits."

Harry rolled his eyes. Most cops hated the liberal, four-term governor, felt he didn't have their backs. "Who do you have on the Nathaniel Caruthers case?"

"Joe Johnson. He was on patrol when you left. Made detective a year ago."

"I remember him. Sharp guy. Is he around?"

"Yeah, in his office. What's this all about, Harry?"

"Oh, nothing. Maybe I can help Joe connect a few dots."

"Any help is appreciated. This disappearance has us stumped."

"Thanks, chief. I hear you're thinking about pulling the plug on the search."

"More like scale it back. The helicopter and dive crew are in demand elsewhere, as are Buddy Olsen's tracking dogs. But we're not going to stop looking."

"Good to hear."

"When you're done with Johnson, stop by. We need to catch up."

The chief squeezed Harry's shoulder then returned to his office.

The retired cop walked down the familiar hallway, decorated with framed portraits of former chiefs going back 80 years. He stopped at an open doorway.

"Harry! So that was what the commotion was all about," Johnson said from behind a scratched metal desk littered with files. "Come on in. Take a seat."

Harry settled heavily into a utilitarian chair and looked at the young detective. Johnson's badge dangled on a chain around his neck. He wore a plain white shirt with the sleeves rolled up and a cheap striped tie. He had narrow eyes and dark-brown shoulder-length hair that was perfectly straight. A stubbly beard paired with the bags under his eyes made him look like he'd been on a three-day bender.

"Congratulations on the promotion," Harry said.

"Thanks in large part to you. You were always encouraging me to move up the ranks."

"Nice of you to say."

"What brings you here? It must be something serious."

"It is. The Caruthers case."

"Ah, yes," Johnson said. "The boy who left home and never returned."

"Are you investigating it as a disappearance?"

"More like a suicide. I'm sure the body will turn up eventually. But why are you asking?"

"I think it may be a homicide. And if we don't find the person who did it, more kids may turn up dead."

Johnson leaned back in his chair, making the springs creak. "What evidence do you have?"

"None. It's just a hunch. But I'm convinced the Sam Mendez suicide and the Nate Caruthers disappearance are linked."

"Well, they went to the same school, were both 14 and failing their classes. But beyond that, there's nothing."

"So, no suicide pact?"

Johnson laughed. "What a bunch of horseshit. I called the Messenger to complain after that crap ran. No, those boys weren't close as far as we can tell. Rode the bus together, that's about it."

"What about Sam's sneakers?"

"What about them? He set them on fire. So what? He was depressed. Depressed kids do stupid things."

"Those Air Jordans cost 150 bucks. The mom didn't buy them. She had no idea where they came from."

"Go on."

"So, the Caruthers boy had expensive video games hidden in his room. Did the mother tell you that?"

"Yeah, we know all about it. We even ran the games for prints. It was just the kid's."

"Joe, can't you see what's going on? Two boys from Sunny Slope, both groomed with expensive gifts, both turn up missing or dead."

"Groomed for what?"

"I don't know. Whatever it is, it must be horrible."

"All right, Harry. Maybe it's more than a couple of suicides, but officially there's no connection. Come see me when you have something I can go on."

"What about this man that Mrs. Caruthers caught a glimpse of one night? She's convinced he was watching her."

"She's lost it. Half of what she says makes no sense. She's here every day, you know. Most of the time she just sits out there, mumbling to herself."

Harry shook his head. "Maybe it's better than sitting home alone."

"Yeah, maybe. Look, I know you're trying to help, but we got this. We're running down leads, and we haven't given up searching for the body."

Harry nodded and rose to his feet. The last thing he wanted to do was become a pitiful pest like Mrs. Caruthers.

"Thanks for your time. Good luck with the investigation."

"Take care, captain. Good seeing you."

Harry walked out, doing his best to control the worsening tremors in his right hand. In the hallway, he saw Huggins, who was on the phone but beckoning him to come to his office.

The ex-cop tapped his watch and mouthed an apology.

There was no way he'd shake in front of the chief.

CHAPTER
NINE

With much dread and after several reminders from his physician, Harry had started the more powerful Parkinson's medication. He was pleasantly surprised to discover that it made him feel less befuddled.

He didn't know why that was happening or how long it might last, but he didn't complain. He couldn't wait to try out his newfound clarity in a chess match.

Fred had won four of the first five games and Harry was itching to restore his honor as a skilled amateur.

At the park, Harry was the aggressor from the start, keeping his opponent on his heels. Coordinated attacks came from multiple angles, catching Fred off-guard more than once.

As the German continued to shed pieces, he looked up and saw the intensity etched on Harry's face.

"Someone had an extra cup of coffee today, it seems," Fred said. "There is no stopping your onslaught."

"I can't count my chickens yet. Not with you."

"What an odd expression. Please don't explain it."

After more small talk and another crushing advance by Harry, Fred graciously conceded. As usual, they shook hands across the table.

"There's something I've been meaning to ask you, Fred," Harry said after they tossed the pieces into the frayed shoebox. "Now that we've gotten to know each other."

"By all means," the man across the table said, drawing on his pipe. The aroma of Frosty Mint, Fred's latest tobacco blend, filled the air.

"It's about the war, so you don't have to answer. I won't be offended."

"I'll answer what I can. It is not a pleasant subject, yes? There are some things that the mere passage of time cannot assuage."

Harry nodded. He'd been thinking about the whole Nazi thing, obsessing really.

He couldn't be friends with someone who aided and abetted genocide. He had to know the truth. As a former cop, he believed he could tell if a person was lying by the look in their eyes.

For once, there were no children trailing them like ducklings. With a confirming glance around, Harry posed his question.

"During the war, what the Nazis did to the Jews … did you have a part in any of it?"

Fred seemed taken aback by the bluntness of the query. He looked at Harry intently for a few moments, searching for the right words.

"In the final year of the war, I was just 18 and … what is the American word? A 'grunt.' They assigned me to an artillery unit on the Western Front, but we were already retreating. The war had been lost, everybody knew so.

"What happened to the Jews during the war – and really for many years before – was an abomination. The dehumanizing, the death camps, the depravity of it all. Insanity, really. And, just to be clear, I was never a Nazi, although all boys of school age were indoctrinated, myself included. The Hitler Youth, it was mandatory. Anyone who refused was rounded up for punishment or worse.

"But, I digress. To answer your question, I never saw the camps during the war, was not involved in that in any way, but I was once ordered to stand guard over a cave filled with Jewish plunder.

"The sight of it, the vastness of it all, made me sick. That's when I knew the rumors of mass genocide were true. When the war ended, I discovered that my father had some plunder of his own and I objected strongly. It led to me being banished from my own family.

"Many years later, I visited Auschwitz like any tourist. I had to see one of the camps with my own eyes. What I saw repulsed me, filled me with rage. So, no, I had no role in the extermination of millions of innocent people. But I did nothing to stop it, and so I am haunted by it just the same."

"What did you mean about your father's 'plunder?'" Harry asked.

Fred sighed heavily. "Someday I will tell you that story, you have my word on that. But not today, my friend."

"I'm Jewish," Harry said, watching Fred's eyebrows rise. "That's why I'm asking."

A heavy silence hung over them. "I enlisted at 18 in hopes of killing all the Nazis I could," Harry said after a while. "They sent me to the Pacific instead."

"A crushing disappointment?"

"Not really. On second thought, I figured it might be safer fighting the Japs in a bomber. Less resistance. I was wrong about that – until the very end."

"So, you flew in a B-29?" Fred asked, remembering the grandson's model.

"That's right."

"As a pilot?"

"No, no. Gunner. A grunt, like you."

Fred nodded. "I naively thought I was more fortunate than most. I didn't see the faces of the soldiers I killed, not with artillery shells fired from six kilometers away. But it was gruesome just the same."

Harry, who dropped his bombs through the clouds, said nothing.

His B-29 wing firebombed Japanese cities without military targets, slaughtering civilians by the thousands in one of the most savage ways imaginable. He didn't have to see their melting faces to know how they died.

The justification was that it would hasten the end of the war, like the atomic bombs that soon followed. So why did his nightmares never end?

"I'm sorry, I still have a hard time talking about it," Harry said, suddenly looking pale. "After all this time."

Fred gave his new friend a knowing glance.

"I told Hildy almost nothing about the war," he said. "And to her credit, she never asked. She just knew not to."

"Yeah, Buster keeps asking for more stories, more details. Most of the time, I just say I can't remember."

"Even though you can."

"Yeah, especially when I can."

They sat quietly for a while, watching parents push their preschoolers on the swings. Then Fred suddenly gasped, placing his hand over his gaping mouth.

"*Mein Gott!* You're Jewish! I fed you pork at my house!!"

The comical look on Fred's face lifted Harry's spirits.

"I've never kept kosher," he said, chuckling. "No worries."

"Are you sure? I didn't offend you?"

"Actually, you did a little."

"*Oh no!*"

Harry gave his pal a sly wink.

"By not offering me any leftovers to take home."

CHAPTER
TEN

"Brooklyn, got a smoke?"

Harry shook his head. He was on his cot, writing another reassuring letter to his mother. His kid brother would read them to her, back in their East New York brownstone so many miles away.

In his neat mechanical script, he wrote about the people he flew with, where they were from, the lives they had back home. He didn't write about the missions or the many airmen who'd crossed his path and perished. He didn't write about death, never about death.

He wrote to prove he was alive.

"Sorry, Cap. All out."

Monroe shrugged and sat on the cot next to the newly minted staff sergeant. They were in their makeshift barracks, a short jog from the runway at the airbase on Saipan.

Waiting faithfully was Dancing Damsel, her silver hull patched up yet again.

It was shortly after midnight, another humid night in the tropics. In the distance, they could hear the chatter of Chinese workers in their conical bamboo hats digging drainage ditches. As usual, they were doing the work by hand, using the light of a full moon.

"I hear you don't like this mission," Monroe said, studying Harry's face. "Can't say I blame you."

Harry, clutching his half-finished letter, looked up at the sturdy Iowan, admiring the farm boy's movie star profile – the jutting chin, the distinguished nose, the thoughtful brow, the smoky eyes. He couldn't find any traces of emotion. Before a mission Monroe was a brick wall.

Afterward, it was a different story. Safely on the ground, he'd be the life of the party, telling bawdy stories and drinking everyone under the table.

"Well, for one thing, do you know it's Friday the 13th?" Harry asked.

"Yeah? So what?"

"So, it doesn't seem very lucky to me."

Monroe tilted back his cap. "Ah, come on, you're giving me superstition nonsense? What's your beef? Spill, or I'll have them take back those sergeant stripes."

"But I like them," Harry said, grinning. "It makes me feel kinda special."

He carefully folded the letter and pushed it under his pillow. *I'll finish it later, God willing.*

The airmen looked each other in the eye. There was trust there, forged out of facing death together. Harry knew that whatever he said, Monroe wouldn't take it the wrong way. He just didn't want his captain thinking he was going soft. Or on the verge of cracking.

"It just doesn't seem right," the New Yorker said quietly, so others in the tent catching a pre-mission nap wouldn't hear. "*Civilians?*"

A truck drove by, its headlights briefly washing over the captain's face. He suddenly seemed much older than his 35 years. The wavy blond hair was streaked with gray, and there were leathery creases in his cheeks Harry hadn't noticed before. He had aged five years in 11 months.

"This is a first for me, too. For all of us. But orders are orders."

Normally it wouldn't be the smartest idea to criticize a mission before it was flown. But the pilot asked, so the young gunner decided to go for it. It felt good to release the anxiety that had been building up since their morning briefing.

"I don't mind bombing the hell out of Jap soldiers, or taking out their factories," Harry said. "I mean, they're asking for it the way they dig in and fight to the death. What are we supposed to do, right? But when we're asked to kill thousands of civilians to send a message to their emperor, well, it doesn't seem right. Not *morally* right. All those women and children. They don't deserve to die. Not like that."

Monroe grunted and looked through the open tent flaps into the darkness. A sudden heavy rain had started, chasing away the laborers and tiger mosquitos. The raindrops tap-danced on the camouflaged canvas above their heads.

"It's not that simple," he said in his honeyed farmer's drawl. "It never is. Not in war. There are no more military targets on that damn island. We've hit them all – most more than once. And still they won't surrender.

"So, maybe we have to take out a city or two or three – who knows how many? – until the Jap generals finally understand it's over. You talk about morality, but it wasn't moral to do a sneak attack on Pearl. And you know what the Japs have done to civilians in China – and to our own POWs. No way *that's* right. I'm sorry about those civilians, but my moral compass says let's just get this damn war over with. Whatever it takes so I can go home to my wife and kids."

Monroe pulled a picture out of the breast pocket of his brown leather jacket, showing a woman with twin girls at her feet. Molly Monroe was sitting on the front porch steps of a turn-of-the-century farmhouse with a pretty smile and red-painted lips, or at least that's the color Harry imagined. Her shoulder-length hair was freshly curled. She looked beautiful.

The captain didn't have to explain why he wanted the war to end so badly. It was all there – in a frayed Kodak snapshot.

Harry didn't carry any pictures. He thought it was something of a jinx, and he refused to take any more risks than he absolutely had to. In 15 months of combat, he'd flown 33 missions, including a dozen terrifying bombing runs over Japan itself. He watched in horror as B-29s around him burst into flames and plunged into the icy depths of the Sea of Japan or into buildings, entire crews wiped out in seconds.

He'd escaped death many times in the belly of a flying metal beast, and he didn't know if he could take it anymore. Every morning, he'd get up, shower and listen to the radio for the latest news, hoping and praying for a Japanese surrender. It never came.

This time, the Damsel had been tapped for a pre-dawn raid on Osaka, Japan's second-largest city, with some 2 million inhabitants. Their payload: a few thousand pounds of M69, the latest napalm bomb developed by the scientists at DuPont and Standard Oil.

Harry and his crew knew what to expect from their briefings. Recent raids over Tokyo had reduced a quarter of the capital to scorched rubble, killing thousands. A million people were left homeless.

A mix of jellied gasoline and magnesium, the bombs burst into massive fireballs on impact. Even modest winds cause the blazes to unite, strengthen and move with terrifying speed – a tidal wave of hellfire. People unable to outrace the roaring flames on city streets were instantly burned alive, down to the bone. Those seeking refuge in their homes or in makeshift shelters smothered to death. The heat was so intense, water in streams and rivers boiled.

With reverence, Monroe slipped the photo back in his jacket. He stood to leave and patted Harry's curly black head.

"At least they've pretty much run out of fighters. We go in, drop our bombs and get the hell out."

"Thanks for listening, sir."

How much terror could a young man witness and still be the same kind-hearted, trusting soul afterward? That's what Harry really wanted to write in his letters back home.

Less than an hour later, they were in the clouds, bound once more for Japan.

Looking through his bubble, Harry couldn't help but be awed. There were more than a hundred B-29s in his group, flanked by protective Mustang fighters. Ahead of them were two other waves of similar strength – 300 in all.

God help the people of Osaka.

The crew didn't need its sophisticated radar and navigation systems. As they neared the target, the sky turned a sickly red.

It looked as though the entire city was burning. The first waves had done their job well.

They flew in at under 5,000 feet and locked in on their targets, a pair of residential districts.

Harry looked down. He could see the raging firestorm below, fanned by the wind. He could see tiny homes burning.

The young sergeant shut his eyes, felt the blood drain from his cheeks. Somewhere nearby, he thought he heard a member of the crew retching.

"Bombs away!"

The bombardier's voice boomed as hundreds of napalm bombs began dropping through the bay doors.

Moments later, the plane rocked hard. Harry thought at first it was anti-aircraft guns. Then he realized it was the force from the fire erupting below, the sheer power of the mushrooming blasts buffeting the heavy bomber.

"Christ have mercy," Smitty muttered over the intercom.

"Roger that," Monroe said in a choked whisper.

When they were done, headed safely back to the base, there were no cheers, no high fives. Each man was left to his own thoughts, his own conscience.

Monroe, who'd hidden a bottle of whisky in the cockpit, took a long swig and passed it to the co-pilot, who passed it on. When the bottle returned, it was nearly empty. Not a word had been spoken.

Back at the base, they received a hero's welcome. The raid had been a tremendous success, they were told. The B-29s had dropped 1,732 tons of firebombs on Osaka, turning a 25-square-mile area into a smoldering desert of ash and ruin. Only a few bombers had gone down. Enemy resistance had been minimal. Monroe had been right about that.

Nobody said anything about the civilian death toll, but they all knew it was massive. More than 100,000, most likely. All in a single night.

Harry walked slowly with Monroe toward the tents that served as barracks. Neither man said a word. Behind them dawn was breaking, the first rays of sun gilding the fringed leaves of the coconut palms.

Both men performed a silent, hopeful calculation.

Another day, another mission, another step closer to going home.

"Who was that bastard who said 'war is hell'?" the captain drawled.

"Sherman, I think," Harry said.

"Sherman, huh? God almighty, he sure was right."

With a weak wave, he headed toward the sun, a worn photograph next to his heart.

Harry threw up behind the nearest tent he could find.

This was a story he'd never tell his grandchildren.

CHAPTER
ELEVEN

This time, all of the bleachers on one side of the high school gymnasium were rolled out and packed with people.

Concern was written on the faces of the parents, grandparents, students, school employees and community leaders huddled together on a Friday night. A Portland television news crew was on hand, along with a reporter and photographer from the Two Rivers Messenger. KTWO "Coastal Community Radio" sent someone to record the event.

Maria and Harry scanned the crowd, feeling the anxiety running through it.

"There's a lot of fear," the ex-cop said under his breath.

"Hopefully, we'll get some answers," his neighbor replied. "We need them."

Harry spotted Johnson, the detective, in the front row and pointed him out to Maria.

"If anybody has answers, it would be him."

Even the school board trustees looked nervous. They sat behind their folding table, fidgeting in their seats, as they waited for Rose to start the special meeting.

Finally, she stood, microphone in hand, and the murmuring crowd hushed.

"Thank you all for coming." Her smile had abandoned her, making her appear older and beleaguered. "We don't normally have such big attendance outside of a bond election, but … these aren't normal times."

Rose paused and lowered her head for a moment. Seeing that, many in the crowd did the same.

"We are in shock," she said. "The entire Two Rivers community. In the past six months, we have had a 14-year-old boy take his own life and now another boy from the same school has gone missing. We are all aware of the massive search that has been conducted. Many of you participated as volunteers in that effort, as did every member of this school board.

"Two Rivers is a small town filled with loving and caring people, and the news has hit us all hard. Our hearts go out to the mothers of the boys, Maria Mendez and Carla Caruthers, and we ask God to soothe their aching hearts. We have recently sent to parents a letter explaining that grief counseling is available to all students and their families, either through in-office visits or by phone.

"Tonight, we will do our best to update you as fully as possible on the status of the police investigation and afterward we'll try to answer all of your questions. I'd like to start by inviting Detective Johnson to speak. Thank you."

Johnson, wearing a rumpled navy blazer, accepted the mic from Rose. His blank expression was hard to read: somewhere on the scale between annoyance and boredom.

He opened with a monotonal recap of the month-long search for

Nate Caruthers, reciting the number of officers involved, the massive staff hours and overtime, and the specialized equipment and teams called in, ranging from the chopper to the dive boat and dog handlers.

The detective said no evidence had surfaced to date about the boy's whereabouts after he stepped off the school bus in Sunny Slope that fateful afternoon.

"We had forensic teams comb the boy's bedroom and the rest of the home and found no indications of foul play. There was also no note left behind that could offer clues," he said, scowling slightly. "But we do know that he was depressed and possibly suicidal, based on his mother's account, drawings we found and searches he made on his computer shortly before he disappeared."

Johnson scanned the crowd and saw Harry. The two locked eyes for a moment.

"Some people have speculated that the two cases are related," the cop said. "One theory presented to me by a well-intentioned person has it that the boys may have become involved in some kind of criminal activity and that it led to Sam Mendez's suicide and Nate Caruthers' disappearance ... or 'homicide,' as this individual described it."

There were rumblings in the crowd, prompting the detective to quickly continue.

"But we have zero evidence of a homicide and after many weeks of investigation have found no credible links between the tragedies. In the meantime, we are asking the public to use our toll-free hotline to call with any tips or information. I can promise you that all leads will be pursued."

Johnson returned to the bleachers as one of the trustees rose to his feet.

"I'm Herb Brooks with an update on the district's internal investigation. At the previous board meeting, you may recall, Ms. Mendez urged the board to investigate whether there are other students, particularly in our middle school, whose academic performance may have suddenly declined.

"We were disappointed to learn that approximately six students, all boys between 12 and 14 years old, were in danger of failing, and we have immediately responded by making tutoring services available to those families at no cost. While some of the teachers involved did notify parents of the slip in performance, that was not true in all cases, and we are changing district policies to make such notifications mandatory in the future. I would like to thank Ms. Mendez for bringing this to our attention."

Harry looked at Maria, who was shaking her head.

"They're sweeping it under the rug," she whispered. "Tutoring? *Notifications?*"

Rose invited people in the audience to ask questions. "Please raise your hand and Lucy here will bring the portable mic to you."

Scores of hands waved in the air. Lucy, a dimpled high school senior who was a school board intern, started with the first row on the far right.

A man dressed in his blue janitorial service coveralls stood and glared at the trustees.

"All due respect, but those two boys knew each other and attended some of the same classes. Them both gone months apart? *Seems connected to me.*"

The man sat in a huff, and Lucy, moving fast enough to make her ponytail bounce, dashed up several rows to a thirtyish woman in a pink pantsuit.

"The Mendez boy's note said 'I hate what I've become.' That sounds like he was caught up in something very bad."

A pale man in a brown sport coat added: "What aren't the police telling us?"

There were shouts of agreement from the crowd, prompting Johnson to again stand. His scowl was now plainly evident. He didn't wait for the mic.

"When a young teenage boy says he hates what he's become, it could mean anything. Boys that age are learning about sexuality, dealing with massive peer pressure. ... We can't let fear lead to rampant speculation," he said in a booming voice.

Members of the school board were nodding in agreement when, at one end of the gym, there was a commotion. Carla Caruthers emerged, striding across the polished wood floor to the center of the bleachers. Harry, watching, remembered that powerful stride. And the slap to the face that followed.

"I wasn't going to be here today. I've done enough crying," she said. "But I decided to come because I still have hope that we'll find out what happened to my son, and that whoever did this will be arrested and sent to prison for the rest of their life."

She surveyed the crowd, eyes burning with heartbreak and anger.

"I believe Nate was murdered. And I believe the killer lives here, in Sunny Slope."

"Oh my God!" a woman in the crowd exclaimed. Others, shocked, covered their faces with their hands. The average annual murder rate in Two Rivers was a hair over zero.

Rose stood in hopes of calming things down, but Caruthers wasn't finished.

"The police aren't telling you this because they don't want you to panic," she said, her face now contorted with rage. "But you deserve to know the truth. Maria Mendez is right. Someone is preying on our children and we have to stop it. We have to stop it right now. *Now!!*"

She stormed out, brushing past the shocked intern and the reporters, who pressed forward hoping to snag an interview.

"Wow," Harry muttered as the gym's big glass doors slammed shut.

He turned to Maria and saw a tear rolling down her cheek. Her hands were trembling, mirroring his own.

"Let's go," he said. "You've heard enough."

CHAPTER
TWELVE

The first thing Harry thought as he and Honey crossed the street was that he must have the day wrong.

It couldn't really be noon on a Saturday. The playground was half empty.

Fred was at the chess table waiting for his friend, newspaper opened on his lap. Smoke curled lazily from his pipe.

"Where are all the kids? What's going on?" Harry asked, wrinkling his brow.

Fred tossed the paper on the table. The headline on the front page of the Messenger was "Two Rivers Neighborhood Fears Child Predator."

"I believe there is a panic going on," the German said. "Parents are not letting their children play."

"Oh no," Harry said, dropping onto his stool. "This may be partly my doing."

"How so, my friend?"

"My next-door neighbor Maria lost her son to suicide, and she's convinced he got into some trouble that drove him to it. A few months later, the Caruthers boy vanished. He had been depressed and suicidal, too. I talked to that mother and she also suspects foul play."

"I see. And how are you involved?"

"I promised Maria that I'd help her get answers. Unfortunately, I may have contributed to this panic."

He looked around and saw only a handful of children on the swings and slide. The adjacent lawn area was still filled with sunbathers, but they were adults.

Fred took a drag on his pipe and studied Harry's face.

"Hand me the shoebox. I think more clearly when we play."

They set up the pieces and Fred made the first move.

"Tell me everything you know. Perhaps I can be of some assistance," he said.

Eager for some feedback, Harry told his friend the chilling details of how Sam hanged himself, the contents of his note, the coveted shoes that had been set on fire.

Then he gave a thorough, policeman's recap of his meeting with Carla Caruthers, including the constant looks over her shoulder for the shadowy figure she believed was watching her, and how she told the crowd at the emergency meeting that she was certain her son had been murdered.

Harry then recapped his frustrating meeting with the local detective, who resisted the notion that the cases were connected.

When he was finished, Fred set his pipe down.

"You were a policeman for 35 years?"

"That's right."

"And do you trust your instincts when it comes to criminal behavior and such things?"

"I do."

"So, why then are you not doing so now? Two boys may be dead. Others may be in danger as we speak. Parents are afraid. The police department is failing to act. Something must be done."

"What are you proposing I do?"

"Not you, my friend. *Us.* I propose that we investigate. If the police cannot find the villain, then we shall."

Harry grunted. "In America, we don't believe in vigilantes."

"Ah, but true vigilantes mete out justice in their own perverted way, yes? They are too consumed with vengeance to know when to stop. We would not make such a mistake. We would find the suspect, collect the necessary evidence and present it to the authorities. Justice would be served, and our part in it need never be disclosed."

"You have no training. I don't want to involve you in this."

"It's true that I am no policeman. But it is not true that I have no training. Don't forget – I am a veteran of combat, just like yourself."

Harry shook his head. He was tempted to enlist Fred, use his keen intellect to bounce off his ideas and information as they developed, but he didn't want to put his civilized friend in harm's way. Just asking questions the wrong way and of the wrong people could do that, he knew.

"I'm doing this for my grandson, to protect him. You have no children. This isn't your fight. And besides, this isn't some graffiti artist we're looking for. It could be a stone-cold killer. A very dangerous man."

Fred slapped the chess board hard enough to upset some of the pieces.

"Did you not hear me when I explained why I come here, to this playground? The innocence of these children must be protected. I will investigate on my own if I must, but I prefer to be your partner."

Harry was taken aback by the fiery look in his friend's eyes.

"Okay, okay," Harry said, waving both hands. "We'll do it together. But promise me one thing."

"What is it?"

"That we won't become vigilantes. We won't cross the line."

"I promise."

"Oh, and one more thing."

"Yes, Harry?"

"I'm in charge."

"I assumed so," Fred said with a wry smile. "You out-rank me, after all."

———

Harry had reached the age where birthdays seemed more frivolous than festive, but he consented to Charlie's party plans for his grandson's sake.

Buster loved Harry's birthdays because they always featured floppy New York-style pizza imported from Benino's two towns away and prodigious quantities of Tillamook Udderly Chocolate ice cream.

They could have celebrated at a nice restaurant, as Charlie and Liz suggested, since 75 was a milestone and, quite frankly, the prospect of Harry reaching 80 was less than certain. But he insisted on having an intimate family get-together at his home where Honey could be part of the action. She loved ice cream, too.

During a chess match in the park a few days before, Harry casually mentioned his birthday and Fred seized on it, thoroughly delighted.

"Oh, how fun!" he declared. "You must celebrate!"

"I'd rather not, truth be told."

Fred laughed. "My dear friend, we are of a certain age that requires celebration of each passing year. It may be our last."

"If you love it so much, why don't you come?"

"Truly? I shall be there! Oh, how exciting!"

"That's enough. It's just pizza, beer and ice cream. And probably one of Liz's cakes."

"Delightful!"

Harry shook his head and turned to point to a friendly white house with silver trim across the street. "That's the one. Saturday at 6. Bring nothing."

"*Wunderbar!*"

"Knock it off. Just play."

The day of the party, Fred arrived at the house precisely at 6, ringing the bell and greeting Charlie at the front door with a big smile.

"Hello. Fred, right? I remember you from the chess game."

"Yes, that's right. Nice to see you again, Charlie."

Fred, who was wearing a suit for the occasion, saw that the other guests were wearing jeans but was unfazed. He looked around, admiring the home's broad moldings and built-in bookcases.

Charlie saw the present in Fred's hand and guided him to the guest of honor. He and Buster were in the kitchen playing with the B-29 model, the grandfather recounting the time one of the bomb racks got stuck, putting the crew in a panic.

"We could have blown to pieces right over the ocean," he was saying.

"But you saved everyone, right Grandpa?"

"Well, let's just say we lived to fight another day."

Fred tapped his friend on the shoulder and handed him a small box wrapped in shiny purple paper with a matching bow on top.

"Happy 75th birthday, Harry," he said, and everyone in the room erupted into cheers.

"Calm down, calm down. I told you not to bring anything."

"I couldn't resist," the gentleman replied.

Moments later the doorbell rang, and Charlie glanced at his father, who responded with a shrug.

The son opened the door. Maria was standing there with a smile.

Harry caught a glimpse and walked over. She gave him a hug, then handed him a gift bag with a chilled bottle of Champagne and a card inside.

"I can't stay, Mom and Dad are in the car. We're going to the movies, apparently. There aren't many theaters in their part of Costa Rica."

"Nice of you to stop by. I hate this kind of fuss."

She rolled her eyes. "I wouldn't have guessed. Well, at least try to have some fun. Talk to you later."

Maria kissed his cheek and waved goodbye.

When Harry closed the door, Charlie was standing a few feet away.

"She seems okay. I'm glad."

"Her parents have distracted her a little from her grief, I think. That's a good thing. I remember when you did that for me."

"And vice versa."

Charlie draped his arm over Harry's shoulders and they walked back to the kitchen linked.

"Time to eat," Liz announced, and in a flash everyone was at the table salivating over a pair of giant pizzas – one plain cheese, the other topped with sausage and pepperoni. Harry's purist sensibilities wouldn't allow any more exotic toppings.

"I didn't know they made them that large," Fred said in amazement, drawing laughs.

Harry surveyed the people gathered at his table, the happy faces enjoying the moment, and realized he'd been thinking about birthdays the wrong way. It was a moment that simply had to be shared.

I hope I can have a few more.

"How did you and Pops meet?" Charlie asked Fred as the table was being cleared for dessert.

"He challenged me to a chess match. The day Buster showed his grandfather the model."

"Oh right. Sorry about intruding like that. You two should have kept playing."

Fred smiled and looked at Harry. "We've played many games since then, haven't we, my friend?"

"That's right. I've even won a couple."

"Pops says you're quite the player," Charlie said.

"He is being generous. I would say that our matches are highly competitive. We have learned each other's favorite moves, so now it is even more challenging."

"Well, take it from me, Pops hates to lose. When I was in high school, our driveway basketball games were brutal. People would come over from the park to watch."

Harry chuckled. "I was just toughening you up. Your defense stunk."

The lights dimmed and Liz walked over, carefully carrying a cake dripping with chocolate icing. There were two lit candles on top – one shaped like the number 7, the other a 5. Buster had been charged with filming the moment.

"Happy birthday to Harry," she began to sing, and everyone

joined in.

Harry blew out the oversized candles, privately relieved that his lungs cooperated instead of contributing to a videotaped blooper.

When the lights brightened, his end of the table was stacked with presents.

Liz brought out Champagne glasses and handed the bottle from Maria to her husband.

"Ooh, French," Charlie said, reading the label as he loosened the cork. "The public defender's office must pay better than I thought." He turned to Fred. "How's the bubbly in Germany?"

Fred made an ugly face.

There was a pop and Charlie began filling the glasses as Liz started taking orders. "Who wants ice cream, cake or both?"

"Both!" shouted Buster.

"I know what *you* want," his mother said, smiling. She looked around the table. "Let's see, Harry, ice cream only; Charlie, a little of each. Fred, what about you?"

"I must try that delicious-looking cake," he said.

Harry raised his glass and offered a toast. "To friends and family."

The first present he opened was the purple box from Fred. He removed the lid and was surprised to see a silver pocket watch similar to the one the German carried.

The message engraved on the back read "Count Your Life By Smiles Not Tears."

The watch made the rounds and everyone looked at Fred in admiration. He blushed and said softly, "It's an old saying."

After a while, Charlie noticed that his father's tremors were worsening. His right leg was making a thumping sound under the table and the spoon in the fingers of his right hand was shaking.

Charlie gave his wife a look – the kind of clandestine communication only longtime couples share. "Well, we should let Pops rest. It's getting late."

They pulled on their coats and Buster gave Harry a squeeze.

"Thanks for everything," the 75-year-old told his guests as Honey worked the room, making her own goodbyes. "More fun than I thought it'd be."

Fred, the last to leave, slapped Harry on the back.

"Good night," Harry said. "Thanks for coming."

"My pleasure," the German replied.

Harry closed the door and walked back to the dining room, where he expected to find a mess to clean up. Somehow, Liz had already done it all. Everything was rinsed and neatly packed into the dishwasher. The leftover cake was in Tupperware he'd never seen before.

He saw Maria's gift bag on the counter and fished out the small white card. The message inside read, "Dear Harry, thank you for helping me find the truth. I know God is watching over you."

She added: "Happy hunting."

CHAPTER
THIRTEEN

Harry's first move as a clandestine investigator was to tap into the gossip spreading through Sunny Slope like an electrical current.

He'd start with the neighborhood mailman

Lou Esposito knew almost everyone in Sunny Slope from his rounds, which made him an ideal source.

Harry waited for him one afternoon, pretending to be trimming the boxwood hedges by the mailbox.

Right on time, Esposito materialized, wearing his regulation blue shirt and shorts, a bulky mail bag slung over his right shoulder.

"Hey Lou, how's it going?" Harry said with a smile.

"Not too bad. Weather's nice."

Esposito was an agreeable sort, of average size and build, with a round belly, curly brown hair and a jovial face sporting a dark goatee. He reached into his bag and handed Harry a couple of home décor catalogues that Bonnie had signed up for and he hadn't gotten around to canceling.

"What's the scuttlebutt on this missing boy situation?" Harry asked.

"People are scared," Esposito said, shrugging. "That's about it."

"I saw you at the school board meeting."

"Yeah, I had to check it out. Feel pretty bad about poor Mrs. Caruthers. And your neighbor, of course."

"What are you hearing?"

"Not much." He looked at the mostly deserted playground across the street. "It's probably all overblown. Things will get back to normal soon, I think."

"What's overblown?"

"Oh, this nonsense about a killer on the loose. It'll probably turn out to be a coupla suicidal kids. Maybe they're gay. Or bipolar. Who knows?"

"Yeah," Harry said, trying not to argue with his source. "Guess we'll know more when Nate's body is found."

"Don't hold your breath."

"Well, it's hard to commit suicide *and* hide your own body. Takes planning that I think the average 14-year-old isn't capable of."

"Interesting way to look at it. Figures that you, being a former policeman, would suspect the worst."

"I do."

The mailman leaned in and lowered his voice, even though they were alone. "If I were investigating, I'd take a hard look at Melvin."

"The Vietnam veteran?"

"Yeah. I've heard him yelling some pretty terrible things at kids passing by his house. Sexual stuff."

"Word is he's suffering from PTSD."

"That makes him dangerous in my book. But, hey, it's only what some people are saying. Have a good day. Gotta keep walking."

"Thanks, Lou. If you hear anything, can you let me know? You also live in Sunny Slope, right?"

"Sort of. The newer section, but still an easy walk. Are you helping your pals at the police station?"

"Nah, I'm just doing Maria Mendez a favor. She wanted me to ask around."

"Doubt if I'll come across anything useful, but if I do, you'll be the first to know," he promised before walking away. A few seconds later Harry heard the postman whistling.

With Honey leashed and ready, Harry was about to take a walk when Fred suddenly appeared on the sidewalk. He was wearing spotless deck shoes, pressed black jeans and a cream-colored turtleneck.

"So that's how you look when you dress casual," Harry said with a smirk. He glanced down at the wrinkled yellow polo shirt he'd been wearing for three straight days and frowned.

Fred ignored the remark. "Ready to get to work?"

Harry nodded. "Let's go see Melvin, the local Vietnam vet."

"Is he a suspect?"

"No, but his name came up when I was chatting with the mailman. We can start with him. He's always home, maybe he saw something."

———

Melvin Mathers lived with his disabled mother in one of the only houses in Sunny Slope that wasn't properly maintained.

It desperately needed a coat of paint, one window was boarded up, and several roof shingles were missing. The yard was overgrown with weeds that were a foot high.

On warm, sunny days, Melvin often sat on his porch with a bottle of booze, rocking in a chair and hurling insults at passersby. Schoolchildren knew to either bypass the home or scoot past it as quickly as possible.

But it just so happened that Melvin lived between the school bus stop and the Caruthers residence, a fact Harry passed on to Fred as they approached.

"What is your plan?" Fred asked.

"Dunno. I'm winging it."

"I think I see him on the porch."

"Great." Harry checked his watch. "Bus should be arriving any minute."

"Good thinking."

They stepped over to the edge of the park, directly across from the bus stop. Harry pulled a rubber ball out of his pocket that was dotted with tooth marks. He unhooked Honey and tossed the red ball high in the air.

The graceful golden dog raced after the ball, tracking it in the sky. It rolled to a stop in the grass and Honey snatched it in her mouth and began trotting back, tail wagging.

"Reminds me of Bruno, my German shepherd," Fred said wistfully. "Such a great companion."

After a few more tosses, the men heard the rumble of a big yellow bus. They watched as a dozen kids got off at one of Sunny Slope's four stops. They scattered on the sidewalk, book bags strapped to their backs.

"There's usually twice that many," Harry said. "Parents must be picking them up. Let's get closer and see what Melvin does."

Melvin was standing up and leaning over his porch railing. He began screaming obscenities at the passing children.

"Fuck you!"

"And fuck you, cocksucker!"

"Fuck you and your mother, too!"

Avoiding eye contact, the children pretended not to hear and hustled down the street.

Harry approached warily, but when Melvin saw the dog he launched into another foul-mouthed tirade.

"If that fucking mutt craps in my yard, I'll shoot it! Do you fucking understand me?!"

"That's enough, Melvin. Calm down."

"Shove it up your ass, old man! Who the fuck are you telling me what to do?"

"A combat veteran like yourself. Someone who knows what it's like to suffer from the past."

Melvin, silenced by the unexpected retort, sat down heavily in his wooden rocker. He had a long ponytail and a scraggly beard streaked with gray. He was wearing a tattered camouflage T-shirt, faded jeans with holes in the knees and bright blue flip-flops.

"I don't mean anything by it," he said in a quiet voice. "Just letting off steam."

"Mind if we talk for a few minutes?" Harry asked. "This is Fred, he's another war veteran."

"Okay, but if that dog shits in my yard ..."

"She won't."

There was only the one chair on the porch, so Harry and Fred leaned casually against the railing. Melvin slipped inside the house without any explanation and returned moments later with three cans of cheap beer.

Harry breathed a bit easier when his friend, an admitted beer snob, cracked open his can and took a drink. He did the same.

"So, you served in Vietnam?" Harry asked.

"Yeah, '68. Got me really fucked up." He tapped his forehead. "Doc says it could be Agent Orange. All I know for sure is I came home different. Still am."

He looked Harry up and down and guessed, "Korea?"

"No, I fought the Japanese in the Second World War."

"The fucking Japs?"

"Yeah."

"That's cool, man. At least we won that war. You came home a goddamn hero."

"We all did what we had to do. Just like you."

Harry hoped Melvin wouldn't start quizzing Fred. The German soldier thing would almost certainly set him off.

Melvin's appearance softened as a melancholy mood came over him. His eyes morphed from glazed to focused.

"I don't want to scare the kids," he said. "I-I don't know what comes over me."

Fred gave Harry a nod. It was time to start asking questions, while this veteran was lucid and self-aware.

"A 14-year-old boy who lives two blocks from here went missing a while ago. He would have passed by this place," Harry said.

"He did."

"How do you know?"

"I was sitting here, just like now. I know Nate. He's one of the only kids in the neighborhood who talks to me. I remember him looking at me when he got off the bus."

"He disappeared somewhere between the bus stop and his house. Did you see anything? Anything out of the ordinary?"

"Nah, he just looked at me and I gave him a nod, and then I went inside and grabbed another beer and he was gone. You sound like a cop. I fucking hate cops."

"I used to be one. Now I'm just looking out for the kids. If you hear anything unusual, anything that could be related to Nate, could you let us know?"

"Like, be your fucking snitch?"

"More like a concerned citizen."

"Why the fuck would I do that? I keep to myself and I like it that way."

Harry nodded. He knew he'd get nothing more out of this tortured man. "Thank you for your time – and the beer."

The visitors turned to leave. Before they reached the broken gate, Melvin blurted, "Watch that fucking dog!"

They looked back and the man on the porch was grinning. Both middle fingers were extended.

"What do you think?" Fred asked as they headed toward the playground.

"We can cross him off our list. The poor SOB is crazy, but he wouldn't harm children. Besides, they wouldn't want anything to do with him. I think the only person he'd hurt is himself."

"Agreed."

"I'm hungry. How are you at making grilled-cheese sandwiches?"

"It's one of my specialties, with tomato-basil soup, of course."

"Of course."

Harry gave Fred a friendly slap on the back.

"This partnership is working out just fine."

FOURTEEN

They were playing chess in the park when Fred suddenly said, "That's interesting."

"What's that?" Harry said, moving a bishop. Each player had only six pieces left and the game was getting fairly intense.

"Don't look, but there's a white van that's been circling the park. It's behind you now. You'll see it in a minute."

Fred pondered a counter-move as Harry looked out of the corner of his eye. Sure enough, a white van slowly drove by. The driver appeared to be fixated on a handful of children in the playground.

"That *is* interesting," Harry said. "Unmarked van, suspicious man behind the wheel …"

"What do you propose we do?"

"Let's get the plate number and if it stops, we can have a little chat with the driver. We'll say we're with the block watch."

"Is there a block watch here?" Fred quickly answered his own question. "Of course not. No need."

"Now there is."

"True. Let's finish this game and if the van is still cruising, we'll take action."

Fred moved his queen aggressively, imperiling Harry's king. "Check."

"Damn."

Harry began to retreat, but it was too late. Fred quickly had several of his pieces in position to win the game.

"I concede," Harry said.

He extended his hand and Fred grasped it.

"A valiant effort, my friend."

They dropped off the shoebox and board at Harry's place and then stood on the front porch. There was no sign of the van.

"Looks like he moved on," Harry said. "False alarm."

"Yes, perhaps. Still, I … *oh, dear.*"

The van had returned. The men observed as it made yet another slow circle around the park.

Harry dashed inside the house and returned with a piece of paper and a pen, which he handed to Fred.

"When it comes around, I'm gonna stop the driver. You go around back and write the plate number down. Take a peek in that rear window, too."

They stepped over to the curb and waited, watching as the older model Dodge Econovan made a 20 mph loop. The vehicle finally turned the corner and headed toward them. The driver appeared to be a man in his late 20s with bushy black hair and a full beard.

Harry stepped into the middle of the street and began waving his hands.

The driver, paying no attention, nearly ran him down.

He slammed on the brakes, stopping the van just a few feet from Harry, who didn't flinch. He stepped over to the driver's side.

"What the hell you doing?" the man behind the wheel snarled, rolling down his window.

"That's what we want to know. We're with the neighborhood watch. Why have you been circling the park and staring at children?"

"Fuck you, *pendejo*. I do what I want. It's a free country."

Harry felt a familiar torrent of rage building within him, reaching up to his eyes and ears, clouding his senses.

"One more time. Tell me what you're doing here," he said.

"Fuck you! Get out of my way."

Powerless to resist his tidal wave of white-hot anger, Harry yanked open the door and punched the man in the face in a fluid motion.

As the man slumped over, holding his broken nose, Harry hit him again on the back of the head with enough force to sound the horn. Then he unbuckled the man's seatbelt and dragged him out, onto the grassy fringe of the park.

As Fred stood there gawking, Harry said simply, "Check the back."

Then he turned to the man on the ground, who was bleeding and writhing in pain.

"One more time. Why are you cruising this park looking at little kids?"

"I paint houses! I'm just killing time! Stop hitting me!!"

Fred came over in a hurry. "Harry, stop. There's just paint in there."

"What's your name?" Harry asked the man, who was sitting up. His T-shirt was now soaked with blood.

"Enrique … Enrique Sanchez."

"Enrique, listen carefully. If I ever see you cruising this park again, I will break both of your legs. If you touch one of the kids, I'll shoot you. Now get the hell out here."

"You're *loco*, man," the painter said as he limped over to the van.

"The only danger here is you."

"Have a nice day," Harry said as the Econovan sped away.

Harry didn't know that the man he'd just beaten was working for Portland police as an informant in major drug cases. His record was far from clean, but he'd never been charged with a sex crime.

Moments later, a Two Rivers patrol car pulled up. The officer who stepped out recognized Harry immediately.

"We got a report about a disturbance at this location. Know anything about that, captain?"

"Just a suspicious vehicle cruising the park. We asked the driver a few questions."

"And did you also punch that driver a few times, like the caller said?"

"Of course not."

"That's good. Tensions are high enough. We don't need anyone making things worse. Understood?"

"Absolutely."

Scowling, the cop returned to his shiny black cruiser. He immediately called the chief.

Huggins listened for a few minutes then hung up.

"Damn it, Harry," he said.

———

A few years after Harry joined the force, Huggins had saved the captain from himself.

The chief had known all about the scandal in Miami, going so far as to call Harry's former boss and review the investigative findings and news reports. There had been red flags, but Huggins hired him anyway, because Harry was an experienced cop who had demonstrated courage in the field and came highly recommended.

Then one day, at the local supermarket, between the meat counter and the potato chip aisle, Harry had a meltdown.

A man was berating his 7-year-old stepson over some silly thing – a striped plastic ball that he'd plucked from a barrel and bounced too many times on the linoleum floor. Harry was off-duty but still in uniform, picking up a few things for dinner on his way home.

He saw the tattooed man in the grease-stained flannel shirt slap his stepson in the face, leaving a red mark. Moments later, he saw the man place both of his hands on the boy's shoulders and shake him violently when he didn't stop crying. Then he saw the man make a fist.

"Don't do that," Harry said.

The man paused to eye the burly cop standing less than 10 feet away. "Fuck you, I know my rights," he said.

"Get your hands off the boy, or I'll show you what that feels like."

The crying boy looked up at Harry with wide eyes. He'd suffered his stepfather's wrath before. The man shoved the child roughly out of the way, causing him to fall to the ground.

"I'd like to see you try," the man snarled, daring Harry with slitted eyes. "I'll have your badge."

Something flashed in Harry's brain, something he hadn't felt since Miami. Adrenalin began pumping, supercharging his muscles. Everything around him swirled but he could see clearly. He was in the eye of his own private hurricane.

He took one long stride and then left the ground as if propelled by an invisible force. When Harry came down he punched the man hard enough to crack his jaw and send him rolling backwards.

A woman entering the aisle with her shopping cart screamed.

Employees came running over. The boy began shaking in fear.

Harry, stunned by his sudden violence, staggered away. Outside the entrance, the hurricane fading, he pulled out his phone and called the chief.

"I've screwed up," he said.

Huggins rushed over and hustled Harry into his brown Buick.

"Wait here," the chief said. "I need to talk to a few people."

Twenty minutes later, Huggins returned, a serious look on his face. He stared at his highest-ranking officer, who was in the passenger seat shaking his head.

"It's the children, Barry. I-I can't stand watching them get hurt," Harry said, his voice scarcely audible.

"None of us can. I have three of my own. But what you just did … it's wrong. Do you see why it's wrong?"

"Yeah. I shouldn't have hit him. I … just get so filled with rage."

Huggins nodded but couldn't hide his disappointment. "Look, the guy you hit has a long rap sheet, been in and out of jail. He may sue, but it'll go nowhere. And I made sure the supermarket manager will keep this incident out of the paper."

"If you want me to turn in my badge, I will."

"No, Harry. That's not what I want. But there is something I need you to do."

"Sure, anything."

"I want you to see a psychiatrist that I've used in the past, mostly to help officers deal with trauma. She's good, and nobody else needs to know."

Harry gulped. He'd never been to a shrink. Lay down on a couch like a damn wimp while a stranger dissects the most personal details of your life? He always thought he was too tough, too resilient, to need anything like that. But after what just happened, after crushing bones in a man's face, he knew he had no choice.

"If you think it'll help."

"It will. It has to," the chief said, starting the car. "For you, it's Strike Two."

———

Strike Three would have been an older version of Harry roughing up the painter in the van, Huggins knew.

Harry wasn't a cop anymore, but did he pose a danger to the community? With the panic going on in Sunny Slope and children at risk, would he be able to keep it together?

Huggins grunted. He had his doubts. All those triggers. All that rage bottled up, ready to explode.

He picked the phone back up. A woman answered.

"Dr. Brentwood, this is Chief Huggins," he said. "I have another problem with Harry."

CHAPTER
FIFTEEN

The grimy white van pulled over by the swings. The driver stepped out.

He grabbed a little girl, the one with blonde pigtails and a pink frilly dress who'd just come from church.

The sinister man with shark-like eyes was grinning as he dragged the girl toward the van. She was screaming, but her mother and the other parents didn't notice.

Why couldn't they hear the screams?

But The Protector could. He rose from the chess table, pulled a revolver from his trench coat.

He jogged across the lawn toward the van, the barrel of the gun shining like a cross on a steeple.

No children would be harmed on his watch. *Not today.*

A warm rain was falling as he took aim.

The Protector squeezed the trigger.

And the gun … barked?

———

Harry opened his eyes and saw Honey licking his cheek.

She jumped off the bed, anticipating movement. Someone was knocking at the door.

Why so damn early? Harry glanced at the alarm and saw that it wasn't early at all. He'd seriously overslept.

Rubbing sleep from his eyes, he yawned, slipped on his plaid robe and looked out the window. He could see Charlie staring up at him from the front yard.

Pulling up the sash, Harry called out, "What the hell's the matter?"

"We need to talk, Pops. It's important. You're not answering your phone."

"Okay, okay, give me a minute."

Cursing under his breath, Harry put on his slippers, paused to touch Bonnie's picture and headed down the stairs a bit too fast. His knees ached a little when he reached the bottom.

When the door opened, Charlie didn't wait to be invited inside. He hustled past his father and made a beeline to the breakfast table.

"You know it's 10:30, right?" he asked, taking a seat.

"Yeah, I overslept. Probably the new medicine. What's so damn important?"

"Make your coffee first. I need your brain working."

"Good luck with that."

Charlie knew what his father was like first thing in the morning – grumpy and obstinate, until he had his first sips of espresso-grade coffee and became someone who could be reasoned with.

When Harry sat down with a steaming mug, Charlie cut to the chase.

"There's something wrong with Buster," he said. "It's like those other boys."

"Okay, slow down. Take it from the beginning." Harry liked his stories told in chronological order.

Charlie took a deep breath. "Do you remember when you were at the house and Buster was building that tank model?"

"Sure."

"Did you buy it for him?"

"No."

"That's what I thought. The other day, I saw another model in his room, still in the plastic. A stealth bomber."

"Didn't buy that either."

Charlie cradled his head in his hands. "Jesus," he muttered.

"Did you talk to him about it?" Harry asked, stirring his coffee. The spoon in his quaking right hand began clinking against the ceramic mug.

"Did you take your medicine?"

Harry shot his son a nasty look. "How can I when you're pulling me out of bed? Did you talk to him?"

"Not yet. I wanted to see you first, figure things out. But there's something else."

"Go on."

"His grades are starting to slip. His teacher called Liz yesterday. Buster's always been on the honor roll, a top student. Pops, I'm worried. His best friend Chase was over the other night, and he looked morose. He's usually a chatterbox and I couldn't get a single word out of him. What's going on with these boys?"

"I don't know, but it's good you're on top of it."

"What if Buster becomes suicidal? What if he suddenly disappears?"

Tears flooded Charlie's eyes and Harry slid his chair over to wrap a beefy arm around him.

After a few minutes, Charlie gathered himself and Harry got up to get a coffee refill.

"I'm afraid that if Liz and I question him, he'll clam up," Charlie said. "We might have better luck if you tried first."

"Dunno about that. Maria asked me to try to get Sam to open up. We all know how that worked out."

"Yeah, but wasn't that after he'd become seriously depressed? As far as I can tell, Buster is still happy. At least I think he is. We watched a baseball game last night. He seemed okay."

"Son, I'm not good at that kind of stuff. You, of all people, should know."

"What stuff?"

"Emotions. Tears. All of that."

"Well, you just comforted me – despite yourself."

Harry sighed. "Maybe I'm getting soft in my old age."

"*Please*, Pops? Do it for me. I'm scared. Liz, too."

Harry could see the panic in his son's eyes. There was no way to refuse. "Okay, I'll do it. Just don't count on any major revelations."

"You think this may be all connected. Four boys?"

The ex-cop rubbed his whiskered chin. "Hard to say. I mean, the ages are similar. They go to the same school. There's that whole gift thing. But the other boys live in Sunny Slope. Buster doesn't."

"True, but he's at your place several times a week, and he likes hanging out at the park. That may be how the kids are getting targeted."

Harry shook his head. "What am I missing?"

"Pops, I know you and Fred are doing some kind of investigation," Charlie said. "I heard about the painter in the van. Did you really break his nose?"

Harry exhaled loudly. "If you'd have been there, you'd have done the same thing. Circling the playground, eyeing the kids … disgusting."

"You think roughing him up is a good idea … *after Miami?*"

Harry winced, stung by the reference.

Years ago, he was a sergeant out on patrol in a tough part of Little Havana when he saw a Hispanic man dragging a young boy into a car. It was the middle of the afternoon. The boy was screaming in Spanish. Harry didn't know the language, but he knew panic when he saw it. He stopped his car and came running over.

Letting his emotions get the best of him, Harry tackled the man and clubbed him in the head with the butt of his gun. Several times. It would turn out that the 10-year-old was the man's son and the father, a Cuban, had just caught him spray-painting graffiti on the side of a neighborhood bakery and was taking him home to be disciplined.

Outraged, the Cuban-American community demanded that Harry be fired. Protests fueled by the victim's prolonged hospital stay didn't help. An internal investigation was launched and Harry was suspended with pay. He resigned before the findings were completed.

While the review board ultimately found he had used excessive force in repeatedly striking the man, it determined that the officer had made a split-second judgment call, reasonably convinced that a child's life was in imminent danger. Had he stayed in Miami, he would have been reinstated. Maybe even praised by his fellow officers for being a tough guy.

Deep down, though, Harry knew he was wrong. The boy was his son's age and seeing him being dragged into a car like that unleashed a hidden fury – one he hadn't realized he harbored. It clouded his judgment, obscuring the fact that he should have shouted a command before resorting to violence.

"Miami was a long time ago. I have nothing against Hispanics," Harry told his grown son across the breakfast table. "I'm protecting little kids."

Charlie reached out and put a hand on his father's vibrating knee. "I'm glad you're doing it," he said. "The kids here need protecting."

"So, you believe me – about a predator?"

"I always did. I just was hoping it wasn't true."

———

Two days later, on a breezy Sunday afternoon, Harry and Buster strolled over to the lawn area of the park.

In Buster's hands was a big blue kite with a long white tail that Fred had made using some mysterious Bavarian process.

Charlie had taught his son the basics, so it was no surprise that on the first try, the kite took flight, soaring and dipping on the wind currents.

"Wow, thatta boy! Fly that thing!" Harry enthused.

"It's a beauty, Gramps. Look how it moves."

"Let it out a little. Let's bump that cloud."

Buster smiled as he let out more string. Harry studied the joy on the 13-year-old's face and relaxed a little. There was no comparison to Sam's grim demeanor.

Chase soon joined them and the trio took turns with the kite for a while. Harry showed the boys a couple of dramatic dive-bombing tricks that could have shattered Fred's handiwork but instead drew a smattering of applause from a group of sunbathers nearby.

After about an hour, Chase, sadness filling his face, said in a tiny voice that he had to go. He walked off without saying goodbye.

"What's that about?" Harry asked, watching the young teen cross the park. "Where's he off to in such a hurry?"

Buster shrugged. "Don't know. Probably going home for dinner."

Harry glanced at his watch, saw it was 2 p.m. *Charlie was right to worry. What's going on with these boys?*

They decided to reel in the kite and play a little chess. Harry was teaching his grandson the game.

When they reached the table by the playground, Buster tried to hand Harry the kite. The grandfather refused.

"That's yours. Fred made it for you. He'd be upset with me if I kept it."

Buster gave Harry a hug. "Awesome! It's such a sweet kite!"

"Glad you like it. Now you have to name it."

The boy thought for a minute, then brightened.

"I got it! The Blue Baron."

Harry grinned. "Perfect. German like Fred, but fun like an old-fashioned biplane. Help me set up the board. Let's see if you remember which pieces go where."

As they played, Harry eased into a gentle interrogation.

"Your model-building skills are getting really good. No excess cement, extra plastic trimmed out … And it looks like you still have all your fingers."

Buster laughed. "Just a few nicks."

"That Israeli tank. Must have been tough."

"Really tough. Those treads! They're supposed to move, but I put a little too much glue on the other parts."

"Well, it looks great."

"Thanks, Gramps."

"Hey, you've heard about those boys from your school, right?"

"You mean Sam and Nate?"

"That's right."

"I knew them. We rode the same bus. Something bad happened to them, didn't it?"

Harry nodded sadly. "Yes, Buster, and I'm trying to figure out what it was. I was hoping you could help me."

Buster, saying nothing, plucked the black king from the board and began rolling it in his palm.

"Just tell me what you know, that's all," Harry continued. "Maybe you can help me protect other kids, yourself included."

"Okay, I guess."

"Did Sam or Nate ever say anything about what they were into? Anything strange?"

Buster shook his head. "They just bragged a lot."

"About what?"

"About their stuff. Sam had these awesome Air Jordans, and Nate always seemed to have cool video games."

"Bet that made you a little jealous."

"A little. I asked Dad if I could get those Jordans for Christmas. He said they were too expensive."

Harry knew that was true. He was the one who had advised Charlie not to spoil his son with such an extravagant gift.

"Sam and Nate's parents didn't buy them those things. They don't know where they came from. Do you know?"

Buster suddenly looked pale. He put the king on the table and began studying his feet.

"No."

"There's a man in the neighborhood, isn't there? A man who gives gifts to kids."

"Maybe."

"Buster, I need you to tell me who that person is. I need to talk to him, make sure everything is okay."

"I can't."

"I just want to ask him a few questions. He may be able to help us find out what happened to Nate."

"I can't."

"Why not?"

"Because he made me swear to keep it a secret. He said people wouldn't understand. I won't give you his name. You can't make me."

Harry nodded. "I won't make you do anything," he said. "I promise. But that man, that's who gave you the models, isn't it?"

Buster suddenly burst into tears and jumped to his feet. He began running through the playground as fast as he could.

Harry gave chase but after a few minutes, he had to stop. He leaned over, chest heaving, trying to catch his breath.

Seeing no trace of his grandson, he grabbed the kite and chess pieces and went home. He called Charlie's office number.

"Pops, what's up? Did you talk to him?"

"I did, but he got upset and ran off."

"Ran off?

"Yeah, I couldn't catch up to him. Sorry."

"He's probably running home. He's done it before for track practice. I'm leaving work now, I'll pick him up. What did you learn?"

"I think he got those models from a man in the neighborhood, but he took off before I could get it out of him."

"Jesus."

"Don't say anything to Buster. I'll come over tonight."

"He won't say anything more now."

"Maybe not, but I have an idea. An old policeman's trick."

"Do I want to know what it is?"

"Probably not. Just let me know that he's safe."

CHAPTER
SIXTEEN

"He's out back, on the deck. I think he's waiting for you."

Charlie was hugging his wife tightly when Harry arrived.

"You told him I was coming?"

"No, he just knew somehow. He came home out of breath, went up to his room and smashed his models to pieces, even the new one in the box. He's been sitting outside ever since."

"Poor kid. Let me see him alone."

"Okay, Pops."

"Please be gentle, Harry," Liz whispered with frightened eyes.

Harry nodded and walked down the hall and through the kitchen to the French sliding glass door. The outdoor lights were off, but the glow from the house was enough to put Buster in silhouette.

With a hard pull of the door with his trembling right hand, Harry stepped onto the cedar deck that overlooked a wide expanse of lawn sloping down to the river. The sky was turning from blue to black. The first stars were twinkling.

"Hey, Buster," Harry said, settling into an Adirondack chair about five feet away from his grandson, who was perched on a chaise lounge. "Sorry if I scared you earlier."

Buster kept staring straight ahead at nothing in particular. He had a defiant look in his eyes.

"I'm not going to answer any questions," he said. "Mom and Dad already tried."

"I didn't come here to ask you anything. Besides, that doesn't matter anymore."

Harry let those words hang in the air for a minute or two. He watched as Buster slowly made eye contact.

"Why not?"

"It's all over, Buster. The police are on to him."

"Who?"

"The man who gave you and the other boys those gifts."

"Really?"

"Yeah. You have nothing to worry about now."

Without saying a word, Buster walked over to the shed where his parents kept their lawn and garden tools and supplies.

A few minutes later, the boy reappeared with a shoebox. He placed it on the table next to Harry and opened the lid. Inside were new Nike basketball shoes in red and black, the colors of Buster's favorite NBA team, the Portland Trail Blazers.

Harry eyed Buster, who had returned to the chaise lounge. The boy suddenly looked much older than 13. The aura of innocence that had enveloped him like a warm blanket was gone.

"Nate told me about him one day, said he was a professional photographer who also made movies," the boy said in a far-away voice. "Nate said if I posed for him or acted in a movie, I'd get this really cool stuff.

"He brought me and Chase over to the man's house one day after school. I'm not going to tell you his name, but I recognized him. The man told us that if we posed for a few pictures in his basement studio, he'd give us a present. So we did. When we were done, he said we could take anything we liked from his stash of games and toys and stuff. So, I took the tank model. Chase took a shooter game.

"A few days later, Nate handed me a note at school. It was from the man, asking me to come back for more pictures. I did, because I really wanted the stealth fighter I saw the last time. He had me put on a swimsuit."

Buster gulped and stared into the dark.

"The last time, he said he had a really special gift for me if I did a short movie with him. He showed me this rack of awesome new basketball shoes, told me to find my size and I did. Then he asked me to take off all my clothes. … I knew it was wrong. … I ran out of there, but I kept the shoes. I-I shouldn't have."

Harry shook his head. "How long ago was that?"

"Last week – Wednesday."

In a sudden fury, the young teen jumped up and threw the box off the deck. The shoes tumbled out onto the lawn.

Then he crumpled weakly into Harry's arms.

"I'm sorry, I'm sorry," he sobbed as the old man wrapped him up. "I didn't do anything bad, but Chase … he went back."

"It's okay," Harry said, his big hand cupping Buster's head. "It's all over now."

Minutes passed before Buster got up and wiped his eyes. Harry stood next to him and said, "Will you go with me to the police, tell them what you just told me?"

The boy stepped back. "No!" he shouted. "And you can't make me!"

"Nobody's making you do anything, Buster. But can you tell me why? Why won't you talk to the police?"

Buster turned away, looking toward the river. "Because of Chase. His parents don't know. And, besides, you promised me."

Harry nodded. He had indeed assured his grandson that he wouldn't drag him down to the police station, as foolish as that now seemed.

"Pick up those shoes," he told Buster. "I think we need to send a message."

"What do you mean?"

"Do you trust me?"

"Yeah, sure."

"The police haven't made the arrest yet. They're still gathering evidence. But we're going to put those damn shoes in this man's front yard and set them on fire."

Sam had set fire to his sneakers shortly before taking his own life. He was trying to set things right, cleanse himself of as much evil as he could, Harry figured. While tragic, there was a touch of courage in that act.

What the old veteran was about to do, there was nothing secretive about it. It would be a threat made in public and written in fire: I'M COMING FOR YOU.

"What if he gets mad?" Buster asked, looking frightened.

"He won't. He'll know he's been caught. He'll stop what he's doing."

"But what if he doesn't?"

"Then I'll make sure he does. Me and the police. I still have friends down at the station."

"Okay."

"Buster?"

"Yeah?"

"Sometimes in life, it takes guts to be honest," Harry said, brushing his grandson's cheek with his fingers. "Thanks for being brave – for telling the truth."

———

Minutes later, Buster guided his grandfather to the house with the studio.

It was about a half-mile from the park, in a newer subdivision built in the 1940s that Harry seldom visited. The large front windows were bracketed by white shutters. A stone path led to the curved front door painted fire-engine red. A small lawn flowed around a Japanese maple and some azalea bushes, all neatly pruned.

Harry had always imagined the house of the neighborhood's predator would be more like Melvin's – a shambles.

The downstairs lights were off, but Harry saw a glow coming from an upstairs bedroom. The curtains were drawn. He stepped out of his idling black pickup, the never-worn shoes in his hands. He laced them together, then soaked them with lighter fluid.

Glancing at Buster, who was watching nervously from the passenger seat, Harry said, "Stay here. I'll light this, then we'll take off. No sense being around when the fire truck comes."

Harry hung the shoes over the home's belly-high wooden front gate. He struck a match.

Flames were leaping a foot in the air as he returned to the truck. Buster looked at the fire and nodded.

"Message delivered," Harry said, driving away.

His policeman's trick had worked. He now knew where the suspect lived. Whoever it was.

Justice will soon be served, he thought.

CHAPTER
SEVENTEEN

"You want to do *what?*"

Fred stared at his friend in disbelief.

"You heard me," Harry said.

"I thought you didn't want to be a vigilante. Breaking into a house sounds like crossing that line, yes?"

They sat across from each other at Harry's breakfast table, sipping coffee.

"The police are doing squat," Harry said. "Kids are being harmed and they're doing nothing. It's up to us. We need to see what this man with the movie camera is up to – then the detective and the chief have to take us seriously."

"Or we can search property records and give the detective a name."

"What if he's renting the place? Besides, we need to check out that basement. Sounds like a porn studio. Maybe we can find some evidence."

Fred frowned in a stern way. "Now you want to break into this man's home *and* steal things?"

"Quick in and out. Just a few minutes. To confirm what Buster told me."

"You told me to warn you about turning into a vigilante, yes? I'm giving you that warning."

"Look, I know how the investigative process works. Maybe a stakeout, followed by a voluntary interview of the suspect at the station, followed by a search warrant. It could take weeks, with the suspect given every opportunity to conceal or destroy evidence. And that's if they believe us. How many kids may be harmed in the meantime?"

"Buster could identify him."

"Yeah, but his photo sessions were consensual, and he says there was nothing sexual about it. He ran out before it got that far. But I am certain this man is linked to Sam and Nate. It's up to us to find the proof."

"Why didn't you get the name of the man from Buster?"

"I promised him I wouldn't ask him any more questions, and besides, I tricked him into taking me to the house."

Fred grinned, making his green-gold eyes shine. "I'm glad it didn't burn down."

"Yeah, me, too."

"The item in today's paper blamed 'hooligans.' It didn't name the homeowner."

"I saw that. I knew the fire department would respond quickly. It was worth it to see Buster smile."

The aging veterans drank their caffeinated brew in silence for a few minutes, thinking things over.

"We're a little long in the tooth to become burglars," Fred said.

"You don't have to join me," Harry said. "I can do it alone."

"And what kind of partner would I be then? I think we should do this thing together or not at all."

"So …?"

"So, we become burglars for a night," Fred said, relenting. "When?"

"Tonight. Wear black."

———

Hours later, they sat in Harry's Chevy Silverado, parked on the street.

There was no sign of activity in the blue house, no lights on in any of the rooms. The driveway was empty.

Harry checked the miniature flashlight in his lap, turning it on and off. He pulled on his black leather gloves.

"Have you done this sort of thing before?" Fred asked, watching.

"Never," Harry said, handing his accomplice a matching flashlight and pair of gloves.

"That's a relief."

"Come on, let's go. Let's see if we can get in through that basement window on the side there."

"Won't the neighbors see?"

Harry shook his head. "Looks like a perfect blind spot."

They stepped out of the black truck and rushed over to the side of the house. Harry pulled hard on the window and it groaned, opening about an inch.

"It's not locked, just stuck. Probably painted shut. Give me a hand."

After a couple of tries, the window swung toward them with a loud creak.

"I'm going in," Harry said, turning onto his stomach and pushing his legs through.

Moments later, Fred saw the beam of the flashlight.

"Come on," Harry whispered. "We have to move fast."

By the time Fred made it into the basement, Harry was already off exploring what appeared to be some kind of home recording studio, complete with a stage, lights, props and a video camera mounted on a tripod.

"Hey, come over here," Harry called out.

On the other side of the stage were built-in shelves filled with dozens of shoeboxes. It looked like a mall sporting goods store.

"Jesus, they're all in youth sizes," Harry observed.

Fred opened a large chest and saw it was brimming with a variety of toys, all new and still in their packages. There were Nerf guns, models, tennis racquets and other prizes that young teens might desire. Next to the chest was a zippered sports bag.

"Wonder what's in this," Fred said.

"Open it and see."

Fred pulled the zipper and was astonished to see video games still wrapped in plastic. He held one up to Harry.

"There must be dozens of them," the German said.

"This isn't normal."

"Definitely not."

Harry used his light to check his watch. The plan had been to get in and out as quickly as possible. "We have a couple of minutes left," he said. "Let's find some kind of evidence."

The men searched around the studio and then suddenly Harry broke the silence.

"Got it!"

He hustled over and Fred saw him holding a videotape labeled

"Vol. 19."

Harry stuffed it inside his sweatshirt and turned toward the window. Then they heard the sound of a car pulling up in front of the house.

"Crap!" Harry said under his breath. *"Go!!"*

As they dashed to the window, they could hear the front door open and close.

"I'll give you a boost," Harry said, linking his hands and pushing Fred up through the gap.

There was the sound of heavy footsteps above, and then the basement door opened with a squeak.

"Pull me up," Harry whispered, putting his hands up through the window.

He could hear someone coming down the stairs, less than 20 feet away.

Just as Fred pulled his friend out on the grass, the basement lights switched on.

The men gently closed the window and ran to the pickup.

"Think he saw us?" Fred asked.

"No, we're good."

"Thank God."

Then the color drained from Harry's face, giving him a ghostly pallor.

His flashlight was missing.

———

"There's a problem," the man said into his phone.

He stood in the basement, next to the shelf of pre-edit videotapes he'd meticulously arranged. One was missing; he knew right away.

Traces of dirt stood out on the pristine gunmetal gray concrete floor. He followed the trail to the window. When he looked down and saw the flashlight, his suspicions were confirmed.

Someone had broken in. *Someone knew.*

That person was undoubtedly Harry Bolden, the man who'd set his grandson's basketball shoes on fire. He watched the pickup truck drive away, but when he called 911 he kept that knowledge to himself. He didn't want any cops around asking questions.

Now, though, things had changed. The intruder had to be silenced – quickly, before things spiraled out of control. Before Bolden convinced the police to investigate.

The man had made the call in a cold sweat. The people he worked for were savages. He knew everyone was expendable to them, even him.

He'd made them huge amounts of money on the international black market and this was his first time seeking help. But being needy was risky. Nobody had to tell him that.

Over the phone, he could sense the silent cost-benefit analysis being done by the boss he knew only as D.

He wouldn't tell D about the charred high-tops. They'd assume he'd lost control of the operation and would order him to shut it down. Instead, he did his best to speak calmly.

"Do you have a name?" D asked. There was no discernible emotion, just an eerie, gravelly voice created by a computer.

"Harry Bolden, an ex-cop. He broke in, stole a tape."

"Has he gone to the police?"

"Not yet." The man was only guessing, but in situations such as this it was best to project a level of certainty.

There was a long pause.

The man in the basement gulped and suddenly regretted making the call. He should have handled the situation himself, quietly, like he did the last time.

"We will send someone," the voice said.

PART TWO

BAVARIAN IN EXILE

CHAPTER
EIGHTEEN

Friedrich Von Stiller sat at his piano and played one of his sonatas, composed shortly before his wife died.

While the music was meant to be festive, he played it in a mournful way, like someone turning "Happy Birthday" into a dirge.

As he caressed the keys, the polished Sauter upright translating his every touch into sounds dripping with emotion, he gazed through the window of his penthouse and realized just how lonely he was.

He didn't see the happy people below, strolling along the waterfront on a sun-drenched morning. He didn't notice the lovers walking arm in arm. He didn't enjoy the otters floating playfully on the river.

All he saw and felt was misery and gloom.

After a menacing ending flourish, Fred found himself holding back tears. He sat on the padded bench, frozen, for several minutes.

It wasn't until his thoughts turned to Harry and Sunny Slope that he managed to summon the strength to stand.

He had discovered a new purpose in helping his friend fight the evil that had taken root in the tranquil hilltop neighborhood. And even though inner voices strenuously warned him of the risks of getting too involved, of sinking too deep, he'd defied them to the point of interrogating people and breaking into a home in search of evidence.

But they found the proof they were looking for, so Fred told his voices to quiet down. He had work to do, to protect innocent children.

Harry had called first thing in the morning, urging him to come over as soon as he could. Buster's parents would be there.

But Fred was afraid. He knew his friend would want him to see what was on the videotape and that was something he didn't think he could stomach. He wasn't as tough as Harry, the hardened former cop. Whatever was on that tape would likely give him nightmares, and he already had enough of those.

And yet he managed to rise from the piano, brush his mane of silver hair, pull on a burnt-orange windbreaker and step out the door. He descended the two flights of stairs as if gently pushed by an invisible force. He'd see this thing with Harry through. He owed the children that much at least.

As he left the lobby and spilled onto the sidewalk, a man of about the same age stopped and tipped his fedora.

"Morning, Mr. Von Stiller," the man said, quite formally. "I will have your rent today. Slide it under your door?"

"That would be fine. Thank you, Peter. Have a good day."

"And you do the same."

It was exactly a half-mile walk up to Sunny Slope, with some of the streets steep enough to cause his thighs to burn. But Fred had come to enjoy the exercise and fresh air that filled his lungs. He folded the thin local newspaper under his arm and began walking in his usual loping strides.

He had discovered the neighborhood shortly after moving to Two Rivers, drawn by the views and shrieks of children at play. Soon, instead of reading and smoking his pipe alone in his apartment, he claimed a seat on one of the benches at the playground. The one closest to the swings.

There, in that special place, the pain lingering in his heart would melt. There, he could be Fred, the refined gentleman with trusting eyes and a kind smile. The assumed grandfather.

Not the miserable man who lost the only woman he'd ever loved and was living thousands of miles away in a rain-washed land, banished by his own family.

A Bavarian in exile.

On this morning, his hopes for a tonic were dashed. As he neared the swings, he could see they were still. There were no children waiting impatiently for a turn on the twisty slide or the springy horse. There were no parents to urge caution or kiss a scraped knee.

The playground was deserted despite it being a pleasant summer day. Fred could feel the void, as if he'd become connected to the community's beating heart and was now experiencing its sickness.

He pressed Harry's doorbell and took a deep breath. He'd do what he could.

For the children.

Hildy had lifted him from his gloom the first time.

It was her surprising announcement that she wasn't merely pregnant. She was going to have twins.

Friedrich heard the news and smiled for the first time in a long while.

The composer had weathered a dozen surgeries on his shattered right hand and taught himself how to play the piano again, only to discover his inspiration had abandoned him, rendering him unable to write music. His album went unfinished, concert dates unfulfilled. His promising career was over. The surgeons couldn't save it. All it had taken was a slip in the wildflower-dotted Bavarian hills. A cruel slip of fate.

But his joy had returned after he dropped to his knees, pressing his head against his wife's swollen belly.

"There are really two babies in there?"

"Yes, darling. Your two daughters."

"Daughters," he repeated dreamily. "Your intuition is never wrong, my love."

"Elsa and Emma."

Friedrich rose to his feet and kissed his wife's soft lips.

"And you are feeling well?" he asked.

Hildy laughed and ruffled her husband's dark hair. She was wearing a cotton-and-lace maternity dress that had been tailored to accommodate an extra-large bump. The pregnancy had brought out the beauty in her round face, making her creamy skin glow.

"Yes, I am well and the babies are, too, the doctor says."

"You should rest."

"Hmm. Now that you know I am carrying twins, you are twice as concerned about my health, it appears."

Friedrich bowed. "As it should be, my lady."

"Well, I'm going to the benefit tonight. It may be the last thing I do before I get too fat to move about in public. You promised to get the nursery ready, remember?"

"Ah, yes, the nursery. Shall we expand the room?"

"No, silly. Just arrange for a second crib. Set them close to each other. Twins cannot be separated. They are connected emotionally, or so I have read."

"Twins," he said, drinking it in. "What a marvelous gift. Soon, we will be a family."

"And you will be a most excellent father," Hildy said, squeezing him tight. "Just don't spoil them too much."

"That, my love, I cannot promise."

———

They lived in a stunning Tudor home best described as a small mansion in a wooded oasis south of Munich that Hildy had inherited from her wealthy family.

The house boasted six bedrooms and four bathrooms. There was also a stable with several horses and 10 acres of grounds that included a majestic fountain decorated with cherubs and a rose garden that painted rainbows with its blossoms. Behind the main house was a small structure of similar design with quarters for the butler, housekeeper and gardener. A gourmet chef and veterinarian visited often.

Hildy, a talented interior designer, had been very much in demand among Germany's rising post-war elite. A striking blonde with long, toned legs, she could have any man she desired. The fact that she was also rich made her even more attractive in the eyes of potential suitors.

The night she met Friedrich, she was in her mid-30s, fiercely independent, and not at all looking for love.

It happened at a classical concert held at the Munich opera house. Hildy was seated in a luxury box above and to the right of the stage.

Friedrich had just finished performing one of his original works to a standing ovation from the capacity crowd. When the pianist took his bow, he saw the beautiful woman in the box, on her feet, clapping.

He smiled and she felt her pulse quicken as if he'd shot a miniature lightning bolt at her heart.

Before the opera house emptied, an usher delivered to her a note that read, "I am entranced by your exquisite beauty – The Pianist."

Hildy allowed the barest trace of a smile to flicker across her painted lips.

She bid goodbye to the others in the box and slipped the note into her clutch. As she stepped into the carpeted hallway, Friedrich was standing there, breathing a bit hard after dashing from the backstage area. He was still wearing his bow tie and tails.

"Madam, it is a pleasure," he said, bowing slightly.

"Is this how musicians flirt?" she asked. "With notes like Cyrano?"

He laughed. "No, I do my own writing. I just wanted to create this moment. Is it working?"

"It's too early to say. You could do this sort of thing regularly, in which case it would be quite boring. Although, I must say, it seems risky to be so forward. I could be married or engaged. My betrothed could be punching you in the nose right now."

"Ah, but you are Hildy Steggar, are you not? And by some miracle, I am told you are not married."

"I see you've done your research. I don't know whether to be flattered or frightened."

Friedrich gave her a wink. "Actually, it's common knowledge in the orchestra that the Steggar family owns that box. And when I saw you, I knew who you were. … But, to your point, no, I don't make it a habit to write notes to beautiful women."

Hildy folded her arms across her chest and gave the handsome pianist an impatient look.

"Could you get to the point, sir, while we are both still young? What are your intentions?"

Friedrich stepped closer and gazed into her ocean-blue eyes.

"Would you give me the pleasure of your company this evening? I know a wonderful bistro a couple of blocks from here that stays open late."

"No, sir." Her half-smile, equal parts mysterious and mischievous, had returned. "I have plans. But you may call me later."

She wrote her private number on a business card and handed it to him, then began walking away.

Pressing the card against his heart, he shouted after her.

"I will! *I will!*"

———

He did call. And, to his great relief, she answered.

Two days later, they were seated at the bistro by the opera house sipping French wine and sharing a platter of gourmet cheeses and bread.

A whirlwind romance soon began, with Friedrich proposing at a resort in the Swiss Alps, where they had gone for a weekend of skiing.

Their wedding a year later was an extravagant affair, with vows exchanged in the biggest church in Munich and the reception for nearly 200 people held in the countryside inside a 15ᵗʰ century castle with thick stone walls and an actual drawbridge.

Magazines wrote about the wedding, gushing about the promising young musician who was taking the nation by storm and the gifted designer with Hollywood looks who was the granddaughter of Arthur Steggar, the publishing magnate.

No one from Friedrich's family attended the nuptials but that didn't mute his joy. He had married the woman of his dreams and they were already planning a large family.

When he broke his hand and his inspiration abandoned him, she did her best to nurse him back to health both physically and emotionally. Even in his darkest hours, she refused to give up hope. And finally, so did he.

He was finding new happiness in teaching music when she told him about the twins. He'd never forget the date: Nov. 20, 1965.

When the doorbell rang that evening during a thunderous rainstorm, he'd expected to see his wife, returning from the benefit.

He opened the door and saw a policeman instead.

"I have terrible news," the man in the soaked blue uniform said. "There's been an accident."

"Oh my God, Hildy?"

"She's gone, Mr. Von Stiller. Along with the driver. The car slid off the road, down a hill and into some trees. There was a fire. It was too hot for the rescuers, even with the rain. I'm so sorry."

Friedrich's knees buckled. He gripped the door frame to keep from falling.

"The babies," he groaned.

"I'm so sorry," the policeman repeatedly helplessly.

In the days of grief that followed, he wished he had a family to lean on – his two older brothers, his mother. Even his father. The tragedy drew national headlines for days, building into a fervor that ended, weeks later, with a formal inquest posthumously absolving the man behind the wheel. But even then not a single person named

Von Stiller reached out.

Months passed and Friedrich's misery only grew. His moans at night echoed through the near-empty home.

He ordered the housekeeper to lock the door to the nursery and never go inside again. He removed the framed photographs of Hildy and him from their wedding and honeymoon and placed them in a box, hoping to ease his pain.

But it was no use. The house and everything in it reminded him of Hildy.

On their anniversary, after having the cook make her favorite meal, he decided to put the house up for sale. Weeks later, everything but his books and piano, which he had crated and stored, was sold at auction.

Friedrich spent many years traveling, searching for a refuge where he could live again without anguish. He had become a wanderer on a quest cursed to go on forever, it seemed. Along the way, there had been a few women, but never a promise of love. That was reserved for just one. It would always be so.

But in America's Pacific Northwest, amid the ancient woods that blotted out the sky, he experienced a stirring in his heart that he hadn't felt since before that tragic night.

A grove of massive sequoias became his cathedral, ferns the size of cars his altar. He prayed and Hildy came to him, filling him with hope at long last.

He soon discovered a small town off the northern Oregon coast that was nestled at the confluence of two rivers. Walking around the town's quaint downtown, he saw The Commodore, a historic apartment building that happened to be for sale. He immediately arranged for a tour. When he reached the third-floor apartment with the handsome wood floors, built-in cabinets, wainscoting and amazing views, he bought the place on the spot.

He hired contractors to renovate the building and give it a fresh coat of paint, then moved in – reserving the entire top floor for himself. After arranging to have his beloved piano shipped thousands of miles by boat, he began renting out the other four units. He became a landlord in residence.

After a while, on a particularly lovely day, he sat before his piano for the first time in many years and played. His tears stained the ivory keys, but he made it to the end – the final notes of the composition that she had liked best.

Months after that, he accepted a part-time job at a small community college, teaching music. He saw the light in his students' eyes, felt their passion. Slowly, the walls around his heart began to crumble. His own light had returned, however faint.

And then, in the hills above Two Rivers, he met a trembling man who played chess.

CHAPTER
NINETEEN

There was only one way in or out of the old mine the German soldier was guarding: a pair of massive wooden doors fit for a giant, each ten feet high and six feet wide.

The doors were chained together and from the chain hung a steel padlock that was the size of a man's head.

The entrance to the long-abandoned salt mine was carved into a hillside south of Salzburg, Austria. Friedrich wondered how deep the mine went and what it was being used for now that required such security.

Hours passed with only the sounds of chirping birds as the sun slowly set. His relief would come soon, he hoped. His legs ached from so much standing. He set down his Gewehr rifle and leaned against the doors, looking far too casual.

He was debating whether he could risk a short nap when he heard a woman's voice through the pines.

Friedrich grabbed his rifle and straightened, trying to resemble a military man and not who he really was – a privileged 18 year old who prayed every night that the war would soon be over. He knew he would soon have to report to what seemed like a suicide mission: an artillery unit on the collapsing Western Front.

Out of the darkness came two figures: an officer and a woman in a black cocktail dress and heels wrapped in a fur stole. She was pretty, in her early 20s, with dark, curled hair and pouty pink lips.

Friedrich, a lowly private, gulped as the pair drew closer. The officer was a colonel. His tunic was unbuttoned at the top and there were lipstick smudges on his cheek. He held a half-empty wine bottle in one hand.

The colonel fished into his trouser pockets clumsily, producing a set of keys.

"Aha!" he declared. "Now we shall begin your tour, mademoiselle."

The French lady giggled as the colonel grabbed the padlock in a beefy hand. After several failed attempts punctuated by drunken curses, the lock snapped open. With some effort, he pulled the doors apart a few feet.

"Stay here," he told Friedrich. "Let no one else inside."

"Yes, colonel."

The heavy doors closed with a thunderclap, followed by the echoes of footsteps and laughter.

An hour or so passed before the doors groaned and began to swing open. Friedrich, who had been dozing on his feet a few feet away, started. He quickly straightened his helmet.

The couple staggered out. The officer's tunic was now nearly unbuttoned. The woman, her hair mussed, wove her way down a path cut through the woods, admiring her wrist.

Were those diamonds glinting in the moonlight?

Pretending not to notice, Friedrich muscled the doors shut. The colonel surprised him by draping a hand over his shoulder.

"Do you know what you're guarding, son? Any fucking idea?"

He appeared to be in his early 50s, with buzzcut yellow hair and an athletic build. An Iron Cross dangled from his right breast pocket.

"No sir."

"That's gooood," he slurred. "Well done."

The officer scuttled off into the dark, calling after his lady friend. "Mademoiselle! *Mademoiselle!*"

Moments later, Friedrich heard the sound of a car driving off, spitting up gravel, before the stillness returned. When he turned, he noticed that the doors hadn't been locked.

After what the colonel said, his curiosity was at a fever pitch. He wanted nothing more than to look inside.

Just a quick peek.

What could possibly be in there that would interest a high-ranking officer and his guest, likely a prostitute imported from occupied Paris? It surely had to be more than ammunition and food rations. And where did that woman's bracelet come from?

Risking a court martial for deliberately disobeying orders, Friedrich opened the doors just enough to slide through and walked briskly down the main tunnel, following rusted steel tracks embedded in the rocky floor. The air inside was cool, like a morgue.

Just as the trail began sloping sharply downward, he saw the glow of lights ahead.

Rifle slung over a shoulder, the soldier began to jog. He soon found himself in a large underground cavern with rugged rock walls. It had been converted into a modern storage facility, complete with towering racks of steel shelving and long tables covered with scores of boxes, bins and crates.

Amazed, Friedrich peered into the nearest bin and was surprised to see a collection of leather-bound books. He picked one up and saw it was "David Copperfield," a prized first edition.

The next bin held more classic books, as did the bin after that. For some odd reason, they hadn't been burned in the streets for all to see, as had been the Nazi custom.

Stepping further inside, he saw fur coats – dozens of them, neatly hung on wires as if ready for a fashion show. He brushed his hand along them to prove to himself they were real.

Propped against a long wall was a dizzying array of artworks, from statues on marble pedestals to huge oil paintings in gilded frames. Behind them were many more paintings, packed in wooden crates.

Enough art to fill a small museum, he thought.

He stepped to his right, drawn by the glint of polished gold. As the treasure came into focus, he staggered as if punched.

Mein Gott!

Hundreds of gleaming menorahs were in a huge pile on one of the tables.

The soldier stumbled backward over a box and saw it was filled with gold and silver pocket watches. Other bins were filled with wedding rings, necklaces and other jewelry stripped from necks and fingers.

Eyes wide with fright, Friedrich began to run, past the paintings and sculptures and furs. Past everything of value that could be stolen from a condemned people.

He raced to the entrance, then hurriedly locked the doors, as if trying to contain the angry ghosts swirling inside.

It was the summer of 1944, and he knew then for certain that the mass slaughter of Jews was real.

What he couldn't know was how much his life would change as a result.

———

Friedrich returned home to Bavaria after the war expecting to see smoldering ruins.

Instead, he found the postcard-worthy region where he was raised remarkably intact, largely spared the concentrated Allied bombings that had devastated more industrial areas.

The biggest change was his family's wealth. It had grown tenfold in five years.

His father, a well-regarded judge, had purchased homes and businesses for a fraction of their value from Jews who'd been desperate to flee. He acquired their diamonds and gold for a pittance as well.

Klaus Von Stiller had convinced himself that he was being kind – even generous. If not for him, the Nazis would have simply seized the properties and belongings, leaving the Jews with nothing. At least he was giving them the money they needed in order to escape.

In 1945, as the rest of the war-torn nation struggled to rebuild under Allied occupation, the judge emerged as a millionaire with considerable real estate holdings.

In his alpine village alone, he owned nearly a quarter of the businesses, ranging from a medical building and small bank to a bookstore and butcher shop. He gave the finest homes to his three sons, sold or rented out the rest.

The diamonds and gold, later transferred to a safe deposit box in Switzerland, had been appraised at more than $10 million. The buildings were worth millions more.

But Von Stiller's conscience was clear. In his mind, he had merely made sound business decisions, and, like any skilled businessman, had profited. Some of his former high society friends even suggested he was something of a hero for quietly helping dozens of Jews flee persecution or death.

Nobody in the prominent family complained about their newfound prosperity – until Von Stiller's youngest son returned.

Still haunted by what he'd seen in the salt mine, Friedrich demanded that his father return his bounty to the Jews fortunate enough to have survived the death camps, or to the families of those who had perished.

He volunteered to help track down survivors through relief agencies and refugee services, in Europe, America and Palestine. He reminded his father that many of those people had been the family's friends and neighbors, even trusted lawyers who worked in the same courthouse.

The judge was unmoved.

He demanded that his son drop the matter, reminding Friedrich about the high price of his music education and how easily he could lose his rent-free home and inheritance.

The ultimatum worked.

Rebuffed, Friedrich focused on his studies in Munich and Berlin, and on his budding career as one of Germany's brightest young artists. Years later, he would meet Hildy and fall deeply in love.

One day, while retrieving the last of his belongings stored at one of the homes owned by his father, he discovered a message painted under the basement stairs.

Dear Home, We must leave you. We pray we will return someday soon and be happy again.

A Life Interrupted

Under that a Star of David was drawn.

Friedrich read the words and cried, knowing how complicit he had been.

That night, he drove to his father's home in the richest part of the village. When they were alone, in a paneled office lined with towering bookcases, the son pleaded one more time for justice.

"Father, we must return what we can to the families forced to flee," Friedrich said.

The elder Von Stiller, now retired, scowled. He narrowed his eyes under bushy white eyebrows.

"This again? I thought you had come to your senses."

"Today, I saw a message written in the basement of the house where I once lived – one of the homes you bought during the war. The message was from the previous owners, a Jewish family. They were praying to return someday. Father, we have to find them. We have to at least try."

"I paid them for that house. I paid all of them. Nothing was taken."

"You paid them next to nothing. You took advantage of their desperation, of their fear. Our family now must make amends."

Von Stiller pounded his mahogany desk. His wrinkled cheeks flushed with anger.

"I don't need to make amends. I helped those people. Do you know what would have happened to me if the Gestapo learned what I was doing?"

"My noble father. How many Jews did you hide in your many buildings? Whose lives did you spare?"

"I helped many."

"I have heard you say that before, but who did you help without first taking everything they had?"

"They were business transactions, nothing more."

"You were a rich man before all of this. You could have given them all a fair price. An honest price. So why didn't you?"

"I don't have to explain myself to you. I'm giving you a final warning. Stop this nonsense, or you will no longer be a part of this family."

Friedrich stared at his father and shook his head sadly.

"When I was young, I looked up to you. You were respected as a judge who dispensed justice fairly, who understood the value of mercy. But the person I see before me is an empty husk, a man who would profit off the damned. Your wealth is poison, and you deserve to choke on it."

"Get out of my sight, insolent creature. Never come back here again!"

Friedrich turned and walked away, his father's screams echoing off the walls.

"You'll never see a *pfennig* more! *Do you hear me?*"

"Nothing more!!"

CHAPTER
TWENTY

The day he met Harry, Friedrich was sitting on his bench by the swings, reading a gourmet cooking magazine and smoking his pipe.

He watched as the shaking man approached and immediately recognized him as the chess player from the other side of the playground.

He'll be challenging me to a game.

When he looked into Harry's eyes, he sensed a steely determination softened by kindness that was intriguing.

"You may call me Fred," the German said, and the friendship began.

They were both war veterans and widowers who lived alone, both still mourning their loss but carrying on as best they could.

That they fought on opposite sides in the war only seemed to make their unlikely friendship more valuable, like an unearthed relic that slowly reveals itself to be much more precious than it had seemed.

Fred had heard about a group of American veterans who fought in the Battle of the Bulge reluctantly agreeing, decades later, to meet some of the former German soldiers who had been trying to kill them. Surprising everyone, close friendships were forged.

Harry and Fred didn't fight in the same battles – he was engaged in a hopeless war in Western Europe while the American was bombing the Japanese in the Pacific, but that hardly mattered. The fact that they had both endured fierce combat was enough to bind them.

On the park's concrete chess table, Fred enjoyed their games but quickly realized that his rival had an unfair handicap: Parkinson's and the drugs required to control its ravages.

Fred didn't go easy on his friend, because even under the influence of the brain medication he was still a dangerous opponent. But he came to know which victories seemed legitimate and which deserved asterisks.

Winning didn't matter, really. It was the conversation that Fred cherished. The men soon began trusting each other enough to delve into matters of the heart.

Harry told him the story of his wife's sudden terminal illness, and Fred, in turn, offered a brief description of his wife's accident, omitting the details about the babies and the fire.

"She died terribly, and I still can't talk about it," he said over the chess board one day.

"I understand," Harry replied.

"Yes, I suppose you can, more than almost anyone."

"Every day I touch my wife's photo."

Fred nodded, a solemn look on his face. "As do I. And, in return, I sometimes hear her voice."

"No kidding? Me, too. I thought … I was going a little nuts."

"Nonsense, my friend. These are the ghosts we know. The ghosts who loved us, who still wish to guide us out of the darkness of despair."

"You have a good way with words. That's exactly right. Bonnie appears to me when I'm most in need."

"She is trying to help you, yes?"

"I think so."

"They are in the spirit world but they can appear in our minds much like angels." Fred smiled. "At least that's my belief."

"Spirits, angels, that's all very good. Just no demons, please."

Harry reached over to tap the top of Fred's hand. "When I do start losing it, will you let me know?"

"What do you mean?"

"I mean, if I start seeing things that aren't there. Not my Bonnie, more like horrible hallucinations."

"Is that a side-effect of your medications?"

"Yeah, it's what scares me the most. One time, I thought I saw troops in the street coming toward the house, rifles pointed at me, but I closed my eyes for a few minutes and when I looked again they were gone. Just an illusion, but scary all the same."

"I can't even imagine what you felt. I promise that if you start seeing things that aren't there, I will let you know."

"Thanks."

"Of course. Checkmate."

"Why you sneaky SOB!"

"Not at all. I'm just thirsty. Loser buys the beer, right?"

———

Fred was preparing a special dinner honoring the memory of his late wife when the phone rang in his apartment.

He expected the caller to be Harry, his lone invited guest, asking again for directions.

Instead, he heard the voice of his brother Hans, who was two years older and still living in the same village where they'd grown up.

"Friedrich, is that you?"

Fred was stunned silent for a moment or two. He hadn't expected to ever hear from his family again.

"Yes, Hans, it's me."

"How long has it been?"

"Forty years, give or take," he said dully. They were speaking in German. "Why are you calling?"

"It's Mother. She's taken ill. She's 95 and wants to see you before she dies."

The request came as another jolt. His father died a few years ago. He had only learned of his passing through a friend of the family, weeks after the patriarch was buried.

"Why now, after all these years?"

"My brother, we all had to follow Father's strict orders. We wanted to reach out to you, but if he found out …"

"I was asking about Mother. Why see me now?"

"We don't really know. She just asked me to contact you. Somehow, she knew you lived in America – in Oregon. Thank goodness your number is listed."

Fred made a mental note to change that.

"Please come," Hans continued. "She doesn't have long to live, and Kurt and I want our brother back. I would be happy if you stayed with me. I've remarried, but I'd like you to meet my wife. Her name is Gerta."

There was a long silence as Fred debated what to do. The death of the old judge had softened his heart toward his family, but only a little. It would be best to continue to ignore them all, but that would only be perpetuating his father's punishment.

"Friedrich, are you there?"

"Tell Mother I'll see her – one last time."

"She will be so happy. Thank you, Brother!"

"Hans?"

"Yes?"

"Don't call me 'Brother.' A brother would have offered condolences after my wife and unborn girls were killed."

"I'm so sorry. I wanted to … so very much. Father wouldn't allow it."

"Hans?"

"Yes?"

"Fuck you for being such a coward."

———

Days later, as Fred walked up the long, curving staircase to his mother's bedroom, he felt neither angry nor sad.

It had been decades since he'd seen her. She'd never called or written during that time, but then again, neither had he. It had been a thorough divorce, the judge had seen to that.

He resolved to grant her this one wish and then leave. He would not return for the funeral. He would not pretend to be a loving son. Not even now.

Fred entered the room and saw a shriveled figure encased in a goose-down comforter in the middle of a huge bed. Thick, gleaming maple posts, ornately carved with leafy vines, rose from each corner.

As footsteps on the wood floor signaled his approach, sunken eyes in an ashen face popped open.

"My son," Ursula Von Stiller croaked.

"Mother."

"Please sit."

Fred pulled up a chair and looked at his mother, instantly knowing that her death was indeed imminent. Her breaths were labored. Her eyes were rheumy, and she winced with every word she uttered.

And yet she managed a small smile.

"My baby has returned. Thank you for that."

"I don't hate you, Mother, if that's what you're thinking. Not seeing you wasn't my idea. I was banished."

She reached out with a frail hand, but Fred didn't take it.

"I don't have much time, the doctors say," she said. "First it was cancer, then a stroke, then pneumonia …"

Fred watched as his mother lapsed into a coughing fit that caused her entire body to spasm. A nurse in a white uniform hustled into the room, but the patient managed to wave her off.

"I am sorry that you are suffering," the son said, speaking the truth.

She grinned in a way that brought a touch of color back to her fissured cheeks.

"You have a tender heart," she rasped. "From the time you were a little boy. Remember the wounded birds you mended?"

Fred sighed. "Is that why you asked me to come? To reminisce?"

"I asked you to come because I love you. I wanted to see you, before … before I'm gone from this Earth."

There was no reply for a moment.

Fred felt emotions within him stir. "I suppose I wanted to see you as well," he said finally.

Using all her strength, she pulled herself into a sitting position.

After gasping for air for a full minute, she locked her red-rimmed eyes on her son.

"My boy, I need your help."

"Help with what?"

"Just before your father died, he confessed something to me. He said 'Friedrich was right.'"

"About what?"

"He didn't say, but I knew what he meant just the same. It was his way of saying he was wrong in cutting you out of the family." She paused to take a deep breath, her diseased lungs making a rattling sound. "Now, it's my turn – *my deathbed* – and I say, Friedrich, it's time to return the diamonds and gold, and anything else that we can."

Fred leaned back as if struck.

"You're 50 years too late. The Jews Father cheated, they're all dead."

"Many, but not all. You once offered to search for survivors, for their families. I am asking you to try."

"Why, Mother? So you can clean your slate before you die?"

"Yes, son. But also clean the slate of this family. Before word gets out and our reputations are destroyed. Forever."

"I'm not part of this family, remember?"

"When your father died, his curse against you ended as well. Last year, I restored the will to what it was before your rightful inheritance. You coming here to see me proves I was right. You are part of this family."

"I don't know what to say. This is unexpected, to say the least."

"Say you will do what I ask. Return what was taken. As much as you can. Restore this family's honor."

Fred leaned over and squeezed her limp hand.

"I will, Mother. At long last, I will."

And with that, the matriarch lay down and closed her eyes.

He pulled the comforter to his mother's chin and, as he walked out the door for the last time, she smiled.

CHAPTER
TWENTY-ONE

Fred learned of his mother's death shortly after returning to Two Rivers with a briefcase filled with financial records that included his father's old, leather-bound ledger.

When Hans called with the news, he wasn't in mourning. He was seething.

"The gold, the diamonds, the properties – it's all being given away?"

"Yes. As much as possible."

"And you persuaded Mother to change the will? To give you a third of the estate?"

"No, that was her idea. That's one of the things she wanted to tell me before she died."

"I don't believe you. And I don't trust you with Father's fortune."

"You're welcome to help. It's going to take many months to track down the people Father exploited, or at least find their kin."

"Kurt and I, we're hiring a lawyer. This won't stand. Mother was not well. You took advantage of her."

"She told me she made the changes more than a year ago."

"Liar!"

"It's true and rather easy to verify, but that's not important. Mother's dying wish was for me to return as much to the Jews as possible. To restore the family's honor."

"Nothing will be given back! *Nothing!* Our lawyer will see to that."

"Do what you will, but understand that if a lawsuit is filed, this whole ugly business will be exposed. The truth will come out. Stories will be written. Reporters will knock on your door, asking what Father did during the war. They will ask you what is in the safe deposit box in Geneva, how the Von Stillers got so rich."

"You wouldn't dare."

"Oh, I would," Fred said, marveling at the resolve he had found. "I would indeed."

"I'll see you in court, Brother."

Hans hung up and Fred stared at the phone before setting it down. Part of him had hoped his brothers would lend a hand, if only to distance themselves from what their father had done. But greed, once aroused, was a difficult beast to tame.

Eager to get his family off his mind, he slipped on a blue cashmere sweater and began his hike to Sunny Slope. When he got to the nearly deserted playground, Harry was sitting alone at his chess table, looking forlorn.

"Welcome back," the American said in a wistful voice. "How did it go with your mother?"

"I'm glad I went. She passed the day after I left."

"I'm sorry."

"She was very sick, but on her deathbed she ended my banishment. So that's something at least. But now my brothers are fighting over the will and ... other matters. They don't want me to get anything, it appears." *Not a single pfennig!*

"Ah, money. The root of everything evil."

"Some valuables are more evil than others."

Harry shot him a puzzled look but Fred didn't elaborate. He had decided not to tell his Jewish friend about the gold and gems obtained by his father during the war. Even though he was on moral high ground, he didn't want Harry to get emotionally involved in his project. Not yet anyway.

"So, where does our investigation stand?"

Harry briefed Fred on the latest developments, which included the announcement by Huggins that while the intensive search for Nate had ended, the investigation was ongoing and all credible tips from the public would be examined.

The panic in the community, meanwhile, was growing. Fretful parents no longer allowed their young children to be outside by themselves. The Sunny Slope custom of residents waving warmly to strangers ceased. Police patrols were stepped up, but the attempt at reassurance only served to underscore the new grim reality. Fear hung thick in the air.

Worst of all, Harry's grandson was in a sudden, alarming tailspin. It was the chief reason for Harry's sad state.

When Harry said he was planning to get Buster alone for a crucial chat, Fred suggested they could start by flying a kite together. He offered to build one by hand.

Amused by the look of surprise on Harry's face, Fred said: "In Bavaria, we often made our own toys. It's a tradition, you may say."

"Well, thanks."

"There is a hobby store that sells what I need two blocks from my building. In my basement, there is a workbench and tools. I'll have it ready for you in 24 hours. What are you going to ask him?"

"I need to know if he's been approached by anyone unsavory, and if so, try to get a name and address."

"Will Buster do that?"

"Dunno," Harry said, shrugging. "Maybe. If he's not too scared. But I have to try."

CHAPTER
TWENTY-TWO

Dressed entirely in black, wearing knit caps and gloves, Fred wondered why his gung-ho friend didn't also insist on face paint and camouflage.

They were about to become burglars, breaking the law in pursuit of justice. The irony of the moment would have amused the German if his nerves weren't so frayed.

"Are you ready?" Harry asked.

Fred nodded soberly. They left the Silverado and hustled to the side of the blue house – the side that Harry said couldn't be seen by the neighbors.

As Harry began pulling at the basement window, Fred kept watch for passing cars or people out taking a stroll. He was thankful for the breadth of a Japanese maple in the front yard that provided some concealment.

It was a moonless night and the lights in the house were off. Fred felt his heart pounding in his chest. He had been a law-abiding man his entire life. Never cheated on his taxes, drove drunk or punched anyone. Hell, he'd never even cut in line. But all that was about to change.

"It's just stuck. Give me a hand," Harry whispered.

They both pulled and seconds later the window opened, swinging toward them with a loud protest. Harry crawled in first and Fred, after another anxious look around, followed.

He switched on the miniature flashlight and looked around. He found himself in some kind of film studio.

An expensive-looking video camera attached to a tripod was aimed at a small stage that featured a red-velvet loveseat and several large white throw pillows. A painting of a nude woman hung on a wall erected behind the loveseat. A Persian-style carpet and a small table with an empty flower vase rounded out the set.

On a desk nearby was a laptop and an assortment of camera lenses and filters. A box of new videotapes was on the floor. Just off the stage was a microphone on a telescoping boom arm that sprouted off a wheeled base. Above, an array of sophisticated lights worthy of a Hollywood studio hung from the ceiling on tracks.

There was something unsettling about the basement set-up and its obvious sophistication. But the fact that Buster had led Harry to this place made it downright ominous.

Harry called out from the other side of the stage and Fred rushed over, fearing the worst.

His flashlight illuminated a wall lined with shelves that were filled with basketball shoes of all styles and colors, price tags still dangling. When he opened a duffle bag stuffed with video games still wrapped in plastic, he gulped.

We've found our predator. In Sunny Slope, just as Harry thought.

"Here it is," Fred said. "The gifts used to pay those poor boys."

Harry nodded. "But we need to find actual evidence of crimes.

Look around," he said, his voice thick. "We only have a couple of minutes."

Fred returned to the camera on the tripod and turned it on. Maybe the most recent recording would reveal something. Nervous about what he might see, he hesitated for a moment before looking at the small screen used to review footage.

He saw the back of a naked boy. The boy turned and dropped to his knees. Then he smiled, looking up at the camera, before unbuckling the belt of the man standing before him.

Fred recoiled in horror.

It was Chase, Buster's best friend. He'd seen the boy a few times at the playground. He seemed so innocent.

As Harry hustled over with a videotape in his shaking hands, Fred quickly turned the camera off. He'd seen far too much.

"We have what we need," Harry said with a triumphant grin. He couldn't see how pale Fred had become. "Anything on that camera?"

Before Fred could answer there was a sudden noise – a car pulling up outside.

"Go, go!" Harry whispered.

Fred raced to the window, and with Harry giving him a boost, wriggled his way through. He could hear the front door closing as he grabbed Harry's hands and pulled him up.

They were closing the window as the basement lights turned on. Feeling lucky, they hustled to the pickup and drove off.

Harry steered the pickup down the hill to The Commodore and parked, keeping to himself the fact that he'd dropped the flashlight.

"Better that we stay here for a little while, in case he caught a glimpse of the truck. Got anything to drink?"

"What a silly question," Fred said.

Harry stuffed the videotape in the glove box. "I'll look at that tomorrow," he said. "Don't have the stomach for it now."

"I may not tomorrow either."

Fred wondered whether Buster would appear on the tape. What would such a stunning revelation do to his friend's already fragile state of mind? He wished he could take the evidence somewhere and burn it, prevent it from ever being seen. He wished he hadn't gotten in this deep, but then he thought about the children. About keeping them safe.

"I hear ya," Harry said, "but if it's evidence of crimes, we can go to the detective on the case and put an end to this nightmare."

"I'm all for ending nightmares. Let's have that drink."

They walked up the two flights to Fred's apartment. He poured them each a cognac.

Fred took a drink and felt his anxiety ebb.

"Harry, I must say that I was impressed with how you handled yourself tonight. During your law enforcement career, have you had occasion to break into other people's homes?"

"Never did, but then again, I went straight from patrol to an office. Good stuff," he said, tasting the liquor.

"Do you think we found our predator?"

"Absolutely," the former cop pronounced. "Now we have to bring the bastard to justice."

Fred nodded, but he was thinking more about the collateral damage. About how he'd find the strength to tell Harry the truth about his grandson's best friend.

Justice, but at what cost?

CHAPTER
TWENTY-THREE

The next morning, when Harry opened his door, he had a steaming cup of coffee in his hand and a fierce look on his face.

"Come in, come in," he said impatiently, motioning with his free hand.

Fred stepped inside, a bit warily. He heard other voices and saw Buster's parents seated at the dining room table. They looked as anxious as he was.

"Sit down, Fred," Harry said. "I haven't told them anything yet. Coffee?"

"Already had some, thank you."

The truth was Fred had woken with his stomach in a knot over the videotape that he now saw on the table in front of Harry. There was no way he could eat or drink anything without immediately throwing up.

Harry looked at Charlie and Liz and said matter-of-factly, "Fred and I broke into a house here in Sunny Slope the other night."

The couple exchanged worried glances.

"We went into the suspect's basement to find proof," Harry

continued. He patted the tape. "And we did."

"You know who this person is?" Charlie asked.

"Not yet, but it won't be hard to find out."

"Where did you get this information?"

"From Buster."

"Buster told you his name?"

"No, but he led me to the man's house. He doesn't want any more boys to be harmed."

"Why didn't you go to the police? Why break in?"

"That's right," Liz said, looking alarmed. "I don't understand why you two would break the law like that."

"Because I know that without evidence, the police won't act. And I'm trying to protect Buster from what I know will be grueling interviews. I made him a promise."

Charlie nodded. "So, what's on the tape?"

Fred's gut flopped in dire anticipation. He silently prayed that Buster's name would not be mentioned.

"It's Sam Mendez and another boy having sex, and Sam and a middle-aged man. About 45 minutes of it. It's disgusting stuff, but proof positive that there's a child porn operation right here."

"Poor Sam," Liz said, shaking her head.

"What else did you find?" Charlie asked, recovering from his initial shock.

"Lots of other videos, a professional studio in the basement, and all kinds of toys and games and sneakers that young teenage boys would want. That's how they're being paid, I guess."

"Christ," Charlie said. "You and Maria were right all along. What's the next step?"

"Fred and I will go visit the detective on the case, show him the tape. Hopefully, that will convince him to put the man under surveillance and get a warrant. When they get a look at all the tapes, they'll have enough to put this bastard in prison for life."

Charlie squeezed his wife's hand. "I hope so, Pops."

"How has Buster been?" Fred inquired. That question had kept him awake all night.

Liz turned to look at the gentleman to her left. He seemed pale and anxious, but his expression was kind.

"We've kept him out of school the last few days," she said. "Charlie and I are taking days off. We're all sort of rallying together. This has been hard to take. But he seems to be okay, thank you for asking. He's turning 14 next week."

Fred wondered if he should tell the boy's parents what he saw on the video camera, then quickly ruled that out. He wouldn't add to their worries. He'd tell Harry later somehow, when they were alone.

Harry, shaking, rose to his feet and addressed the group. "Well, that's about it. I'll have to tell poor Maria at some point, but that can wait a bit. Fred, if you'll join me at the police station …"

"Of course, Harry. But I don't know how much help I can be. I can't even bear to watch the tape."

"Two heads are better than one. I'm not thinking so clearly these days."

Charlie stood and patted his father's shoulder. "Everything you've done … Liz and I are proud of you. Even that thing with the shoes."

Harry allowed himself a thin smile.

"For Buster," he said, raising his mug.

"For Buster," they all said.

———

On the short drive to the Two Rivers Police Department, Fred noticed that Harry seemed unusually tense.

The last time he'd been inside, Harry was given a hero's welcome. Patrol officers slapped him on the back. The chief offered to buy him a drink.

But now he was more of a headache than a distinguished former captain, he told Fred. He had to make an appointment to see Johnson this time, and it took several calls to do so.

"Word spread pretty quickly about that tussle with the van driver," Harry said. "They know I've been asking around, too. I think they've pegged me as a troublemaker, and that goes for you, too."

Fred studied the anxiety on his friend's face and nodded. "So be it. When we talk to this detective, we will let him know our true intentions, yes? Protect children. Seek justice."

Harry parked the truck and took a deep breath. "Let's seek some justice," he said.

They walked inside and Fred could see the expressions on the people with badges immediately change to one of concern.

"Joe's waiting for you," Marjorie intoned before Harry could say a word.

"Thanks."

They walked down the hall lined with portraits. When they got to Johnson's office they could hear him talking on the phone in a low voice.

He hung up as soon as the men entered.

"Afternoon, detective," Harry said. "This is Fred."

"The Dynamic Duo," Johnson said sarcastically. "Take a seat."

Fred looked over at Harry and gulped. The videotape was on his friend's lap.

"You said you had some important information for me about the Sunny Slope investigation? I'm all ears," the detective said, locking his hands behind his head.

Harry placed the tape labeled Vol. 19 on the cluttered metal desk.

"That should be all you need to get a warrant."

Johnson stared at it as though it was a contagion, eyes wide in alarm.

"What the fuck is this?"

"It's child porn, filmed in the basement of a home in Sunny Slope. It features the late Sam Mendez," Harry said.

The young detective leaned back in his chair and glared at Harry and Fred.

"I don't know how you two got this – I don't want to know – but I would bet that the owner didn't just hand it over. There's no way this could be introduced in court. I can't even watch it without getting embroiled in something illegal. Jesus Christ, Harry, you're way out of line."

Fred gulped. What was supposed to be an encouraging conversation was fraying quickly. He didn't expect the hard-bitten detective to be grateful, or even mildly appreciative. But this sudden anger?

"Calm down, Joe," Harry responded. "We're not asking you to introduce it as evidence. We just want you to get off your ass and make an arrest."

The perpetual-hangover look on Johnson's face hardened. "I should have you both arrested for this. Breaking into someone's home?"

Fred politely raised a hand. He began searching for words to help defuse the situation.

"Please, I believe you are missing the point. We know who the predator is and the proof is on that tape. If you act swiftly, you will be applauded, and rightfully so, as the man who cracked the most sensational murder case in the history of Two Rivers. If you don't, and other children are hurt or killed, I'm afraid that will be your legacy."

Johnson scowled at Fred, then faced Harry, giving his former colleague a withering look.

"So, you bring me tainted evidence and demand that I run out and arrest somebody? Do you know how crazy that sounds?"

"Not as crazy as waiting for another kid to go missing," Harry said, refusing to back down. He reached in the pocket of his coat and pulled out a slip of paper.

"This is the address. There's a goddamn porn studio in the basement, filled with evidence. All you need is a judge to give you a warrant."

"You're giving me advice? After you assault a man, set a fire outside a home and now steal so-called evidence? I've been vouching for you, Harry, but no more. That's it. You either stand down and let us do our job, or I'll have you locked up."

Harry glowered at the detective.

"My grandson is being groomed by this monster. If he gets hurt, I'm holding you responsible."

"Okay, that's it. Nobody threatens me, and nobody gives me orders except the chief. Get out and take your friend with you. Meeting's over, boys."

"We didn't mean to—," Fred began.

"*Out!*"

As they left the station, drawing still more stares, Harry looked at Fred and quipped, "That went well."

"Will he at least look at the tape?"

"Hard to say, but if he does, he'll get that warrant somehow."

"What if he doesn't?"

"Then, my friend, we'll do his job for him. Tail that pervert, see where it leads."

As they drove away, Fred looked apprehensively at his friend.

"Harry, I have something to tell you. Something rather distressing."

"Go ahead."

"When we were in the basement looking for evidence, I saw something on the camera set up on the tripod."

"Oh yeah? What?"

"There was footage of Buster's friend."

"Chase? They've been best friends since 3rd grade. What was he doing?"

Fred gulped. He didn't want to inflict this kind of pain. "He was naked. I'm sorry, my friend."

"What?" Harry nearly lost control of the truck. "Naked? What was he doing?"

"I think he was in one of those sex movies. I was shocked. I didn't want to see any more. I turned the camera off – and then we heard the noise and had to flee."

Harry, stricken, pulled into his driveway. He slumped over the steering wheel.

"I'm so sorry," Fred said.

After a couple of minutes, Harry straightened. Tears stung his eyes.

"If this predator can get to Buster and Chase, get them to do sick things …" Harry turned to face the playground where children no longer frolicked.

"Then no kids here are safe."

CHAPTER

TWENTY-FOUR

Hildy came to him in his sleep, as she sometimes did when he was terribly troubled.

She appeared in a silvery light, but he could see the outline of her face – her shining eyes, her tender smile, her long, golden hair floating on an invisible current.

He felt her presence pass over him like a summer breeze, comforting and warm. Her lips didn't move, but he heard her words in perfect clarity.

"The ledger," she said.

Fred opened his eyes and sat upright in his bed, waving his arms frantically in a desperate attempt to see his love again, to bring her back somehow. He called her name, pleading, nearly begging. But there was only darkness.

It was well before dawn, and yet there was no use trying to return to sleep. He walked down the hall to his study, plopped into the padded leather chair facing the oak rolltop desk. He rummaged through papers until he found what he was looking for.

Opening his father's dusty ledger, he flipped through the pages, looking for anything unusual.

What was Hildy trying to tell me?

Fred was about halfway through when he came across an old photograph paperclipped to one of the entries.

The hairs on the back of his neck stood up. It was a picture of a ring unlike any other.

The entry described it as a flawless 21-karat blue diamond mounted on a white-gold band engraved with a pair of noble lions – one on each side.

According to the ledger, the elder Von Stiller paid the equivalent of $75,000 dollars for the ring during the war. Next to that notation, he gleefully penned: "Appraisal, $5 million American!"

Fred wondered who could have owned such a magnificent jewel. Given his father's dark history, one of Germany's wealthiest Jewish families, no doubt. Likely an heirloom, handed down through generations.

According to the ledger, the ring of rings was sitting in a Swiss bank vault – one that the judge's youngest child could now access. It had to be the single-most valuable item obtained from the scores of desperate people trying to flee Germany.

Fred hadn't given back any of his family's ill-gotten riches yet. His mother had only recently been buried. But he suddenly knew where to begin.

Studying more recent pages in the ledger, those from the 1950s and '60s, Fred shook his head. There were numerous entries in a shorthand he didn't understand. The sums involved were large, ranging from $50,000 to a quarter-million. His father conveniently listed the sums in both Deutschmarks and dollars.

Fred was not aware of any business dealings by his father after the war, when he was officially retired, but the ledger seemed to suggest otherwise.

What had the old man been up to?

Rubbing his tired eyes, Fred looked up at roughly the spot where Hildy's spirit, if lingering, might be present.

"I'll start with the ring, my love," he said.

———

After making a few calls to leading gemologists, Fred quickly learned that the diamond was more valuable than his father knew.

Mined in South Africa, the dazzling gem arrived in Europe in the early 1700s in the possession of German nobility, namely an affable Jewish baron with an affinity for fine clothes and bushy mutton chops named Moses Gittelbach.

After Gittelbach's death, the ring was passed to his son, who passed it on to his. By the time the Nazis came to power, the famed Gittelbach Blue was in the hands of 45-year-old Herman, the great-great-grandson, who in 1942 was making arrangements to sail to America with his wife and three daughters.

Troubling Herman Gittelbach, a former bank executive, were two facts: One was that the power and influence of what remained of the Jewish elite in Germany was over; the other was that the once-opulent Gittelbach home would soon be seized and with it the diamond in the steel safe in the master bedroom.

Gittelbach had a seamstress sew a secret pocket in his suit coat where he could carry the ring undetected. But days before the family planned to flee, he realized it was too risky to try to get both his family and the ring out of the country. If they were caught, they'd be taken to concentration camps, where what remained of their possessions would be stripped away and either confiscated or burned.

There was also another matter. He had quickly become mired in debt, the direct result of being fired by the bank, having his financial accounts frozen and continuing his habit of betting on horses.

Desperate, he paid a visit to the friendly judge he had met socially, before such contacts with Jews had been outlawed. Sources had told him that Von Stiller was willing to pay Jews cash for their valuables – even homes and businesses.

In the judge's home office, Gittelbach placed the Blue on the mahogany desk.

He looked at Von Stiller with sad eyes. "It's a family treasure," he said.

"And you want me to buy it from you?"

"I understand you will offer a fair price."

"I am not a diamond dealer."

Gittelbach sighed. "There are no dealers willing to take the risk of working with Jews. I've tried."

Von Stiller knew that was true. He examined the diamond for a minute, twirling it before his eyes. Light from a window struck the gem, causing the judge's face to turn blue.

"It truly is extraordinary. Makes the ring I gave my wife look like a trifle. Given the circumstances, I won't ask for an appraisal, though that would be customary."

"It's been in our family for nearly 250 years, but I would rather sell it to a friend and see it survive the war, than let the Nazis get their hands on it. So, go ahead sir, make me an offer."

"You consider me your friend?" Von Stiller said as he returned the ring to its black box. "Why, we scarcely know one another."

After a long pause, the judge said: "If you come back tomorrow I can round up $150,000. That's the best I can do."

The offer cut through Gittelbach like a knife. He was hoping for 10 times that amount, at least.

But what choice did he have in these perilous times? He would need cash to bribe border officials and secure passage to America. He reached an arm across the desk and shook the judge's hand.

"I accept," he said.

The next day, with his family packed and waiting in an idling car outside the Von Stiller residence, Gittelbach returned to Von Stiller's office.

He placed the box containing the ring on the desk with tears in his eyes. In return, Von Stiller handed yet another panicked seller an envelope filled with cash.

The great-great-grandson of royalty counted the bills and stared at the judge in disbelief.

"There's only $75,000 here. Half what you promised."

"That's all I could get on such short notice."

"But we're leaving … in a few minutes. My wife and children, they're in the car outside."

Von Stiller seemed to enjoy the immense pressure he was exerting.

"Will you wire me the rest, when we make it to New York?" Gittelbach asked, doing his best not to plead.

The judge grabbed the lapels of his wool suit with both hands and leaned back in a hand-carved wooden chair, regal enough for a monarch. He gave the desperate man standing before him a condescending look.

"What do you think the Gestapo would do to me if they learned I was sending money to escaping Jews? Even worse, Jews in America, our enemy?"

"After the war then." Gittelbach clasped his hands together, surrendering the last vestiges of dignity. "Please, I beg you. It's for my *family*."

"Perhaps," said the man behind the desk, savoring the savagery of the moment. "You best leave now – while you still can."

CHAPTER
TWENTY-FIVE

Herman Gittelbach's dark foreboding soon proved true.

The Gestapo stopped his Mercedes sedan less than two miles from the Von Stiller house, acting on an informant's tip.

After a grueling interrogation that left him bruised and bloodied, but merely a prelude to far worse, Gittelbach was loaded onto a train bound for Auschwitz. His beautiful wife and their young daughters, ages 4, 6 and 8, were sent to Buchenwald.

There were no privileges awarded Moses Gittelbach's descendants. As they were herded onto freight cars, local Nazis set fire to the Gittelbach mansion, a formerly magnificent Gothic edifice built in the late 17th century that by 1942 was nearly empty inside and in serious disrepair. The mob used ancient Hebrew prayer books and family portraits as kindling, laughing as the grand symbol of Jewish heritage was reduced to charred ruins.

Fred learned in his research that only one member of the family survived the Holocaust, the youngest child. Four-year-old Anna was protected and fed extra crumbs of bread by other women in the camp after they learned that the child's mother and siblings had been executed.

When Buchenwald was liberated in 1945, Anna, then nearly 7, rushed to the first American G.I. she could find and hugged his legs, using all her remaining strength to hang on as long as she could. Her head was shaved and she wore the striped pajamas of the emaciated prisoners so near death. Tears ran down her cheeks, making wet tracks through dirt and grime. A photograph capturing the moment was published in papers around the world.

A couple of years later, she would join a group of refugees who sailed into New York Harbor, past the Statue of Liberty. She was taken in by an aunt in Brooklyn, a school teacher with a big heart who had better timing than the rest of the family. She and her husband had left Germany in 1938, before the war. They were among the lucky few to get American visas.

Using the computers at his college and assisted by one of his more tech-savvy students, Fred learned that Anna had attended a liberal arts college, became a muralist and then made her way to the West Coast, where she married and opened a modest art studio in Seattle.

Fred tracked down the address of the studio and was amazed to find that it was still operating. Anna, he figured, would be about 65 years old now.

Sadly, he found an obituary in the Seattle Times for her husband of 35 years. He was a philosophy professor, also Jewish, who had met Anna at a community event honoring Holocaust survivors. "She cast a lovely spell over me," he had said at their wedding, according to the obit. "Every time I'm with her, my heart soars."

Fred wondered if that was really true. How could someone who lost so much project such love?

He'd soon know the answer.

On a bright early-autumn day, he got in his red BMW coupe and headed north across the mighty Columbia River and past the bustling lumber yards lining its banks to Washington state. A few hours later, he was in West Seattle, heading down a steep hill to the deep-blue waters of Elliott Bay.

He parked off the long stretch of sand and rock known as Alki Beach and drank in the downtown Seattle skyline shining across the bay. He nodded at the young people gliding by on skateboards and inline skates. Then he turned and smiled.

Across the street was a white-stucco cottage with a pitched green roof. A wood sign planted out front read GITTELBACH ART STUDIO. Above the front door, a banner stretched across the building, offering "Lessons for All Ages."

Fred stepped inside to the tinkle of a small brass bell and was greeted by an attractive woman in her 30s with long, dark hair. She looked to be about five months pregnant.

"How may I help you?"

"I'm looking for Anna, the owner."

"That's my mother. She's in the back teaching a class."

"I don't want to interrupt. I can wait."

"It's ending soon. Would you like to watch? There's a couch in that room."

He gave her a gentlemanly nod. "That's very kind of you."

"Better than standing, at least. I'm Rachel."

"A pleasure to meet you. My name is Friedrich, but most people call me Fred."

"Oh, you're German. Did you know my family?"

"Not myself, but my late father knew your grandfather."

"My gosh, Mother will be so excited to see you. Follow me."

Fred smiled politely. He had no idea what kind of reception he'd receive, or what words he should say to a Holocaust survivor, given the circumstances.

My father stole an immensely valuable heirloom from your family, just before your parents and sisters were murdered.

The front of the business was an art supply store, but Rachel ushered him into a large, sunny room where a half-dozen older men and women were looking out a picture window, painting seascapes. A lively woman with short silver hair walked between them, hands clasped behind her back.

"Betty, what a lovely start!" she told one of the hobbyists. "Your brush strokes are getting so much better."

Fred took a seat on the couch and quickly found himself admiring how the teacher found something encouraging to say to every student, no matter how poorly they painted. That was not an easy thing to do, he knew from his sessions tutoring young would-be pianists.

Anna Gittelbach-Stein glanced at her watch and announced apologetically, "I'm afraid that's all for today, class. See you next week. And be sure to keep practicing!"

Rachel walked up to her mother and whispered a few words, causing Anna to look at the stranger on the couch curiously.

Fred rose to his feet as the woman approached with a warm smile that put a glow on her round, pink cheeks.

"It's a pleasure to meet you," he said.

They shook hands and Fred could see the identifying tattoo the Nazis had scratched into her forearm.

What had been intended as a form of debasement was now a source of power, he could see. Those who survived the worst genocide the world has ever known were revered, respected as guiding spirits of their faith. They felt driven to speak about the horrors they endured and witnessed, so that the Holocaust could never be denied or forgotten. Anna was one of them.

"Please, sit," she said, sliding over a paint-speckled stool for herself. "Rachel, my darling, please bring us some of your lovely mint tea."

Then she looked at Fred and said softly, "You are from the old country, so you must like tea."

"Yes, thank you. I do like tea."

"My daughter tells me our fathers knew each other in Bavaria."

"That is correct."

There was a brief silence as Fred wondered how he should begin such an unusual conversation.

"I don't know quite how to say this, but … I am here to make amends, on behalf of my family, the Von Stillers."

"Amends? What do you mean?"

"My father, the late Klaus Von Stiller, profited during the war by acquiring valuables from Jewish people fleeing Germany. He amassed a fortune in gold and diamonds, as well as hastily evacuated homes and businesses."

Anna's sunny face clouded.

"He didn't steal the gold and diamonds, but he might as well have," Fred continued. "He paid the Jews, his neighbors and colleagues, a paltry sum. A fraction of the true value."

He paused as Rachel arrived with a wooden tray filled with two ceramic mugs decorated with pink flying pigs, a steaming teapot, and milk, sugar and honey. She set it down on a small table and lingered.

"Why are you telling me this, Mr. Von Stiller?" Anna said as she prepared her tea.

"Please, call me Fred," he said, doing the same. "My mother died recently, but it was her final wish for me to try to return whatever I could to survivors. She knew what had been done wasn't right. Immediately after the war, I asked my father to return everything and not only did he refuse, he banished me from the family. I had nothing to do with any of them for 40 years, but this task I gladly accepted."

"Did your father have business dealings with mine? I know we tried to flee Bavaria and were caught by the Gestapo. My memories of that day are foggy. I really only remember the horrors of the camp."

Fred nodded sadly. "Closer to theft than a business transaction, I'm afraid."

"I see."

"Have you heard of the Gittelbach Blue?"

Blood drained from Anna's face. "The family diamond? But I thought it vanished with the Nazis. There were attempts to locate it after the war, none successful. It would be worth millions today."

"Fifteen million, to be precise."

"How do you know?"

"I know because I have the Blue. And I intend to return it to you and your family, where it belongs."

Rachel gasped. "Oh my God!"

Fred reached into the pocket of his button-down sweater and produced the old photograph of the sparkling gem set in the thick band decorated with lions.

"Yes, I remember it more clearly now. It's so beautiful," Anna said, passing the picture to her daughter, whose eyes widened.

"Klaus Von Stiller purchased the ring from your father for $75,000 in 1942, the same day you were all captured. It's in the records I've been given, along with a notation stating that it was appraised shortly thereafter for $5 million. It's since been valued at more than three times that."

"Why would grandfather agree to such a low price?" Rachel asked her mother.

Anna shook her head sadly. "Mother and Father were so desperate to flee, to protect us. I think he thought that any price was better than none at all."

She faced Fred. "I always thought the Gestapo seized the ring when they detained us and ransacked the house. But, based on what you're telling us, they were just a little too late. Tell me, was your father ever questioned by authorities over his dealings with Jews?"

"Not that I know of. Why do you ask?"

"After hearing your story, I think my assumptions were wrong. At the camp, Mother told me and my sisters that Father was tortured after we were caught attempting to flee. She thought they did it in hopes of finding the Blue. Now, I realize that it was much more than that. Father could have led the Gestapo to the ring, to your doorstep, but he told them nothing. In accepting death, he may have spared your father."

"My father did not deserve such a sacrifice," Fred said. "I'm sorry."

Anna took a sip of her tea and her expression softened. "But enough of that," she declared. "You come bearing good news, not bad, after all."

"Yes, I do. Your family's heirloom is in a safe deposit box in Switzerland, just as it has been since the war. It would be my pleasure to liberate this magnificent jewel and return it to its rightful owners, so that it may again be passed down through the generations."

A tear rolled down Anna's face and Rachel rushed to her side.

"They tried to erase us, you know," the survivor told Fred. "They set our home on fire. They stripped our family of its land and titles. They tried to erase our very existence. My parents, my sisters … But then you, a stranger, arrive one day, offering to return a piece of our past."

She leaned forward and hugged the man from Germany, whose own eyes brimmed with tears.

For the first time in many years, Friedrich Von Stiller felt whole.

———

A cool rain was falling when the tall, slender man arrived in Sunny Slope.

He drove slowly by the blue house, then steered the black Escalade with tinted windows past the neighborhood park to the address on the piece of paper resting on his knee.

As the SUV idled at the curb, he could see an old man through the front window. He was sitting in a chair reading a book.

"Harry Bolden," the driver said under his breath.

His flicker of an accent was foreign, possibly Swedish, and his manner of speaking was that of an educated man.

He could be polite and persuasive when the moment called for it, but more often than not he was as vicious as a junkyard dog – with an added dash of cruelty. He was in his 30s and had dyed blond hair cut close to the scalp and calculating brown eyes. There was an old 2-inch scar, visible in the right light, running from his left ear down his neck.

The man was dressed all in black as usual, with tailored wool trousers and a thin pullover sweater that hugged his chiseled torso. His arms were long and sinewy, like the steel cables holding up bridges. An expensive Swiss watch adorned his right wrist, but it was more tactical gear than an accessory, with a built in timer, stopwatch, alarm and depth counter. His shoes were soft-soled for traction. He knew most martial arts, had been trained for combat at an elite level and previously served as a mercenary in hot zones around the world.

The Organization found him in Moscow and offered to double what he was making assassinating dissidents and Western agents. His new employers gave him the initial Q, a random selection that bore no resemblance to his true name.

His assignment in Two Rivers was to wrap up a few loose ends, preventing a budding investigation from reaching beyond the small woodsy town.

Q had planned to make it look like Bolden had lost his mind. The story would be that in a rage, the veteran went after the child porn maker. Then they each pulled guns, and in a frantic shootout, both were killed in the basement. That's what police would assume, once he arranged the bodies correctly and fired a few extra rounds from the guns he would place in their cold hands.

It still rankled him that his superiors had overruled him. They wanted their predator removed but not killed.

If anyone truly deserved to die, it was the hideous excuse for a man who was turning innocent children into actors in porn videos. But he had his orders. He kept his objections to himself.

The morning after he first spotted Bolden, Q watched as the surprisingly fit old-timer sat in the park near his home with a well-dressed man of about the same age.

Their conversation seemed serious. They kept looking around as if they were plotting something.

Was this friend another loose end?

Q checked his pulse, as was his habit before a job, touching his wrist with two fingers. A minute later, he smiled.

Calm and steady.

There was time enough to be careful, he thought, driving slowly away.

PART THREE

A STORM GATHERS

CHAPTER
TWENTY-SIX

Five days had passed since they'd been tossed out of the police station and there were zero signs of a heightened investigation.

Harry and Fred sat at the deserted playground feeling defeated.

"Did you tell Maria about the video?" Fred asked during one of the many lulls in their conversation.

Harry lowered his gaze. "I couldn't. She'd want all the details and I knew if I told her, she'd be haunted by it the rest of her life. She'd blame herself somehow."

"Yes, but she deserves to know."

"I know."

"I can do it, if you'd like."

"No, I made a promise to keep her informed."

"My friend, I don't know her as well as you, but she is stronger than she appears."

"Yes, she is. She reminds me of Bonnie, who refused to show her pain, her fear of death – even at the end."

"Your wife was a courageous woman. Your love must have run deep for her to spare you such agony."

Fred's thoughts were turning to Hildy and her swift but brutal death when he noticed a man hustling toward them. He was wearing worn denim shorts and flip-flops, and had a ponytail and scraggly beard.

"Is that Melvin?"

Harry used his hand to shield the sun from his eyes. "That's him, all right. Heading straight for us."

"I've never seen him leave his house before."

"Me neither."

They watched as Melvin crossed the lawn and strode past the empty slide, stopping abruptly in front of their bench. His head swiveled back and forth, searching the perimeter.

Fred could see Harry tensing, as if he was ready to start boxing the wild-eyed man before them.

"You're Harry and Fred? My memory ain't so good these days," he asked, rapping his skull with his knuckles.

"That's right," Harry said warily. "We chatted with you on your porch."

Melvin looked again over both shoulders. "I heard something, man," he said.

"Oh yeah, what's that?"

"A couple of boys getting off the school bus yesterday. One of them said a man in the neighborhood was giving away video games. That kinda got my attention because of what you said earlier."

Fred and Harry glanced at each other, exchanging puzzled looks.

"Go on," Harry said.

"Well, I don't know these boys, but they looked a little older than Nate."

Melvin, twitching a little, scanned the park yet again.

"Last night, I saw them again, walking past my place, so I decided to follow. A man joined them a couple of blocks later."

"Did you get a good look at that man?" Harry asked.

"I sure did."

An awkward silence followed. "This is when you tell us who he is," Harry said finally.

"Oh, yeah. It's the asshole who drops my mail in the mud, just because I swear from my porch sometimes. It's not my fault. It's the fucking Agent Orange, man."

"Melvin, are you saying it's the mailman?" Harry asked, incredulous. "Lou Esposito, the postal carrier who lives in the neighborhood?"

"Are you certain?" asked Fred.

"Yeah, 100 percent, man. It's fucking Lou, that big-mouth pig."

"Did you keep following them?" Harry asked.

"Nah, I think he saw me and I started freaking out. I went back to my porch, took my meds. But, hey, I remembered to tell you guys, so I guess I'm not too fucked up."

Fred asked Melvin if he'd be willing to report what he saw to Two Rivers police, but the addled man scrunched his nose and spit in disgust.

"Fuck the cops. All they do is hassle me. I'm telling you two motherfuckers instead."

Suddenly, Melvin froze. His eyes grew wide. He turned and ran, headed for the safety of his porch.

"What th-?" Harry began, but Fred saw what had spooked the veteran.

Esposito was making his way slowly down the block fronting the park, wearing his blue uniform shirt and matching shorts.

The men on the bench could hear his familiar whistling.

"What do we do?" Fred whispered.

Harry took a deep breath. "Watch him, I suppose. See if what Melvin is saying is true or some kind of psychotic episode. It's anybody's guess."

"You told me you looked up that address and the owner is a woman, last name Winters," Fred said.

"That's right, Alice Winters. Maybe she's a relative or maybe he's just renting. Could be any number of explanations."

"We should find her. Whatever she tells us could be useful, yes?"

"I thought of that, but nothing would tick our detective friend off more. Witnesses often only give a statement once."

"Ah, you're right."

Esposito had reached Harry's house. He dropped some mail in the pole-mounted box by the gate, then turned and waved at the men watching from the playground.

"Wave back," Harry said under his breath, and they both did.

Minutes later, Esposito turned the corner, headed for his official white vehicle.

"If he's our bad guy, he's acting awfully cool," Harry said. "Maybe Melvin was seeing things."

"I may have an idea," Fred said, his voice just above a whisper. "Please don't laugh, but in detective movies I have seen, they have something called a surveillance vehicle that they park outside a suspect's home or business. This mailman would recognize your truck, so I think we should rent a van. We can park nearby and watch who comes and goes out of that house."

Harry, thinking, stroked his chin. "Better than shadowing him on street corners, I suppose."

"How exciting," Fred said, brightening. "I'll see to the van."

———

It was a boxy white Chevy with no markings on the sides and dark windows in the back. It was conspicuously inconspicuous, but neither man seemed to care.

They were too obsessed with their intelligence-gathering mission to fret about the optics.

They parked across the street from the blue house. Fred was the camera man, snapping pictures of anyone coming and going. Harry had his binoculars. Unsure how long the stakeout would last, they also brought with them a large Thermos of coffee and a dozen glazed doughnuts.

A couple of uneventful hours passed, and then Harry suddenly whispered, "Here we go."

A sporty red-and-white Mini Cooper pulled into the driveway of the blue house. Esposito got out, stared for a few moments at the van, then went inside.

"He looked right at us," said Fred, who snapped a few pictures.

"Hopefully, he'll think one of the neighbors is getting some work done."

"In the evening?"

"Don't worry so much."

"I can't help it."

Minutes later, two boys came into view. They seemed to be between 10 and 12 years old, headed right to the mailman's house.

"Jesus," Harry muttered. "Those boys are young."

Two more boys soon approached from the opposite direction.

They, too, strolled casually down the sidewalk and entered the house.

"Oh my God," Fred said, snapping feverishly. "So many boys. Should we call the police?"

Harry frowned. "Something's not right. Those kids were too happy. And they're showing up in pairs. That doesn't make sense."

The men continued mulling it over as a black Escalade pulled up a short distance away.

The driver sat and stared at the van. Then he began twisting a silencer onto the barrel of his semiautomatic Ruger MK II.

Q was delighted when the van he was tailing parked in front of the blue house. His job had just become easier.

He'd order the old men into the house, where he would kill them in the basement and then create the narrative he wanted the incompetent local police to see: Bolden and his friend had broken in a second time, only to be shot by Esposito, who set the house on fire to destroy the evidence before fleeing.

In this scenario, Esposito, regrettably, would be spared. But no matter where he ended up, he'd be a hunted man. Q smiled at the thought of that.

His new plan would work. He just had to wait for the children to leave. Judging by their ages and the hour of the evening, that would be soon, he thought.

Q glanced at his watch, then something caught his eye — approaching headlights in the rear-view mirror. A police car with two officers. Cursing, he slipped the Ruger inside his coat.

The Two Rivers PD cruiser rolled past, parking directly behind the van. Another last-minute complication.

The assassin checked his pulse, steadied his breathing.

There is still time.

Patience.

———

"What the hell?"

Harry watched through his binoculars as Esposito and a half-dozen boys suddenly poured out of the blue house.

The chubby postal carrier, glaring, was standing on his driveway. He stabbed a sausage finger at the van.

Fred and Harry exchanged glances.

"Our cover is blown, as they say," Fred said meekly.

There was a loud bang on the van's steel rear doors, creating a thunderous echo inside.

"Police! Come on out!"

Harry leaned over to Fred and handed him his binoculars. "Hide this and your camera," he whispered.

Fred stuffed them in a built-in storage box and put a moving blanket over the top.

Another hard rap.

"Come out now!"

Harry pulled the lever and the double doors sprang open. Facing them were two officers with their guns drawn.

"Fellas, I can explain," Harry began with a sheepish grin.

"Step out of the van, put your hands behind your back!" one of the officers commanded.

Both men did and were immediately handcuffed, snared in the spotlight of the police car's headlights.

As Harry and Fred were spun around, they were immediately confronted by Johnson, whose face was red with anger, a purple vein in his forehead looking like it was about to burst.

"The Dynamic Duo strikes again," he spat, stepping closer to Harry.

"I told you if you played vigilante one more time, I'd haul your ass to jail."

"Since you're here, how about searching that house across the street?" Harry asked in a show of defiance. "There's a bunch of young boys there."

Johnson gave a harsh laugh. "Esposito leads a Bible-study group for First Methodist every month. He reported a suspicious vehicle, and I suspected right away it was you two."

Sure enough, Harry looked over and saw that some of the boys gathered outside in the driveway were clutching Bibles. He should have noticed that right away. What other details had he been missing?

His heart sank. It was horrifying that a child pornographer who preyed on vulnerable kids had become a volunteer entrusted with young boys, no doubt grooming them for future exploitation. But who would listen to Harry now?

"Put them in the back seat, boys," Johnson told the officers. "Lock 'em up."

"On what charge?" Harry demanded as he was shoehorned into the cruiser along with Fred.

"We'll think of something."

They rode in silence to the county jail, where they were processed, complete with mugshots and fingerprints. Then they were placed in a large holding cell with steel benches ringing the barred walls. It was big enough to hold a dozen or so people, but they were the only ones inside.

In a way, it was a good thing that neither man had a wife at home who would come rushing over in a panic. Getting jailed was humiliating enough.

One of the corrections officers walked over and studied Harry through the bars. He was a big man with flaming red hair and a thick beard.

Harry recognized him right away.

"Hey, Duane."

"Hey, captain. Looks like you're my guest for the evening."

"Looks like it. This is my friend Fred."

Duane nodded. He lowered his voice to a conspiratorial whisper. "I appreciate what you two are doing. My son is 13. He knew Nate and Sam."

"Must be tough on you and your wife," Harry said.

"We're both scared. A lot of people are. Word in the station is you may know who's responsible."

"Johnson doesn't think so."

"He's useless. A rookie," Duane said, shaking his head. "I trust you."

A door buzzed in the distance and the officer hustled off.

"Wish we had the chess board," Harry said after a while.

"It would help pass the time," Fred agreed.

"Well, maybe the next time we get arrested."

"I'll be sure to keep a travel set in my pocket, just in case."

"Ever been arrested, Fred?"

"No, first time. For you as well, I assume."

"Right. But I did put quite a few behind bars over the years. Drunken drivers, brawlers, wife beaters …"

"A veritable rogue's gallery."

"You got that right."

Hours passed before they heard heavy footsteps approaching. Harry was surprised to look up and see the police chief. The incarcerated former lawman rose to his feet, feeling somewhat pathetic with his twitching right arm.

Huggins exhaled loudly, like a frustrated parent.

"First, I don't see you for eight years and then you end up in my jail. What's going on, Harry?"

"We're just trying to help protect kids. That's all it is."

"Johnson tells me you beat up an innocent man across the street from your home and you've been spying on people. Is that right?"

Harry gave a weary sigh. "The man we're watching makes child porn in his basement. My grandson's best friend is on one of the tapes, for Chrissake."

"So, you broke into the basement and seized some evidence. You took matters into your own hands."

"That's right."

The chief shook his shaved head, which was glistening with perspiration. "Johnson showed me that tape. I watched a few minutes of it. You're right about one thing, it's horrifying."

"So, you believe me?"

"Of course. You're one of the finest officers we've ever had."

"Then what's the problem? Get that sonofabitch!"

"You, of all people, should know why we can't. If we arrested and charged someone, their lawyer would have the entire case thrown out because you stole the evidence it was built on. Fruit of the poisonous tree, it's called. Your little break-in has created a huge headache for this department. And now your surveillance of the suspect? He has a harassment claim if he wants to bring it. So, you see, Harry, you're not helping us at all. In fact, you may have just allowed a guilty man to go free."

"You believe this man is guilty?"

"I believe in you and your instincts. Or at least I did until you let yourself go off the rails. You and your friend here." The chief shot Fred a disapproving look.

Chastened, Harry sat heavily on the steel bench. "So now what?"

"You back the fuck off and let us do our jobs. I want you both to promise me that you'll stay on the sidelines, or I'll have you charged with interfering with a police investigation, burglary, assault and a half-dozen other crimes. I'm not bluffing."

Harry glanced at Fred, who nodded somberly.

"I promise," Harry said.

Fred added, "As do I."

"I will hold you to it."

The chief called out to Duane, who came hustling over.

"Let them out," Huggins said. "They have some thinking to do."

CHAPTER
TWENTY-SEVEN

Harry trudged up the stairs to his bedroom, half his body quaking feverishly.

He downed his medicine, then reached across the dresser to the picture of his wife, clutching it to his chest. He hoped she'd pay him a visit that could soothe his aching soul.

Long minutes passed and there was nothing, just the stillness of dawn. He looked through the window at the playground below. A gust of wind moved the empty seats on the swing set, rattling the chains. It seemed haunted.

The troubled old veteran propped up some pillows and, still cradling Bonnie's smiling photo, laid down on the queen bed they had shared.

"I've disgraced myself," he said aloud. "I did it for Buster, but I've disgraced myself all the same."

Harry looked around, hoping to see an other-worldly pulsing light or hear a few calming words. There were only shadows and silence.

His efforts to find the Sunny Slope killer had skidded to a halt. He'd found a suspect, but he'd been too obsessed with seeking vengeance to see how reckless he'd become. Exactly what he promised he'd never do.

Even worse, he'd just been accused by the chief of dealing a severe blow to the criminal investigation. That meant more kids could be in danger. Because of him.

I've disgraced myself, Bonnie.

He wondered what Fred was thinking at this precise moment. After leaving the jail, they had embraced and gone their separate ways.

What were Fred's parting words? "I'm sorry it turned out like this, my friend," he'd told him.

Harry closed his eyes and lost track of time. Hours could have passed, even days. It was dark out when he finally got out of bed and began to move. Honey was trailing him warily, sensing his malaise.

He felt odd, like he was in the depths of an out-of-body experience. He found himself pulling down the wooden stairs to the attic and climbing up.

He yanked the chain to turn on the light, a bare bulb hanging down, and walked over to the large chest that held his war uniform. He reached around until he found what he was looking for.

He unlatched the box and touched the gun with his fingers, felt the cold steel. Then he lifted the pistol out, appraising it.

Next Harry checked the seven-round clip on the old Colt – the gun issued in case airmen had to ditch their planes behind enemy lines. He had never used it in combat. He'd never even had to fire a weapon in all his years as a police officer.

But now he held the gun, filled with angst and dire thoughts, and still Bonnie did not appear to him.

———

They met accidentally beside a white-sand beach.

There was a sudden tropical downpour – the kind that lasted only minutes before moving on – and they both were in work clothes, taking a lunch break in Miami's South Beach. They sought refuge under a music store's awning, nearly bumping heads.

"Mind if we share?" she said with a smile.

Harry was struck mute. She was the prettiest woman he'd ever seen. She had wavy amber hair and radiant green eyes, pillowy lips and a freckled nose.

He could see from the ID card dangling from her neck that she worked at the hospital a few blocks away, a fact supported by her low-cut Keds in regulation white. Harry was wearing his blue patrol officer's uniform.

"So, I'm stranded with a cop?" Her alluring smile broadened. "I'm Bonnie."

"Harry. And you're a nurse?"

"Good guess." She laughed. "I suppose if disaster strikes, we're poised and ready."

They chatted until the drumming of raindrops on the canvas slowed, and then Harry dialed up his courage. He asked if she'd be interested in having a drink after work.

"I don't usually have drinks on the first date," she said, taking measure of the good-looking, muscular man next to her. "I'm not that sort."

"Well, technically it would be our second," he said, grinning.

"Ah, yes. The 10-minute rain date."

"Exactly. Los Reyes at 7? Their food is good, the mojitos great. I can pick you up."

"I'll meet you there," she said as the sun emerged, warming the street. "Bye, Harry."

It didn't take long for them to fall in love. After six months of dating, Harry screwed up his courage again and proposed, by the same beach storefront where they had met.

Charles Wayne Bolden was born a couple of years later, just weeks after they moved into their first home together, a one-story bungalow painted flamingo pink with an orange tile roof. Everything was wonderful – until Harry tried to save a boy and quickly found himself the subject of an excessive-force investigation.

It was Bonnie who urged him to resign. The stress was taking a toll on both of them and she knew it wouldn't relent. No matter what the investigation found, he would have a tarnished reputation. Certain Cuban restaurants were already refusing to serve him. One bartender spit in his drink and didn't bother to hide it.

They could start over on the West Coast, she told him. Someplace quieter, cooler and far less humid. They could get less stressful jobs and focus on fun and family. Maybe buy his-and-her kayaks and hang them from the ceiling in the garage.

Harry saw the sense in her plan and agreed to give it a shot, though privately he doubted if a big city guy like himself could adapt. Would he go stir crazy in a few months?

They wound up choosing Two Rivers, buying their view home by the park and enrolling Charlie in an excellent public school. Bonnie landed an RN job at a clinic a short commute away. Harry was hired by the local police department, which considered itself fortunate to have snagged a cop with so much experience.

About a year later, the couple was sipping wine on their wide front porch, watching the kids play across the street.

"You were right," Harry said.

"Yes, I know. But can you be more specific?"

"About moving here. About Two Rivers."

Bonnie smiled and stroked his hand.

"That's nice, dear. One of these days, you'll even learn to relax."

———

Harry heard the phone ringing and realized he'd been holding the barrel of the gun to his head.

He lifted his finger from the trigger and lowered the weapon but didn't put it back in the box. He stuffed it in the front pocket of his jeans and headed downstairs.

The ringing stopped by the time he reached the kitchen, but he sat down heavily at the dining room table, tears in his eyes.

He wondered what Sam had been thinking when he slipped the noose around his neck. He figured the teen couldn't live with his disgrace, either.

Harry placed the gun on the table. He was staring at it when the phone came alive again.

"Hello?"

"Pops, how are you doing?" It was Charlie calling, full of concern. "I heard about your arrest. Want me to come over? We can talk."

"No, son. I think I'd rather be alone."

"You sound strange. I'm coming over."

"Please don't. I need to think. About everything."

There was a brief silence and then Charlie said, "You did the right thing. I'm proud of you."

Harry couldn't tell his son about the damage he'd done – that a heinous criminal could escape punishment because he'd taken things too far.

"I'll come over in the morning," Charlie continued. "Try to get some rest."

"Okay, son."

"Love you."

"Love you, too."

Harry hung up. His first thought was that at least his son would find his body before it decomposed. He grabbed some note paper and a pen, and returned to the table to write.

That's when he noticed the giant SUV idling in front of the house, its windows an impenetrable black. He sensed the driver was staring at him.

His mind was foggy from the drugs and his deepening depression, but Harry thought he'd seen the vehicle before, a Cadillac Escalade, unusual for Sunny Slope, where kid-hauling minivans and Volvo wagons were the norm.

A few days ago, he'd been sitting in the living room and looked up in time to see a similar SUV – *the same one?* – drive off.

Harry dialed Fred's number and was relieved when the German answered. He still had no idea what time it was.

"Fred, do you remember seeing a black Escalade in the neighborhood in the last couple of days?"

"Let's see." Fred paused briefly. "No, I don't think so. Why do you ask?"

"It's parked in front of my house. I'm looking at it right now."

"It's probably nothing. Maybe the police are watching you, after … you know, everything."

"Yeah, you could be right."

"You should get some sleep. We both should. We'll talk tomorrow."

"Thanks, Fred. You're right, it's probably nothing. Have a good night."

He put down the phone and took another look out the window.

The Cadillac was gone – if it had ever really been there at all.

———

Fred spent the rest of the night worrying about his friend.

Twice in his life the Bavarian had contemplated suicide. The first period of darkness came after his fall, when he feared he'd never play the piano again. The other enveloped him after he lost his other love, Hildy.

Both times she had saved him. Once in the flesh; then, years later, in the form of a soothing spirit.

There was something in what Harry said on the phone, perhaps the glum tone of his voice, that troubled Fred, reminding him of his own bleakest days.

He would have raced up the hill if he had known Harry had a loaded gun in his hands. But he didn't know, so he poured himself a Scotch on the rocks and sat on his piano bench. He gazed at the freighters anchored for the night on the river, lit up like parade floats.

While their efforts to save the children may have ended poorly, at least they had tried, Fred thought. At least now the police knew whom to watch and where to search. In a clumsy way, they had done that at least.

Will justice be served?

Fred took a deep breath. *If not in this life, then the next.*

He ran his fingers delicately across the keys. It was too late in the evening to play, one of the sacrifices of living in an apartment building, so he did so in his imagination. A mime's symphony.

When he was done he walked over to the kitchen to get some fresh ice. Gazing out the window overlooking the street, he did a double-take.

A black Escalade with tinted windows was parked in front.

CHAPTER
TWENTY-EIGHT

Louis Kelso Esposito hadn't always been a monster. High school classmates in Seaside, Oregon, impressed by his various business endeavors and crazy math skills, named him "Most Likely to Succeed."

The future back then seemed limitless. He was accepted into Stanford, intent on earning a business degree, but despite a generous scholarship that he needed because his parents were in the midst of a highly contentious and costly divorce, he dropped out after a single semester. He found the classes stifling, the professors pompous, the campus boring.

Nobody he knew was alarmed.

By then, he'd already launched several promising start-ups, including a gourmet food delivery service, a computerized investing tool based on his own algorithm analyzing Wall Street trading, and a dating app that referred losers to sex workers.

The ventures were like meteors, streaking across the sky before fizzling out. But the ideas kept coming, with maiden voyages close behind – until he ran out of money.

His handful of investors walked away, as did the women of means he professed to love. Under pressure from his mother, a psychologist in private practice who was his last benefactor, he reluctantly took a day job with the intent of ditching it as soon as he had enough savings to hit it big on his own. He began working for the United States government as a postal carrier.

At the age of 46, single and smoking too much pot for someone with lofty ambitions, he found himself living in Aunt Alice's Sunny Slope home.

After blowing out both knees and cracking her hip, she had moved into an assisted living center an hour's drive away. She stubbornly refused to sell her home, thinking that one day a miracle of physical regeneration would occur and staircases would no longer be a barrier.

Alice Winters agreed not to charge her nephew rent as long as he paid the taxes and insurance, and took care of the yard, specifically her prized vegetable garden. Whenever he visited during the growing season, which wasn't often, she'd demand proof – in the form of tomatoes and string beans – that all was well.

The home on Dover Street was a godsend to Esposito, who fancied himself a gifted filmmaker on the cusp of being discovered. It was only a matter of time, he believed. In the basement, tapping his mother's bank account yet again, he created a professional studio, complete with cameras, editing equipment and a sound stage that he could configure as needed.

He began using his day job to recruit young actors for a variety of films, his most ambitious being an hour-long horror movie based loosely on Edgar Allen Poe's "Masque of the Red Death" in which a modern plague strikes at the heart of a small Oregon town.

Esposito managed to get a screening at a Portland art festival but was devastated when the smattering of people in the audience began to laugh. Although one writer for an alternative weekly would hail it as "dark comedy," the director had no such intentions. He left the festival in tears.

Instead of giving up, he went home and began furiously banging out another screenplay. It was tentatively titled "The Water," a sci-fi tale in which aliens take over a city's water-treatment plant and poison it with a mind-control substance. Two days later, script in hand, he set out to find his cast.

It had become known to neighborhood children of all ages that the mailman with the dark goatee was always looking for new talent for his never-ending slate of movies – and that he'd "pay" with toys and prizes.

When a young girl or boy was reluctant, Esposito would reach into his mail bag and pull out a Tootsie Pop. "Here you go," he'd say with a smile. "Think about it."

"The Water" proved to be too ambitious to get off the ground, but he didn't give up. Far from it, he sent dozens of mini-movies to Hollywood studios and agents with hopes of landing his dream job. It was elementary mathematics, he figured. The more queries, the better the odds.

After 200 or so, he stopped counting. Nobody had written back. There were no offers of movie and TV deals. Not even an apprenticeship.

Instead, perversely, he routinely stuffed his own mailbox with rejection letters.

He had nearly given up hope when one day a man called.

The caller praised Esposito's "eye" and the quality of his work. He told him he had a future in the business and was destined to make a lot of money.

"Well, thanks," the mailman said. He was too flattered to notice that the man had not given his name. "I think I'm getting better with each film."

"I couldn't agree more. So, let me get to the point of this call: I'm a recruiter for a big international syndicate and we can use a man like you."

"Really?"

"Absolutely. As a director, you clearly know what you're doing, and I can see that you work well with children."

"That's nice of you to say. Where are you based?"

"We have offices in many cities. As I said, this is a global operation. Very lucrative. We would pay you $50,000 for a 30-minute film, professionally scripted, filmed and edited. You would have complete creative control."

Esposito nearly fell off his chair. He was producing a half-dozen "practice" films a year. There was a brief silence as he did some mental calculations of his gross earnings, then the caller continued.

"Have you ever done an explicit film?"

"You mean, like a porno?"

The man on the phone chuckled. "Yes, Mr. Esposito. My clients are always looking for top-quality explicit films. Would that be something you'd be interested in?"

"How would I find the actors?"

"That's up to you. But they need to be amateurs and as young as possible."

Esposito suddenly felt nervous. Was this man with the money asking him to do something illegal?

"How young?"

"It's really up to you – the casting director and filmmaker. Keep in mind that in many parts of the world children appear in explicit films and it is not considered a problem in any way. Since you are based in the United States, you would need to operate … discreetly."

"Children? Gee, I don't know."

"Give it some thought. My clients would give you a $50,000 advance, plus purchase any equipment you may need. I'll call tomorrow at this time to get your answer. This is a very time-sensitive offer."

"I didn't catch your name."

"It's J, for short. I'll be calling."

The phone went dead and Esposito found himself standing in his kitchen, stunned.

What the man had offered was definitely illegal. But in less than a year, he'd pocket a boatload of cash. Then he could quit and bring some of his legit business ventures to life.

There was also something else: his admittedly strange sexual appetite. He'd been watching extreme bondage videos and under-age porn for years, hooked up by the man running the local adult video store. Esposito preferred it over normal adult sex, which he found too tame to be arousing.

In his movies, whenever he filmed a cute adolescent boy, so innocent and pure, he felt a stirring. He didn't think he was gay. No, he was absolutely certain he wasn't. He just felt an attraction to young boys. There's a difference, he told himself.

But making child porn? Was he really up for that?

That night he weighed the risk of going to prison against the fact that he had a built-in cover as the affable neighborhood postman, plus a house to himself with a very private downstairs studio.

Best of all, he had access to Sunny Slope's ample supply of kids, both outside their homes on his mail route and at that playground that drew them like a magnet.

The next day when the man called back, Esposito accepted the offer. With the seed money they sent, he upgraded his cameras, lights and editing gear. He went to the Foot Locker at a Portland mall and bought two dozen pairs of basketball shoes in boy's sizes, claiming they were for a church raffle. At Toys 'R' Us, he snapped up an armload of video games, the most violent he could find.

The trap was being set.

A monster that had been caged was now loose.

———

When the old men stalking him were arrested, Esposito knew he'd only bought himself a little time.

At any moment, the bumbling local police would wise up and get a search warrant. And then all his hard work would be wasted.

All his grooming of the young brats. All the fitting-in that required such exertion. The trust he'd developed over years with the people on his route, leaders at his church, even the guys on his bowling team at Two Rivers Lanes.

Delivering mail with a smile and a wave, talking about Jesus like a true believer, high-fiving dim-witted teammates just because they got a strike – he despised it all. It wasn't real. It was someone he pretended to be. He did it because he needed the cover.

His employers paid extremely well. As promised, he delivered one short film every three months, sent by overnight mail to a post office box somewhere in Southern California.

The paper-thin plots lasted only a minute or two – a young teenage boy caught stealing, having to make amends; or a man who finds his 13-year-old stepson masturbating and demands that he continue. The rest of the videos were filled with graphic sex. There were no female "actors," just boys and men – with the men shot in such a way that their faces weren't shown. There were titles and credits, just so it would appear more professional. None of the names scrolling up at the end were real.

Esposito starred in some of the videos, but for the rest he had no trouble finding a few men about his own age with "exotic" sexual tastes. They may have been the only actors in history to pay the director for the privilege of performing.

As he produced video after video, the money poured in, electronically deposited in his account, tax-free.

Feeling rich for the first time in his life, he bought himself a new sporty car, the glittery Rolex he'd always wanted and an expensive wardrobe. He began frequenting trendy nightclubs in Seattle and Portland, dining at the finest restaurants. His recreational drug of choice changed from cannabis to cocaine. Pretty women, who he was not particularly attracted to but needed as escorts in order to maintain his illusion, took notice.

His initial resolve to quit after less than a year evaporated. The underground movie-making was going too well to drop out now, he decided.

Esposito congratulated himself on running an air-tight operation, keeping a firm lid on secrecy and grooming the right boys – the kind who would either be too ashamed of what they'd done or too greedy for prizes and cash to tell another soul, especially their parents.

There was rarely any communication with his mysterious

employers, and he was never given any addresses or names. Just initials.

He never heard from J again, but one time someone called when he was a couple of weeks late in sending a video. The person told him the delay had cost The Organization "a lot of money." Esposito hung up with his heart pounding. There was something about the electronically disguised voice that unnerved him.

He had been given one number with a California area code that he was told he could only use in a dire emergency. He never did, until the events of the past year forced his hand.

One of his boys had killed himself and his mother was sowing panic in the community. Worse still, she had enlisted the help of a retired cop who lived next door.

As bad as that was, Esposito knew he could have weathered the storm. He summoned his gregarious postal carrier persona and did his best to lead the old cop astray.

The real problem was Nate Caruthers.

The 14-year-old was Esposito's most reliable performer, whom he had not only plied with video games and sneakers but cold, hard cash. It was Nate who had recruited Sam Mendez, and when Sam, consumed with regret, hung himself, it hit his friend hard.

One night, Nate told Esposito he was finished with sex videos. He wanted out.

The director offered to pay him more, but Nate wasn't having it.

"I don't want to end up like Sam," the boy said sadly. "I have to stop."

"But you can't," Esposito said, pleading. "The people we work for … they aren't very nice."

"That's your problem. I'm telling my mother everything. I'm sick of lying to her about where I'm going, about what I'm doing. I'm sick of sneaking into my own house at night, with you following me all the time."

"I follow you for your protection. Because I care."

The boy gave the man a withering look. "*Protection?* You've turned me into something … awful. You ruined my life. Can you even imagine what boys my age would say if they knew? Would girls want to be with me?"

"Nobody forced you."

"I don't think my mom will agree."

"You can't tell her. She'll go to the police. Everything will be ruined."

"All you care about is money. What about Sam? What about Chase? Do you know how bad I feel? Do you have any idea what I'm dealing with?"

Esposito moved closer with the intent of giving Nate a consoling hug, but the young teen, eyes hot with tears, took a step back.

"It's over. I can't do this anymore."

"Sure you can. I know you're upset about Sam. I'm upset, too. Just take a break. Get yourself together."

Nate glared at Esposito. "Don't pretend to care. The day after Sam died you were in here filming. I saw you!"

The mailman didn't have a ready retort. The truth was he viewed the Mendez boy's suicide as a setback, a bump in the road, nothing more.

"But … I need you," he said after a few moments. "Name your price."

"I don't want any more of your fucking money. *It's over!*"

Nate headed for the front door.

In a sudden rage, Esposito tackled him from behind.

For a few minutes, they wrestled on the floor, trading blows.

Then Esposito spied his leather bowling bag filled with two custom balls sitting by the door. With his knees in Nate's back, the bigger man grabbed the bag and yanked the zipper. He pulled out one of the balls, slid his fingers into the holes.

Nate caught a sideways glimpse of the ball and began to beg.

"Please, *don't!*"

"You'll go to the police."

"I won't! I promise!!"

"Sorry, Nate, but I know you will."

Esposito slammed the ball into the back of the boy's head. There was a horrible crunch, followed by silence as a pool of blood began to form.

The mailman thought about the killing the night he had Bolden and his German friend arrested. He had bought some time, but not nearly enough.

Things were spiraling out of control, his wall of secrecy teetering. Intruders had broken into his basement and now they knew the truth. He had no choice but to call The Organization and ask for help.

They were sending a fixer, but it was too late now to repair all the damage, the postman knew. Bolden had screwed up, but he still had some credibility. He had sounded the alarm.

Esposito knew he'd need to get rid of all the evidence – the studio in the basement, the treasure trove. Everything.

But even that wouldn't be enough. He'd have to get the hell away from Two Rivers. *Tonight.* While he still could.

Esposito hastily packed a suitcase, then went to the garage, returning with a large red jug filled with gasoline that he used for the lawnmower and weed whacker.

He'd burn the house down, starting with the basement. Then he'd head south to Mexico, lay low for a while. He'd have his investment guy wire him the rest of the money and buy a house off the water with a very private room. Maybe he'd start his own syndicate. It would be a pity to waste his new skills.

Comforted by the plan taking shape in his brain, he thumped down the basement stairs. When he reached the bottom, he flicked on the lights.

Q was waiting.

The assassin, seated comfortably on the love seat in the heart of the studio, casually laced his hands behind his head.

The gun with the silencer was resting on his lap like a well-trained dog.

"Put down the jug," he said. "We need to talk."

CHAPTER
TWENTY-NINE

It took Victoria Brentwood just four sessions to discover the root cause of Harry Bolden's psychosis after that incident in the supermarket.

The breakthrough came when the psychiatrist began probing Harry's war experiences. When she got to the part about the firebombing, the aging veteran suddenly tensed and began perspiring. His heart began thumping, almost loud enough for her to hear.

When she asked about the children, tears streamed down his face.

Harry, she learned, had made the mistake of looking through his B-29 bubble with binoculars. The people down below were just dots, but he could see them running for their lives only to be consumed by waves of fire. The smallest dots, he knew, were boys and girls.

The airman would be back home months later, the war finally over. He returned to Brooklyn a conquering hero, but that didn't stop the nightmares and panic attacks. In his sleep, the children would stare at him with accusing eyes. Then the melting skin on their faces would fall off in big drips, leaving only bone.

He didn't seek treatment, considering that to be a sign of weakness.

Even cowardice. He figured the nightmares would end in time, and they mostly did. But then came Miami and Two Rivers and those flashes in his brain that he couldn't control.

Brentwood had been fully briefed on the incidents and she quickly determined that they were mere manifestations of what lay beneath, buried in Harry's subconscious. She had to dig deeper, possibly into Harry's childhood.

It turned out that his terror as a 19-year-old on a bomber packed with hellfire was deep enough.

It proved to be an unusual PTSD case. Harry's unresolved war guilt and pent-up desire to protect children were like a pool of gasoline. The match was seeing a young child being harmed.

The "flash" Harry felt was his brain shutting down normal constraints dictated by logic, experience and common sense and his most violent self taking over, Brentwood surmised.

The problem wasn't that Harry had an ardent desire to protect children, or even to punish abusers. It was that he couldn't think clearly during his episodes and could one day kill someone.

"Punching someone in the nose is one thing," Brentwood told her client one afternoon. "But what if, during one of your flashes, you pull a gun? Could you stop yourself from squeezing the trigger, possibly killing an innocent person?"

"I don't know," Harry said in a moment of complete candor. "I hope so."

"We can't just hope, Harry. We have to stop these flashes from happening."

Brentwood spent the rest of her time with the captain surgically probing his wartime horrors and was pleased when the veteran finally stopped resisting.

She dragged his long-suppressed emotions into the open, in hopes of addressing his child-in-danger trigger, but while Harry told her he'd been sleeping better of late, she never really knew if the therapy worked.

He had put off her suggestion to join a PTSD support group in the area, saying he might give it a try – once he found the strength to tell his wife he'd been seeing a shrink.

"She might be pleased to hear that you have taken this step," Brentwood said. "Tell her. She deserves to know."

"She does," he said with more than a touch of sadness. "I'll … try."

Harry wanted to tell Bonnie, even silently rehearsed the words that were never spoken. He just was hard-wired to be tough, circuitry that had proved difficult to break.

About a year later, he retired and the risk of him becoming a crazed cop ended.

But then one day the phone rang at Brentwood's desk. It was her friend, the police chief. The hunt for a missing boy in Harry's neighborhood had apparently set him off. He was "flashing" again.

The psychiatrist pulled Harry's file. It had been nearly nine years since their last session. A year after that, after consulting with Huggins, she had written three words on the cover of the manila folder: CLIENT APPEARS STABLE.

Brentwood found Harry's home phone number and made the call. She expected Harry to be hesitant, but when he flat-out refused to see her she was taken aback.

"It's not a good time, Doc," he told her. "I'm in the middle of something important."

"I heard about the man in the van, at the playground," she said. "I really think we should discuss that."

"I know it looks bad."

"Let's talk about it. I think it might help get you back on track. Okay?"

Harry paused before answering.

"I can't do that," he said. "But don't worry, I'm in control."

Days later, he'd be seated at his dining room table next to a loaded gun, writing a suicide note.

CHAPTER
THIRTY

Frustrated by his beloved ghost's refusal to appear, Harry paced the living room floor.

Here he was, on the brink of shooting his brains out and no matter how hard he tried to summon his dead wife, she resisted his call. He placed her framed picture next to the note, even lit her favorite candle, filling the house with a pleasant gardenia scent that clashed with his morose mental state.

And still nothing.

Did she not care whether he lived or died? *Come forth lovely spirit! Show yourself!*

Maybe he was simply asking too much, he thought. Maybe he was beyond soothing. Maybe there were rules in heaven about interfering with the suicidal people down below.

He was 75 and stricken with an incurable disease. More often than not, his brain was fogged by powerful drugs. He didn't have much quality time left. Why not end it now?

"Give me a sign," he pleaded, pausing at the table to stare at Bonnie's smiling face.

At that precise moment there was a loud knock at the front door.

Expecting to see his wife in some form or another, he opened the door and saw Fred and Melvin standing there instead.

"Whoa, dude," Melvin said, looking warily at Harry.

"Put the gun away," Fred said, stepping inside.

Harry hadn't realized that the weapon was in his left hand. His face flushed. He retreated inside and placed it on the table.

Fred scanned the room, saw the note, picture and candle, and knew immediately that his friend had been preparing to take his own life.

"Why are you two here?" Harry asked.

"Nice place," Melvin blurted, taking a seat on the sofa in the front room.

"We have something to tell you," Fred said, also sitting down.

Harry, willing away his dark thoughts, joined them. "Let's hear it."

"It's about that Escalade you saw," Fred said. "I saw it, too – parked in front of my building earlier tonight. And then, coming over here, I bumped into Melvin. Go ahead, tell him."

Melvin, unaccustomed to being helpful, bobbed his head in a nervous way. "Yeah, I was coming to tell you that there's a big black SUV parked in front of the fucking mailman's house. Something's going down."

Harry scratched his head. "I don't get it. What do you think, Fred?"

"I think someone is spying on us, and I don't think he means well. He's probably connected with what Esposito was doing – those dreadful videos."

"Good thing you have a gun, man," Melvin muttered, eyeing Harry. "They took mine away. Still have this, though." He patted the combat knife in the scabbard tethered to his belt.

Harry went to the front window and looked around. There was no sign of a sinister SUV.

"If I was Esposito, I'd be shutting everything down, getting rid of the evidence," the ex-cop said. "Maybe the people he works for sent someone to help him do that and shut us down, too."

"Like a hitman?" Melvin asked. His eyes bulged, making him look even crazier. "That's screwed up. Those fuckers took my guns."

"I know what you're thinking, my friend," Fred told Harry. "You want to go over there and confront them. But we can't. We promised not to get involved anymore."

"That's true. I gave my word to the chief."

"Fuck the pigs, man," Melvin bristled. "Let's go over there now! Let's find out what happened to Nate."

"No, Fred's right," Harry said, shaking his head. "We have to alert the police."

Fred looked at his pocket watch, saw that it was after 10 p.m. "Call at this hour?"

"No call. I know where the chief lives," Harry said, slipping on a lined denim coat, the kind a cattle rancher might wear. "When I made captain, he invited me and Bonnie over for dinner. It's a few blocks away, further up the slope."

He looked at Melvin, who was standing, eager for action. "If you go with us, you need to behave. No insults."

"Yeah, yeah," the Vietnam veteran grumbled. "I'll do my best."

Harry was about to open the door when there was another knock.

Melvin pulled his knife with its six-inch jagged blade, but Fred put a hand over it and shook his head.

Harry looked through the peephole and saw Maria, lips pursed and arms folded across her chest. He opened the door with a lump in his throat.

"Hello, boys," Maria said coldly. "Having a meeting, I see. Care to tell me what's going on?"

"I will, I promise," Harry said.

"Now."

Harry sighed. He knew his neighbor wouldn't relent.

"Okay, Maria. We're going to see the police chief. I'll fill you in on the way."

The four of them walked up the hill as Harry told her about the neighborhood mailman leading a double life, the basement break-in, the botched surveillance op, and the mysterious Escalade that was apparently connected to it all.

Then, in a low voice, he informed Maria that her son was on one of the sex tapes.

"I'm so sorry. I didn't have the heart to tell you earlier," Harry said.

Tears filled her eyes. "You have the tape? I want to see it."

"No, you don't. Trust me. Besides, I gave it to the police."

Maria's body sagged, prompting Harry to wrap her in his powerful arms. Fred and Melvin stood anxiously nearby, unsure what to do or say.

She pushed Harry away and took a couple of steps before looking up at the stars shining in the night sky. Where was God in all of this, she wondered. Why did she bother to pray each night?

"How could anyone harm my Sam?" she asked, her voice throaty and rough. "He was such a gentle soul."

She faced the three men and shook her head. "The mailman. Always praising my rose bushes. And all the while doing such unspeakable things."

Harry nodded glumly. "Let's go see the chief, Maria. We need to let him know that all hell's about to break loose."

Moments later, they walked up a pebbled concrete path to a modern house with a low-slung roof, golden, cedar-shingle walls and huge windows in front designed to capture panoramic views. The oversized front door had a large decorative brass knocker in the middle that Harry used to rap twice.

The door opened, showing Huggins in sweatpants and a polo shirt.

"Well, well," he said. "This is quite the group."

"Sorry to barge in like this at this hour," Harry said. "It's kinda important. Can we come in?"

Huggins groaned but stepped to the side and waved everybody in. He led the foursome to a sunken living room featuring a massive sectional sofa.

"What's this about?" the chief said as they all sat down, though he had a pretty good idea.

Before Harry could talk, Mrs. Huggins arrived with a platter of sliced cheese and crackers as if she had been expecting them all along.

"Would anyone like something to drink?" she asked.

Melvin was about to place an order when Harry cut him off. "No thank you, Wanda. We won't be staying long."

"That's for damn sure," the chief muttered after his wife walked off with a smile.

Harry gave his summary, thankful for the rehearsal he'd just had with Maria. When he was done, Huggins looked at the dark-haired woman with big brown eyes.

"As an attorney trained to rely on facts, do you believe what Harry just said?"

"Yes, I do," she said without hesitation.

"Well, I believe Harry, too. That's why I have my detective watching that house as we speak."

"Thank God," Harry whispered, loud enough for the others to hear.

Fred and Maria looked relieved. Melvin kept scanning the room nervously for assassins.

"Johnson phoned a few minutes ago. He found a piece of paper on the ground by that Escalade you mentioned," Huggins said. "It had your address on it, Harry. I was about to call you."

Maria gasped.

"Am I in danger, chief?" Harry asked, suddenly alarmed. "Am I the target?"

Huggins shrugged. "We know the SUV was rented by a tall Caucasian man at the Portland airport a couple of days ago. He purported to be from California, but his identification proved to be phony. That's all we know right now, but it doesn't sound good."

"He *is* a fucking hitman!" Melvin exclaimed.

Ignoring the outburst, Huggins leaned toward Harry and said, "I can put an officer outside your home if you'd like."

Harry looked at Maria, who nodded strenuously.

"Yeah, sure," he said. "Thanks, chief."

CHAPTER
THIRTY-ONE

Johnson sat in his unmarked car outside the blue house, sipping cheap 7-Eleven coffee.

He was watching Esposito, tracking his movements to the upstairs bedroom and the garage. And then the basement lights suddenly turned on.

The lower side window off a strip of grass had been papered over, but the detective's curiosity was now kindled. What was the mailman doing in the basement that Bolden had been so hot about? Was it as nefarious as the old man suggested?

As badly as Bolden had botched things, Johnson wanted to know for himself. The presence of the Escalade had added a layer of intrigue.

He got out of the car and hustled over to the window, leaning in close in hopes of overhearing something.

There were voices. Two men were talking and it was anything but pleasant.

Did one of them just say "gun?"

233

———

"Why don't you put that gun away?" Esposito said, slowly lowering the two-gallon jug to the floor.

The man on the love seat ignored the request.

"What's your plan?" Q asked with a sneer. "Torch the place?"

"That's right, get rid of the evidence. All of it."

"And then?"

Esposito hesitated. It wouldn't be wise to tell this trained killer about his travel plans.

"I guess it depends on what you're planning to do."

Q smiled in a vicious way.

"Nothing too complicated. I'm going to kill Bolden and his friend, and arrange the bodies so that it appears they died in a shootout with you in this ungodly studio of yours."

Esposito stared anxiously at the gun, which was now in the assassin's right hand.

"Sure, kill them. But you'll help me get away, right? My films have made them millions. I'm too valuable to be … disposed of."

"Too valuable? I'm here because you lost control. You put The Organization at risk."

The mailman thought about running back up the stairs, but he knew he'd be shot in the back before he took two steps. He sat down on the stool he used to edit his cancerous films.

"Just let me burn it down. All the evidence will be destroyed. If you want to eliminate the others, so be it."

Q sighed. This lecherous cretin was giving him orders when he should have been begging for his life.

"I'm not going to kill you," the assassin said after a long, sadistic pause. "For some reason, they want you alive."

Esposito exhaled loudly in relief.

Q examined the wreck of a man and wished he could put a bullet in his sweaty forehead. Left to his own devices, Esposito wouldn't last a day on the run before getting himself caught. Then he'd tell authorities everything. And while he knew little, cooperation in any form was unacceptable.

"Get in your car, drive down the hill. Take the river highway east," Q said. "Someone will be waiting."

"Who?"

"You'll find out. But there is one other thing."

Esposito gave the man with the gun a wary look. "What's that?"

"Tell me where you hid the body of the boy you killed. The family deserves some closure, don't you think?"

"Wh-hat boy?"

Q aimed the gun at the man on the stool.

"*Where?*"

"In the backyard," Esposito answered in a hoarse whisper. "Under the tomato plants."

Q showed no reaction to the grisly detail. "Get out. *Now*. Before I accidentally shoot you in the head."

Esposito scrambled back up the stairs, half-expecting to still be shot. A couple of minutes later there was the sound of screeching tires as the Mini Cooper peeled out of the driveway.

Q checked his pulse and deemed it acceptable. He'd partially unearth the body out back to prove to himself there was still some good in him. Then he'd pay a call on Harry Bolden and his pal.

Maybe they'll put up a fight, he thought. That would at least be interesting.

——

Johnson heard the car drive off in a hurry. Then came a weirder sound: Someone digging in the backyard.

The detective stepped warily toward the noise and caught a glimpse of a tall, slender man wielding a shovel in a raised planter bed. He was illuminated only by a half-moon.

What the hell?

Johnson pulled his gun and crept toward the man, keeping his back to the house. He was about to call out when the man suddenly stopped digging and walked away.

Vaulting a low picket fence, Johnson stepped into the yard just as the spring-mounted screen door at the back of the house closed. He walked over to the mound of dirt. The shovel had been thrust into it like a marker.

He looked in the hole and recoiled. A boy's lifeless face was staring at him, the skin a ghastly pale streaked with mud.

"Christ," the stunned detective said. "Nate Caruthers."

Johnson called for backup in an urgent whisper, then pulled open the screen door as quietly as he could. He entered the kitchen of the house, which was completely dark. With his pistol in his right hand, he switched on a flashlight with the other.

He slowly made his way into the living room. And then he saw him. A man sitting on the sofa, directly across from him. With a gun in his hand.

"Police! Put the gun away!"

The man smiled. "I'd rather not."

"Put the gun on the ground or I'll shoot!"

With lightning speed, the man squeezed off a couple of rounds.

Johnson screamed and fell backward onto a carpet.

"Not if I shoot you first," the assassin said.

He stood over the writhing cop, kicked the man's gun across the room. Q had shot him twice, in the right shoulder and left thigh. Frustrated that his finely crafted plans had been tampered with yet again, he clubbed Johnson hard in the skull with the butt of his gun, rendering him unconscious.

Then he went down to the basement to pour the gasoline, soaking the entire studio. He ran a trail up the stairs and lit a match.

As the flames spread, he paused to look at the cop on the floor.

Q aimed the Ruger at the man's head. He wondered whether it was better to kill him now or let the fire do the work. Either way, it would slow the short-staffed local police department to a crawl. Especially with the body out back.

He decided to go with fire. He'd save his bullets for the old men.

CHAPTER
THIRTY-TWO

The lights were on in the Bolden house when the Escalade pulled up.

There was a uniformed cop sitting on the porch, but Q wasn't deterred. He walked up the driveway toward the front door like a man on a Sunday stroll. He gave a friendly wave to the officer, who was now on his feet.

"That's far enough. No visitors."

"I'm an old friend of Harry's."

"Sorry, not tonight. Chief's orders."

"Well, if the chief says so …"

Q turned to leave, then suddenly spun around, the gun in his hand. He fired once and the cop crumpled to the porch deck, blood flowing from his neck. The assassin walked coolly up the steps and dragged the body out of view.

Careful not to be seen, he moved to the edge of the large front window and took a look.

Harry and his friend.

Perfect.

———

Melvin watched it all go down from a corner of the playground, hidden behind the trunk of a maple tree.

He had left Harry's house in a hurry, sensing that another vivid flashback was coming. He told them he was going home, but he really just walked across the street and waited. He felt a pressing need to stay close, just in case.

For a while he was in the jungle again, on patrol, fatigues soaked with sweat. He was searching for signs of Viet Cong, scanning the dirt path for deadly boobytraps.

He was grateful that the hulking Cadillac thundered by, jarring him back into the present. The jungle flashback didn't end well, and it always left him in a highly agitated state that could only be calmed with the medicine that was back at his house.

The bearded veteran saw the tall man approach the cop in a seemingly friendly way and then suddenly open fire. He saw the cop go down. And he saw the killer look in the window at his new pals, Harry and Fred.

Melvin steeled himself as the man prepared to enter the house. He could see the gun with the silencer.

Without thinking, he pulled his knife. In a trained crouch, he slowly crossed the street.

———

Outside the blue house, officers were holding back worried neighbors as fire crews tackled the blaze.

Huggins stood nearby, his face bathed in pulsing blue and red light.

Still unconscious, Johnson was being loaded into an ambulance. The chief touched the detective's hand.

"Will he make it?" he asked one of the paramedics, who nodded.

"Two gunshot wounds, but pretty clean – no vital organs," the medic said, shutting the back doors.

Moments later, the officer in charge of the scene briefed Huggins.

"Chief, we have a body in a shallow grave out back. Looks like Johnson tried to stop the gunman and got shot. Fire must have been set to conceal evidence."

"The gunman got away?"

"Afraid so. One of the neighbors said they saw a man dressed in black get in an SUV and drive off as we arrived. We've sent out an alert to the sheriff's department and State Patrol."

Huggins' expression darkened. "It's a rented Escalade, black with tinted windows. Johnson sent the plate number to dispatch a couple hours ago. Have them send it out. And alert whoever is guarding Harry Bolden's house. The shooter may go there next."

"Will do, chief."

Huggins went around back to the garden boxes where forensic technicians were unearthing the body. He caught a glimpse of the victim's face and knew immediately it was the Caruthers boy.

They had been searching hundreds of square miles for months, from the river to the forests, and all along he was buried in Sunny Slope, a few blocks from his home.

Huggins shook his head. What a mess.

There hadn't been a homicide in Two Rivers in 20 years. Cannery worker Miles Stimple, having had one too many, gunned down his wife inside their mobile home, riddling her body with bullets fired from his deer-hunting rifle. The phone she was using to chat with her lover was in her lifeless hands when police arrived. It was a simple case, eventually pleaded down to second-degree murder based on a temporary insanity defense. Not at all like this one.

The fire was doused in less than 30 minutes but the house was still a total loss. The officer who briefed Huggins earlier returned from the soaked, still-smoldering basement, shaking his head.

"Chief, something bad was going on down there."

"How bad?"

"Child porn is my guess. There was a whole studio down there. We're trying to salvage what we can."

"Any sign of the man who lives here, Louis Esposito?"

The officer shrugged elaborately. "We haven't found him yet, dead or alive."

The chief took a deep breath. The investigation had only just begun, he knew. While his officers hunted for those responsible, they also had to search for other victims. Undoubtedly, more parents would have to be given bad news.

The first would be Carla Caruthers, who'd accused him of dragging his feet on a criminal investigation. He'd pay her a visit. She deserved that at least.

But first things first.

A gunman was on the loose.

———

Harry and Fred were sitting in the dining room. The chess board was set up in hopes of calming their nerves but neither man was playing.

"Can you put that away?" Fred asked, nodding at the gun.

Harry picked it up and tucked it halfway into the waistband

behind his back. "That better? I kinda want it close."

Fred sighed and got up. "I need a beer," he declared.

"You won't like it. I only have Bud Light."

"How awful. Have you not learned anything about the craft of beer-making since we became friends?"

"They don't sell your precious Spaten at the Safeway," Harry grumbled.

"Or at the 7-Eleven, your other favorite gourmet food store," Fred fired back from the kitchen, his head buried in the fridge. "I suppose these will have to do."

He returned with two brown bottles. Harry twisted the cap off of his, prompting another sigh from Fred.

"No opener required, I see."

"Nope, cheers."

Fred took a gulp and his face turned sour. He examined the label closely. "I can't taste any hops. Can they still call this beer? I mean, legally, can they?"

"Oh, dear God," Harry said, rolling his eyes.

"Seriously, Bavarian hops are world-renowned for their flavor and aroma. But this …"

There was a muffled popping noise outside followed by a dragging sound on the porch.

Harry tensed. "Did you hear that?"

"I'll check," Fred said. "Probably the officer just moving a chair."

Before he could stand, the front door swung wide and a man with a gun walked in.

"Harry and Fred," Q said. "Nice to meet you."

CHAPTER
THIRTY-THREE

Q moved closer, improving his range.

He didn't bother shutting the door. The luxury of time was gone. He needed to kill these two quickly, then slip out of town. The helicopter he'd arranged for would only wait so long.

"You're here to kill us?" Harry asked, gripping the edge of the table with his trembling hands. His wedding ring made a slight tapping sound.

"That's right," Q said with eerie politeness. "It's my job to tie up the loose ends. That's you two."

"To cover for Esposito?"

"Esposito's gone. I'm not covering for that careless idiot. I work for The Organization."

"The mob?"

"Not the mobs and cartels you know. More like a union of highly successful businessmen with, shall we say, exotic tastes?"

"If Esposito is gone, why kill us?" Fred asked, stalling. "What good would it do?"

"Just following orders." He smirked. "A German such as yourself should know all about that. Question time is over, gentlemen."

From less than 10 feet away, he trained the .22-caliber gun on Fred. "You'll be first."

Harry saw the killer's finger tighten around the trigger. All 10 of his own dug into the edge of the polished walnut table. He knew what he had to do; he just didn't know if he had the strength to pull it off. His workouts had been hit or miss lately.

Here goes nothing.

In an adrenalin-fueled burst, Harry flipped the heavy table onto its side, sending chess pieces flying like angry birds.

Q fired two rounds, narrowly missing his targets as Harry and Fred ducked behind the makeshift barrier.

Harry grabbed his gun and fired a shot in the general direction of the assassin. Surprised by the counter-move, Q retreated a few feet into a hallway for cover.

If only he had the time to enjoy this skirmish, he thought. He admired the spunk in these old men.

Q squeezed off a couple more rounds from the Ruger, sending chunks of table into the air, in hopes of getting the men to expose themselves.

Instead, Harry turned to Fred and whispered, "Run out through the kitchen, try to get help. I'll cover you."

He let loose with a hail of bullets, punching holes in the wall a foot or two from Q's head. The distraction worked. Fred slipped away unharmed.

When the shooting stopped, Q stepped brazenly into the open, the sickly grin back on his face.

Harry squeezed the trigger of his pistol, hoping to end the fight. There was only an impotent click.

"You're out of bullets," said the hitman, who'd been counting. "You should know your weapon better."

Q walked over and eyed Harry, whose back was now pressed against the underside of the table. For a man about to die, he seemed strangely at peace. He let the Colt slip from his fingers, then looked up at the killer with a sliver of a grin.

"Goodbye, Harry Bolden." The tall man aimed his gun at Harry's head, directly between his eyes. "I respect you for putting up a fight."

Before he could pull the trigger, there was a thunder of boots and a high-pitched battle cry.

AAAHHHHYEEEE!!!

Q turned, but not quickly enough. A blade pierced his thigh, sinking deep.

"Aaargh!"

The hitman swung his fist into Melvin's face, sending him flying into a wall.

Before Q could fire another shot, Harry tackled him hard, knocking the Ruger loose. The men wrestled on the ground for a few moments before the assassin got the upper hand. He elbowed Harry hard in the jaw, causing the older man to release his grip.

Q scrambled to his feet and staggered toward the front door, the knife still sticking out of his leg.

Harry, who'd fallen on top of the Ruger, grabbed it and fired. It was too late – the intruder had disappeared into the night.

Seconds later, Harry heard the throaty roar of the Escalade's V8 as it raced down the street.

He stepped over to Melvin, who was woozy but otherwise okay. Blood was trickling down his chin from a broken nose.

"You saved me, you crazy bastard," Harry said, handing him a handkerchief.

Huggins and Fred burst into the house.

"Harry! Are you okay?" Fred asked, eyes wide in alarm. "Oh my God!"

"Yeah, yeah," Harry said, exercising his jaw and wondering if it was fractured. "He just drove off."

Huggins nodded. "We're on his tail."

Harry looked up and saw misery in the chief's eyes. "Our babysitter?"

Huggins shook his head. "I radioed him and he didn't answer, so I headed over. Ran into your friend."

"What about Johnson?"

"Wounded, but he'll make it."

Melvin rose slowly to his feet, pressing the handkerchief to his nose. "At least that fucker has my knife in his leg."

"That's good news," the chief said. "He won't go far with that wound."

Huggins cleared his throat and surveyed the three men. "I owe you an apology. You were right all along," he said "This town is under attack."

Harry looked at the bullet holes in the walls, the splintered table on its side. "This guy's a pro. He won't stop until he finishes the job. And me and Fred are on his list."

"I won't make the mistake of doubting you again," Huggins said. "And I'm not leaving your side until that SOB is caught."

The radio on his shoulder crackled.

"Chief, you there?"

"Yeah, what's up?"

"We lost him downtown."

"*What?* How can you lose a giant SUV in a tiny town?"

"He went against traffic, used the alleys. It's like he knew every nook and cranny. Sorry, chief."

"Just keep searching. He's wounded. He won't go far."

Huggins pulled his revolver and checked the chambers. "If he comes back, we'll be ready."

"Fucking police," Melvin muttered.

———

Full of fury, wound throbbing, Q devised an entirely new plan.

He parked the Cadillac in the driveway of a large home by the river. After eluding the cops, he had pulled out the knife, wrapped the wound with a rag torn from an undershirt and tied it tight. The blade had nicked his femoral artery, and even though he was familiar with that type of pain, he wasn't immune to it.

As he stepped out of the vehicle, he grunted and saw white flashes. Harry and his friend will pay for this, he swore.

Q grabbed the roll of gray duct tape he'd packed in his duffle for occasions like this and limped to the front door, Melvin's knife in his hand. He'd much preferred to have his Ruger, so precise and lethal, but he'd have to make do.

He was amazed when he tried the latch and the front door opened. Two Rivers was such a trusting town.

The hitman didn't bother checking his pulse. He knew it was racing. But what he had to do didn't require calm. Just a boiling anger, and he had plenty of that.

He slipped inside the home of Charlie and Liz Bolden, crossing the gleaming, marble-floored entry toward the sound of a TV.

He peeked around the corner and saw a man in the kitchen putting on his coat and grabbing a ring of keys. The local news was blaring on a small TV under a cabinet.

"We have confirmed that there are at least two people dead following a fire and gun battle inside two homes in Two Rivers," a frazzled reporter was saying. "Police are searching for the gunman, who was reportedly wounded in the attack."

"I have to check on Harry," Charlie said, kissing his wife's cheek.

"Be careful, this is horrid," she said, glued to the screen.

But as Charlie turned the corner, he came face to face with a man brandishing a bloodstained knife.

"Take a seat next to your wife," Q said. "You're not going anywhere."

Facing Liz, he ordered, "Turn that off and call your son."

Eyes wide with fright, she said in a choked voice, "Please, don't hurt him."

Q wiped the sweat off his brow and leaned on the granite countertop. He had to fight his body's desire to shut down.

He put the knife to Charlie's throat.

"Do as I say, or you'll watch your husband die. I have absolutely nothing to lose."

"Buster!" Liz shouted. "Buster, come down!"

Footsteps echoed and then a few moments later the boy entered the kitchen. His face instantly filled with fear.

"Ah, there you are," Q said, placing the duct tape on the counter. "Tie them up with this and I'll let them live. If you try to run off and call the cops, I'll kill them both. Understand?"

Buster, pale as a bedsheet, nodded.

The assassin looked at Charlie with slitted eyes.

"Now where's the phone?" he asked.

———

Harry looked outside at the playground, illuminated in silvery moonlight. He wondered if it would ever be the same. Joyful and innocent.

Sunny Slope, long promoted as northern Oregon's "friendliest neighborhood," would need a lot of healing, he knew.

How do people trust each other again after the most egregious breach of trust imaginable?

Fred appeared at his side and, as usual, seemed to be reading his thoughts. "We will survive this, my friend. The children will return."

Harry draped an arm over the German's shoulder. "We'll lead the way. At the chess table."

Fred smiled. "Yes, we will lead the way."

The phone in the kitchen started ringing and Harry headed to it. He figured it was Charlie, checking on him, worried sick.

He picked up the phone and heard a different voice. A wave of panic washed over him.

"Don't hurt him. I'm coming," Harry said.

Huggins, overhearing, rushed into the room as his former captain was putting down the phone.

"That was him," Harry said. "He's got Buster."

CHAPTER
THIRTY-FOUR

Every police car in Two Rivers was outside the house by the river, blocking the street in both directions and sealing off the driveway.

Huggins pointed at the Escalade trapped between the cruisers with their flashing lights and the dimly lit house.

"He's there all right," Harry said.

Fred, wide-eyed in the back seat, filled with dread.

Officers let the chief through. He stopped his Buick within sight of the front door, which was wide open, beckoning. He gave Harry a worried look.

"Sure you want to do this? Go in there alone? At least let us get the snipers set up. The county SWAT team just arrived. They can take him out."

"He's too smart to let your men get a shot. Besides, he's got Buster. I have to do it."

"He's a killer, Harry. He wants blood – *your* blood."

"I'm an old man, chief. He can have my blood, as long as Buster, Charlie and Liz are okay."

"What's to stop him from killing everyone? Changing his mind?"

"That's a risk I have to take."

He patted the chief's knee and stepped out. "Appreciate the concern."

Harry watched as the heavily armed SWAT unit swarmed his son's house, with one officer climbing onto the roof and the others, in their black helmets and body armor, taking positions on either side of the front door.

Harry took a deep breath. He was about to go inside when he heard footsteps from behind.

"I've changed my mind," Fred said, standing beside the grandfather from Sunny Slope.

"No way. I'm doing this alone. This is my family, my battle."

"He's after me, too. I may as well get it over with."

"I can't be worried about you. I have to think about Buster."

"Yes, but two heads are better than one, as you often say."

"Sorry, pal. Not this time."

Fred frowned. There was a defiant look in his eyes. "We face this man together. If need be, we die together. End of discussion."

"Good grief. Are all Germans this pig-headed?"

"Ninety-nine percent."

Harry paused for a moment, stroking his chin.

"Look, if we can get close enough, maybe you can distract him without getting yourself killed. Then I can tackle the bastard."

"So not quite a suicide mission?"

"Not quite."

Harry eyed his watch. "Time's up."

He gave a two fingered wave to the chief, who ordered the cops outside to get ready. Several were leaning over the hoods of their cars with shotguns. Some of the SWAT officers began inching along the sides of the house toward the back.

"We're coming in!" Harry yelled to the hitman lurking inside. "Me and Fred!"

Arms raised in surrender, they walked slowly through the doorway and headed for the light in the kitchen.

When they entered the room, they saw Q standing by the island holding a knife to Buster's throat.

Charlie and Liz were sitting on the floor by the chrome fridge, bound back to back with duct tape. Their mouths were gagged.

"Harry Bolden, perchance did you bring my gun?" the assassin asked.

"No, we're unarmed."

"Pity. I shall miss it."

"You can still surrender. Save yourself," Fred said, trying to hide his panic.

Q laughed, but it sounded coarse, like he was clearing his throat. He was swaying, struggling to stand. Blood from his wound was puddling on the wood floor.

"There's no surrender. Only more killing," he said in a flat tone.

A tear rolled down Buster's cheek. Harry saw it and felt his desperation grow.

"Let him go. Take me instead, like you wanted."

Another grotesque laugh.

"I'll start with your annoying friend," Q said, facing Fred. "Walk backwards to me and I'll release the boy to old Harry."

With a final look at Buster's terrified face, Fred turned and took several blind steps.

The hitman grabbed him roughly, pressing the blade against his neck. Buster started running to Harry, who pushed him toward the front door, yelling, "Run!"

The boy raced out the door. Harry could hear Huggins shouting, "It's the boy! Don't shoot!"

"Harry, the hero," Q said. "I never would have harmed him. I leave that sort of thing to the real monsters. But now it's time to pay the price you agreed to."

"You said 'a life for a life' on the phone. Not two lives."

"Oh well. *C'est la vie.*"

Fred felt the assassin leaning on him like a crutch. If he could punch him hard, right on that deep wound, he'd have a chance. Maybe he could get loose.

He looked at his friend and gave him the slightest of nods.

The boy ran straight toward Huggins, who grabbed him.

"Buster, you're okay. You're okay."

The boy broke into sobs, but the chief didn't have time to waste.

"What's going on in there, son?"

"He's got the knife on Fred," Buster said, sniffling. "He says he's going to kill him and then Harry."

"And your parents?"

"He made me tie them up. Everybody's in the kitchen."

Huggins got on his radio. "Everyone's in the kitchen. Get into position. Wait for my order."

"Are they going to be okay?" Buster asked.

"We'll do everything we can, son," the chief answered, as a cop guided the young teen to a safer spot.

———

Esposito drove through town and turned east on the highway hugging the river, as he'd been told.

A few miles down the road, the Mini Cooper skidded to a halt on the gravel shoulder.

A black helicopter was in a field just off the road, its blades still spinning.

Esposito stepped out of the car, saw the pilot wave for him to come over. He grabbed his suitcase and ran, hunching over to avoid the whooshing propeller.

"Get in," the man at the controls snapped.

"Thanks, man. Am I ever glad to—," the mailman began, but the pilot shot him a dirty look.

"No talking. Say another word and I'll shoot you. Got that?"

"Got it."

Esposito saw the man had a holstered gun on his side. He kept his mouth shut, squirming as the pilot sat there, staring at his watch. Wasting valuable time.

Didn't he know the cops were coming? They'll be here any moment!

A few nerve-wracking minutes later, the copter was in the air, prompting the fleeing man to sigh with relief.

Then his jaw dropped.

Instead of escaping, they were headed toward town.

———

Q stared at Harry like a lion sizing up its prey.

The copter would be setting down on the riverbank behind the home in a few minutes. He just needed to finish his mission and cross the lawn. Maybe dodge a few small-town cops who had little to no experience shooting at a moving target.

He'd never failed before. He wasn't about to start now. Not when all he had to do was eliminate two stubborn old men.

A strange gleam entered his eyes. It was time to finish the job.

"Say goodbye to your friend, Harry," he said.

Then he began slicing Fred's throat.

"No!!" Harry screamed.

As the blade moved, drawing blood, Fred punched the hitman's bloody thigh as hard as he could, causing Q to wail in pain and release his hold.

Fred fell to the floor, clutching his neck.

Q went after him but Harry leaped on the killer's back and chopped down hard with his right hand, sending the knife clattering to the floor.

Despite his pain, the assassin shrugged him off.

Harry was on his back when Q jumped on him and began choking him with both of his powerful hands. Harry's eyes rolled back. His hands grew limp.

Q smiled as his target's life drained away. He could hear the *whoop-whoop* of the chopper's blades. His escape was still possible.

Fred grabbed the knife with one hand, while still pressing the other against his wound. He scrambled to his feet.

"Get off him!" he yelled.

Q didn't stop. He was in a final killing frenzy.

The man from Bavaria saw his friend's lifeless face and roared with a fury that he didn't know he possessed.

He dove at Q, plunging the blade deep into the assassin's back.

With a howl, Q straightened. As surprise filled his face, he slowly tumbled to the side.

"Impossible," he rasped.

The assassin died with his eyes open.

Moments later, Huggins rushed into the house, followed by helmeted cops wielding assault rifles.

"Stop that helicopter! Kill the pilot if you have to!" the chief barked into his radio.

A half-dozen SWAT officers flooded the backyard, taking aim, but it was too late. The pilot had already judged the situation to be hopeless. The chopper banked hard to the right and zoomed off, disappearing into the night.

Fred was on the floor tending to Harry, who was wheezing but very much alive.

Officers cut the tape off Charlie and Liz as Buster ran back into the room. The three of them cried and hugged in relief.

As an EMT bandaged the cut on Fred's throat, saying something about stitches, Harry pulled himself into a sitting position, his back to the sink.

"Not bad for a couple of old men," Harry said in a coarse whisper. He tried to smile but stopped short. It hurt too much.

Huggins walked over and gave the men a nod.

"Esposito?" Harry asked.

"We found his car off the highway. Looks like he got away in that helicopter, if you can believe it. But we'll get him."

"I'm not so certain of that," Fred said, shaking his head.

"Yeah, look who you're up against," Harry added. "An organization with deep pockets that can afford to send a hitman *and* a fucking copter. They'll hide him, give him a new identity."

"But at least Two Rivers is safe," Huggins said. "Thanks to both of you for risking your lives."

Harry climbed to his feet, wincing. Oddly, his troublesome right arm was perfectly calm.

He helped Fred up and the battered friends slowly made their way out the front door.

"Maybe you can give this death wish of yours a rest," the German said. "Tear up that note?"

"Yeah, maybe I should. Chess tomorrow?"

"Certainly."

"Winner buys the beer?"

"Of course," Fred answered. "I'll show you where to buy it."

PART FOUR

BRING FORTH ANGELS

THIRTY-FIVE

Twice, the boy was buried.

Under the pastor's watchful eye, mourners took turns shoveling dirt onto Nate Caruthers' casket, sunk deep in a grass-fringed hole at Two Rivers Memorial Cemetery.

Carla Caruthers watched the sad procession, dressed in black, red eyes hidden behind a veil. In stark contrast stood her husband Hank in his crisp white naval officer's uniform.

Harry accepted the shovel and returned some of the reddish-brown soil to the grave. He uttered a silent prayer and passed the tool to Fred, who nodded to the grieving mother before taking his turn.

The funeral service held earlier at the Methodist church had been a cathartic experience for the community, full of tears and sorrowful hugs.

Harry and Fred attended, along with Charlie, Liz, Buster and Maria. Also present were Huggins and his wife, and Johnson, who was in a wheelchair but expected to be on his feet again soon. Melvin wasn't there, but nobody was surprised.

The pastor, the same one who spoke at Sam's funeral, left many sobbing in the pews. He called for healing and love, urging the people of Two Rivers to renew their faith rather than turn away, feeling abandoned. Then he beseeched God to watch over the devastated town, shield it from the forces of Satan.

"Bring forth your better angels, for they are surely needed now," he said.

Hank Caruthers voiced his deep regret that he hadn't been around to protect his only child, whom he described as "the perfect son, with limitless hopes and dreams."

The fact that the lieutenant was on an aircraft carrier thousands of miles away when Nate fell victim to a pedophile left him feeling powerless.

"It will haunt me for the rest of my days," he told the mourners. "There's no escaping that."

When it was over, Harry and Fred walked up to Nate's parents and offered their condolences.

Carla Caruthers managed a brave smile.

"Thank you," she said. "Thank you for helping find my boy."

"You two are heroes in my book," her husband put in.

The rest of the town thought so, too, especially after the Messenger did a big story on the World War II veterans who exposed a terrible truth and risked their lives squaring off against a professional killer.

Harry and Fred were having a hard time paying for anything around town, no matter how much they insisted.

Unlike Harry, who evaded reporters, Fred loved being interviewed. When they walked into the church, he saw the row of TV cameras setting up outside and told his friend, "Looks like I'll be busy later. Shall I tell the story of how you flipped the table and covered my escape? Or how you tackled an armed assassin – not once but twice?"

Harry shook his head. "Are you familiar with Paul Bunyan and his blue ox?"

"Of course."

"Well, let's not take it to that level. Just the facts. And, no, I won't be posing for any more pictures. I can't believe you talked me into that."

"They're calling you the 'quiet hero,' you know."

"I bet you came up with that."

Fred snickered. "Actually, I did suggest it."

The church was packed for the service but an usher recognized the men and guided them to a reserved section up front, where Maria was waiting.

A few days earlier, she had put her house up for sale. She couldn't do the laundry or go into Sam's old room without breaking down, she said. Fred offered her an apartment in his building and she gladly accepted. Like many people in Two Rivers, she had to rebuild emotionally.

"I may need to lean on your shoulder again, Harry," she whispered as the service was about to start. Just the sight of the polished casket near the pulpit brought a sting of tears.

"You don't have to be here," he said.

"Yes, I do. We all do."

———

The VFW hall was in an old part of downtown, in a square brick building painted white, with glass-block windows.

Veterans smoked inside but for those who followed the rules there was a bench just outside the front door with an old Maxwell House coffee can on the ground for ashes and butts.

Harry and Fred stepped inside, pausing to adjust to the cave-like darkness of the hall.

Before they took five steps, they were hailed by the bartender, who had a dish rag draped over a shoulder and a beer glass in one hand.

"There they are! The heroes!"

Harry cringed as the men playing pool stopped to applaud.

"We're here to see a friend," he told the bartender, looking around.

"Over here!" a cheerful voice rang out. At the end of the bar, a man in a faded olive-drab ball cap with ARMY stitched in front waved.

Melvin drained the last of his beer and quickly ordered another. "It's on the heroes," he said.

Harry and Fred sat down, flanking him. Melvin gave them a look of regret.

"Couldn't make the funeral," he said. "Too painful. Seen too much dying, I guess."

"Perfectly understandable," Fred said.

The German saw the meager array of beer taps and frowned. Noticing, Harry grinned. "Two Bud Lights," he told the bartender before turning his attention back to Melvin.

"We were surprised when we went to your place and your mother said you were here. Come here often?"

"You caught me on the right day," Melvin said with a shrug. "Fifty-cent hot dogs and $2 brews. You guys should join."

"Maybe I will," Harry said, though he knew he wouldn't. Telling war stories or listening to them wasn't really his thing, just an occasional gift for his son and grandson.

He placed Melvin's combat knife on the bar. The jagged blade gleamed and the hilt looked new.

"Got this back from the police," Harry said. "Cleaned it up for ya.

Sharpened it, too."

"Thanks, man. I feel naked without it."

Harry laughed as Melvin returned the weapon to its sheath. "Hey, the doctor did a good job with your nose," Harry said. "It's just as ugly as before."

Melvin's twin black eyes were gone, the bandages also. He no longer looked like a boxer after a 15-round fight.

"That cocksucker really clobbered me, man. Be sure to tell those news bitches that I knifed him good, though."

"Tell Fred, he's the interview king."

Fred laughed. "Melvin, I always mention how you saved poor, defenseless Harry."

The Vietnam vet brightened. "Thanks for coming to see me, fellas. Are we friends now?"

"Brothers in arms," Harry said, raising his glass. Fred nodded in agreement.

"In that case, call me Mel. I fucking hate the name Melvin."

CHAPTER

THIRTY-SIX

When the FBI agents came to town, Huggins was privately thrilled. This wasn't a situation where the feds had to pry the big case away from the small-town cops.

The chief couldn't wait to hand it off.

Days had passed since the deadly spree and not a single clue had emerged about the mysterious crime ring and its hired gun.

The few videos that could be salvaged from the fire revealed that at least a half-dozen Two Rivers boys had been sexually exploited by Esposito going back several years. They ranged in age from 9 to 15.

Huggins fulfilled the promise he'd made to himself and personally visited each of the victims' families. He apologized to the parents for not exposing the insidious operation sooner, confessing that he simply couldn't believe that the swirling suspicions could be true. Not here, in such a pleasant place.

All but Carla Caruthers forgave him. The surviving boys had deep emotional wounds, but at least they were alive. At least with time, they could recover.

Chase's parents told the chief that their son was in therapy and on antidepressants and making progress. His grades were improving and his mood brightening, thanks largely to the support he received from his pal, Buster Bolden.

Buster was also in counseling but he'd been spared the worst of the horrors and rebounded quickly, greatly relieving his parents, who'd been considering pulling him from school. Or possibly leaving Two Rivers and starting over.

Harry and Fred were questioned by the federal agents for several hours. There was little they could tell them beyond what they saw in the basement and their violent encounters with an experienced hitman. A shadowy global consortium of despicable businessmen? Operatives who went by initials? They knew next to nothing.

Q was a ghost, investigators quickly learned. His background had been scrubbed clean. His fingerprints and face had been altered just enough to come up blank on the Bureau's most sophisticated scans. CIA, Mossad and Interpol databases also came up empty.

When agents tracked down the post office box in San Diego that the child pornographer had used to send the films, they learned it had been abandoned. The phone number Esposito called to summon the hitman was disconnected. The off-shore source of the payments to the mailman's account simply vanished.

Harry hated the idea that the people behind the horror might walk away unscathed. Maybe infest another small American town. Destroy more young lives.

Esposito's escape gnawed at him. Despite all the pats on the backs he'd received, despite the news reports hailing his courage, he felt like a failure. He had the predator in his sights, but he'd gone too far. He shouldn't have entered that basement. He knew that now.

He should have taken Buster and Chase to the police station even if it had meant betraying his grandson's trust. He should have had the young teens give a statement, detailing all the incriminating facts.

Then the police would have had to act. They'd have had enough then to get a warrant and make the arrest. *The right way.*

While the rest of Sunny Slope breathed easier, Harry barely slept. He found himself lying on his bed, eyes wide open, wishing for another chance.

One more shot at catching an evil man.

———

Two days earlier, inside the VFW hall, a dapper man sat alone at a round table sipping a beer.

Spencer P. Williams stayed out of view because he didn't fit in and didn't want to attract attention. He was Black, in his early 40s and wearing polished shoes and a pinstriped Brooks Brothers suit.

From a dimly lit corner, he studied the heroes of Two Rivers, Harry Bolden and Fred Von Stiller, making mental notes.

He had followed them inside, watched with interest as Bolden shrugged off the compliments and applause. He saw how the men sat beside the troubled veteran who'd helped them survive the attack on the town.

Bolden and Von Stiller were his kind of people, Williams decided after a while. They'd help him, even if it meant putting themselves at risk again.

He'd done his homework, dug into their backgrounds. He knew about their upcoming trip to Munich, checked the flight itinerary.

He'd approach them separately. Then he'd know if he could trust them to keep his rogue mission secret.

CHAPTER
THIRTY-SEVEN

Williams rapped twice on the door to No. 5.

He offered a pleasant, practiced smile as it swung open. Fred just stood there, blinking. He wasn't expecting anyone and seldom had visitors.

"Friedrich Von Stiller?"

"That is me. What is this about?"

The stranger flashed a badge. "Spencer Williams, FBI. May I come in?"

Still puzzled, Fred opened the door wider. "Certainly, but I don't understand. Harry and I talked to the FBI for some time a few days ago."

Williams' smile faded. He stepped into the luxury apartment, looking around, getting a sense of the European man who lived there.

"I read the Portland agents' report, such as it was. That's why I'm here."

"Please, take a seat. May I offer you a drink?"

"Water would be great, thanks."

Fred went to the kitchen and returned moments later with two glasses filled with Perrier over ice, a slice of lemon in each.

"Nice," Williams said, slightly bemused. He took a sip.

Fred settled into an antique armchair and stared at the trim man in the tailored suit seated on his Queen Anne sofa.

"Mr. Von Stiller, I'm from the Chicago office," Williams said. "I specialize in trafficking cases – the human variety. I've been investigating a criminal enterprise that calls itself The Organization for five years now. Very slippery. Very sophisticated."

"And very dangerous," Fred said, touching the fresh scar on his neck that had required five stitches.

"That's right. I'd say you and your friend are lucky to be alive."

Fred nodded, knowing that to be true.

Williams smoothed his mustache and continued. "So, when I read the report and saw mention of The Organization, well, I guess you can say it piqued my interest. But the other thing that drew my attention was your last name."

The agent gave Fred a probing look but saw only confusion in the German's eyes.

"I suppose a little background is in order. From what we can tell, The Organization sprang out of post-war Germany. A bunch of rich Nazi sympathizers eager to restore their power decided to band together. They began with black market smuggling, then gradually expanded into prostitution, drugs, sex slavery and child porn. We've found traces of their operation across the globe, but every time we move in, they've been a step ahead. They close up shop and disappear like cockroaches in the light. But these people are smart cockroaches."

"Fascinating, but what does this have to do with me or my family?"

Williams took another sip of water. "Not sure I like the lemon," he said, smacking his lips. "Not your family. Just your father. Have you checked the ledger?"

Fred's eyebrows shot up in surprise. "How did you know about that?"

"Your brothers tipped us off, by unsuccessfully seeking an injunction against you. I must say, your Holocaust give-back plan is quite admirable." He cleared his throat and continued. "The court papers detail the financial records belonging to your father that you obtained recently while visiting your mother. Condolences, by the way."

"We weren't close," Fred said in a flat tone. "I'm estranged from my brothers, and my father banished me from the family. So, I don't really know what you're talking about."

"Apologies for not being more direct. We've learned that Klaus Von Stiller was one of five founding members of The Organization, or *Die Organisation*, all of whom are now deceased. But that hasn't stopped the syndicate from operating or recruiting new criminals. I believe the ledger could help us unlock a few secrets, maybe generate a few leads."

"Secrets about what?"

"About the scale of human trafficking they were involved in, where the victims came from, how and when they were taken, how much money changed hands. Have you noticed any strange entries?"

Fred started to shake his head, then caught himself. He suddenly grew pale.

"My focus has been the war years, but looking further, I did see some unusually large transactions, up to quarter-million dollars. The entries were coded. I couldn't make sense of them."

"May I see it?"

Fred rushed off to his office. Moments later, he returned with the book, nearly two inches thick, covered in soft calfskin.

"Where did you find it?" the agent asked. He cradled it in his hands like a talisman.

"There was a locked bottom drawer in my father's desk. I forced it open, and there it was."

Williams nodded. He flipped through the pages until he got to more recent years, then began slowly sliding his index finger down the columns. Finally, he looked up at Fred, who was on the edge of his chair.

"We haven't cracked all of their codes, but we do know this one," the agent said, tapping the notation DOX. "Your father, it appears, was involved in trafficking children. Judging by the amount of money detailed here, he was probably directing it on a large scale."

"*Lieber Gott,*" Fred muttered, falling back into his chair. "Trafficking *children?*"

"Abducting them and literally putting them on the auction block," Williams elaborated, seeing the uncertainty in Fred's eyes. "Sex slaves, mostly."

Fred shook his head sadly. "I wonder if Mother knew."

"Probably not. These people are too secretive to let anything slip. Besides, would you tell your wife something like that? Makes a drug cartel look warm and fuzzy."

A thick silence hung in the room. "I have two young daughters," the agent said after a while, his brown eyes revealing a trace of vulnerability. "This is kinda personal."

"It was to Harry and me as well."

"I understand that you and Mr. Bolden are planning to fly to Munich soon," Williams said, getting back to business. "Something about returning a house to a Jewish family."

"I won't ask how you know that, but, yes, we're leaving in five days."

The agent nodded. On his computer he had their flight information down to their seat assignments. He also knew the room number in their German hotel and the names of the restaurants where they had dinner reservations. He had been trained to be thorough.

"There's something I'd like you two to do for me," Williams said. "Something a bit unorthodox."

"The last time someone told me that, I found myself breaking into a criminal's basement."

"Louis Esposito, the child predator who got away."

"Yes," Fred said, stung by the reminder.

"But maybe not for long."

"I don't understand."

"Mr. Von Stiller, I think I know where Esposito is. And it's close to where you grew up."

"*In Bavaria?* Why don't you get him? Why are you wasting time talking to me?"

Williams sighed. "I may as well level with you. I'm here off the books, so to speak. My investigation into The Organization is on ice – orders from the top. Washington, not Chicago, mind you. Not yielding enough charges, too many dead-ends. I've been told to focus my attention elsewhere: Chinese smugglers, Mexican coyotes … But if you two can help me find this criminal, and he can lead us to his bosses, we can put a dent in their operation. Maybe even shut it down. Protect hundreds of children."

"What do you propose we do?"

"I called in a favor. An intelligence source based in Berlin says someone matching Esposito's description, an American, was spotted leaving the airport in Munich. I have an address for a safe house people in the syndicate have been known to use on occasion when they're fleeing police or rival thugs. I don't know if it's any good, but it's worth a try."

"But he knows us. He'll spot us right away."

"Not if you're careful. Look, I'm desperate. It's a big city and I don't have a team of agents at my disposal. But you know Munich well; you speak the language. If I went there alone, well, I might strike out. Or worse, he might get wise and slip away again. But if you two are willing to help, and don't mind the fact that this is a strictly clandestine operation, we have a chance."

"I see," Fred said, frowning. "So we'd have no back-up from the FBI?"

"That's right. The Bureau wouldn't know anything about it – until we make the arrest. But we can do this if we work together."

Williams had a pleading look in his eyes that stabbed at Fred.

"I'll talk to Harry," he said.

"I already did. He's in."

"I despise being such a foregone conclusion, but so am I."

The men stood and shook hands. Fred escorted the agent to the door.

"How dangerous will this be?" he asked.

"Hard to say, but there's more than one Q," Williams answered dryly. "And they won't hesitate to kill in order to protect themselves."

"This just keeps getting better and better," Fred said, rolling his eyes.

Williams gave a wink as he descended the stairs, the borrowed ledger tucked under an arm.

"And no press this time, before or after," he called out. "That was Harry's request."

THIRTY-EIGHT

Fred paced excitedly in front of the house where he once lived. It was painted a creamy white with chocolate trim and overlooked a winding cobblestone street. Under a steep alpine roof, windows were framed by bright red shutters with heart cutouts. The front door, equally welcoming, was rounded on top.

Nestled in a centuries-old village south of Munich, the home had remained in the Von Stiller family since the war. After Fred moved out, a succession of tenants followed.

It was now vacant, the property manager recently informed Fred, so he moved quickly to have it cleaned and ready – but not for more renters.

He planned to give it back to its rightful owners.

The first thing he and Harry did when they arrived was go down to the basement. Fred had to know if the words painted on the wall under the stairs were still there.

There were stacks of paint and varnish cans in the way. The men moved it all out. Then Fred switched on a flashlight.

The "Life Interrupted" message was there, the Star of David below it. Fred had half-suspected his father would have had it painted over, so as not to trouble future renters. But there it was.

Fred translated the words and Harry's eyes became moist with tears.

"I know this feeling you're experiencing," Fred said, watching his friend's reaction. "It's what drove me to confront my father. But now we can finally set things right, yes?"

Harry nodded as Fred checked his pocket watch. "We should go up. They'll be here any minute. I'm so excited that you will be able to meet them."

"How long did you live here?"

"A few years, after the war. I moved out after I went to Berlin to study, but I really had no choice. I would have been evicted otherwise."

"It's a beautiful home, pretty area," Harry said as they passed through the wainscotted dining room with its dangling crystal light and polished wood floors. "Probably worth plenty."

"It is worth a hundred times what my father paid for it, but that is also why I must give it back. My family must stop accumulating wealth off its wartime thievery."

"And you wanted me here as a witness? *A Jew?*"

"As a friend, nothing more," Fred said, smiling. "But perhaps, when you meet them, you will appreciate the moment better than most."

———

The Hertzogs were respected in their community, until contact with Jews was frowned upon and then ultimately forbidden.

Miriam and Josef had run a pharmacy in the heart of Rosenhatz.

They were known for providing medicine free of charge to those unable to pay and their generosity hadn't stopped there. Their business sponsored a number of community events and benefits.

But on Kristallnacht, in November 1938, the couple's contentment began to quickly drain away. That night, Brownshirts stormed through town, smashing the windows of Jewish-owned shops and defacing walls with hateful slogans. The Hertzog drugstore was not spared.

It was only the beginning.

When the war started, Miriam and Josef did their best to insulate themselves. The couple withdrew from social circles controlled by Nazis so as not to draw attention. Only Jews continued to patronize the drugstore, and the hours gradually shrank, their income along with it.

Their plan had been to ride out the war in their quiet corner of Bavaria, under the snow-capped mountains. But then one of their regular customers rushed into the store in a panic one afternoon. There had been reports of concentration camps being built.

Soon after, they had heard disturbing reports of Jews being beaten or rounded up, businesses and homes looted or burned. Miriam and Josef realized that it could happen in their community next.

Josef paid a visit to a wealthy man he had met at a classical concert. It was a benefit for the regional youth orchestra, in which the man's son starred as a piano prodigy.

The man was Klaus Von Stiller, a judge with a reputation for fairness. After a brief friendly conversation, Josef said he was planning to leave Germany.

"Is this the reason for your visit?" Von Stiller asked.

"Yes, I'm afraid," the pharmacist replied. "Miriam and I would like to ask you a favor. We'd like to sell you our home so that it is preserved by someone we trust. When we return, we would double your investment to show our gratitude."

"I don't manage properties for people," the judge bristled. "I have people manage properties for *me*."

Josef, fearing he'd given offense, apologized. "I do intend to sell. I only wish to tell you that my wife and I very much hope to return after the war. We would then seek to buy our house back at a considerable profit to you."

Von Stiller scowled from behind his imposing desk. "Sell or don't sell. I make no promises. This is wartime and the lives of Jews are forfeit. Consider yourself fortunate to be talking to me now."

Josef left the meeting drained. The judge was willing to buy their home, but only for a fraction of what it was worth. And there was little chance that he and Miriam would ever step foot inside the house again.

He told his wife and she listened carefully at the dinner table, then urged him to accept the offer. She was six months' pregnant. They couldn't risk their baby's life. The Nazis had just ordered them to close their business. Reports of atrocities were now a daily occurrence.

They had an escape plan – if they acted quickly. They knew someone with a single-engine plane, a fellow businessman to whom they had gifted their shuttered pharmacy.

Late one night, the couple made their way to a small private airfield a few miles outside the village. Minutes later, they were in the sky. Miraculously, they managed to cross into neighboring neutral Switzerland without being intercepted by German fighters. All they had with them were their clothes, toothbrushes and a comb.

Unlike millions of other Jews, they were not tattooed. They were not herded like animals onto freight cars, nor were they tortured, starved, shot or gassed.

But they suffered the ravages of the Holocaust just the same. Their money quickly ran out and they found themselves living in a dismal part of Geneva packed with war refugees. Unable to find work as a pharmacist, Josef accepted jobs as a laborer, blistering his hands, while his wife mended clothes on the side.

The baby died at birth, plunging both parents into despair. They dreamed of their former life, before the war, and never gave up hope of one day returning to Bavaria – with the war over and the world a better place.

Josef died of kidney failure, just a year after losing his son. Although she was in her late-30s, Miriam chose not to remarry, plunging herself into self-imposed solitude.

For decades, she lived in a modest subsidized apartment in central Geneva, which she decorated with pictures of alpine meadows sprinkled with wildflowers. At night, her dreams took her there. It was all she had.

And then, as if springing from one of those dreams, a stranger called.

The man on the phone asked if she was Miriam Hertzog, formerly of Rosenhatz.

"I am Miriam," she said in a thin voice weakened by age.

Fred introduced himself and asked if she remembered the writing on the basement wall in the pretty house on Gartenstrasse.

Miriam, shocked, nearly dropped the phone. She hadn't thought of that message for many, many years. "Yes, I wrote that … the day we left. A very sad day. But why do you ask?"

"I am the son of the late Klaus Von Stiller, the man who acquired your home during the war. And, if it pleases you, I would like to give it back."

"Give it back? After all these years?"

"I'm very sorry that it took so long. Belatedly, my family is attempting to set things right."

"Whatever would I do with such a house? I'm too old to start over."

"Not start over," Fred gently corrected. "Resume your interrupted life."

Miriam started to cry and though she tried to conceal it from the caller, he heard.

"I would … at least like to see my house again," she said after a few minutes.

———

Miriam had a younger sister who was living in the country outside Paris, and Fred arranged to have them both flown to Munich.

At the airport, they were greeted by a uniformed chauffeur who guided them to a waiting limousine. When they pulled up in front of the house, Fred and Harry were waiting.

Miriam's eyes were full of tears as her sister escorted her to the porch. She touched the place on the door frame where the mezuzah once hung.

In Hebrew, Miriam whispered, "Blessed are you, Lord our God, king of the universe."

Harry watched the old woman's face light up as she stepped slowly inside, caressing the cool plaster walls, the smooth gray stones framing the fireplace, the doors hewn from the great forests beyond the village.

The American, moved, grasped Miriam's hand like a son.

She looked at him and smiled, knowing she was finally home.

281

CHAPTER
THIRTY-NINE

Across the street, Williams sat patiently in a rented silver Audi SUV. He smiled as the elderly woman slipped inside the house, accepting her gift with apparent reverence.

From his soft-sided leather briefcase, he pulled out the edition of USA TODAY he'd bought at the airport but never read. He flipped to the sports section to see how his beloved Cubs were doing.

A frown creased his face. *Another tough loss. Extra innings.*

Williams read the recap, then looked back at the house. Fred and Harry were walking toward him. He folded the paper and tucked it under his seat.

Harry slid into the back while Fred buckled into the front passenger seat.

"How did it go?" the FBI man asked, even though he knew.

"Just as I had hoped," Fred said with a smile. "My tough policeman friend teared up a bit."

Harry, a dreamy look in his eyes, said nothing.

"I'm glad," Williams said, starting the car. He tossed a folded yellow note to Fred. "That's the address. You navigate."

The building was in the oldest section of central Munich, with narrow streets and tall brownstones squeezed together.

Fred had imagined a seedy hotel or warehouse as the fugitive's hiding place, but when they arrived, he saw a majestic, three-story home with fresh paint and flower boxes tucked under windows on a shady, tree-lined block. People were out pushing strollers and walking dogs.

"Is this where that bastard is? Jesus," Harry marveled. "It's nicer than Sunny Slope."

"We don't know for sure if he's here," Williams cautioned. "Fred, start asking neighbors if they've seen anybody move in recently who matches our fugitive's description. Be as low-key as you can. Speak only in German – they'll figure you to be a native. Harry and I will take a drive, get a feel for the neighborhood. Be back here in an hour."

"Wish me luck," Fred said, opening the door. "*Auf wiedersehen.*"

Harry moved up to the front seat and they drove on, slowly cruising the streets, scanning sidewalks and bistros with outdoor tables for any sign of a murderous pedophile.

"Is he the kind of person who would stay holed up, day and night?" Williams asked after a while.

"Absolutely not," Harry said. "If he's here, he'll be out walking. Just like he did every day delivering the damn mail."

"I agree. But where would he go? Any ideas?"

"The nearest playground," Harry said darkly.

Williams nodded. "Glad to have an ex-cop with me. There's a city map in the glove box. See if there are any parks within walking distance."

Harry scoured the laminated map for a few minutes. "Jackpot," he said. "There's a small park two blocks from here, by the Isar River.

Take a right at the next corner, then a left."

The park was about a third the size of the one in Sunny Slope – a square ringed by more brownstones and a waist-high wrought-iron fence. In the middle was a playground with swings and a straight slide, benches on either side. By the river, there were more benches, a couple of food trucks and a pedestrian walkway.

It was shortly after noon on a cloudy day. The playground was empty, except for a woman trying to coax a little girl into braving the slide.

"School day," Williams said, reading the disappointment on Harry's face. "Let's see what it's like in a few hours."

They drove around some more, then returned to the reputed safe house. Fred was waiting patiently at the curb when they pulled up, leaning against a chestnut tree and smoking his pipe.

He climbed into the back of the Audi. The men in front turned to face him.

"He's here," Fred said, as a vanilla-mint scent filled the car. "Two lovely women were happy to confirm it."

Harry snorted. "I bet. Do you have plans for later tonight?"

"With Gretchen and Gisela? No, my friend. Strictly business. But I had forgotten how fetching German women are."

"How did they confirm it?" Williams asked, returning to the mission.

"They said an American moved into the basement apartment a few weeks ago. They described him accurately, said he always seems nervous."

"Did they ask why you wanted to know?"

"Surprisingly, they did not. Must have been my mesmerizing charm."

"Good. If they don't work for The Organization, we all might just survive the next 24 hours. This is their turf. That apartment may be under surveillance. They may be watching us right now."

Harry groaned. "I wish I had my gun."

Williams patted the holster under his suit coat. "I've got your backs, but let's hope it doesn't come to that. Just a simple grab-and-go. You help me find this guy, I'll make the collar."

"Roger that," Harry said. His stomach rumbled loudly enough for the others to hear. "I'm running on empty. Let's eat."

"I know a good place nearby," Fred said eagerly. "Been around since I was a child. Best schnitzel in Munich."

———

They feasted for more than two hours, emptying large platters filled with tender pork, savory sausages, schnitzel and more, until finally Williams clinked his water glass with a fork.

"That's it. Stop ordering, Fred."

"No dessert?" the German said, looking disappointed.

Williams studied his watch.

"Time to go. Let's take another look at the local park."

Through a gentle drizzle, they walked over, hoping the exercise would aid their digestion. When they got within a block, the FBI agent stopped.

"Harry, take the west side there, by the trees. Fred, take the east. Stay out of sight. I'll go up the middle to the playground and grab a bench. If I see him, I'll light a cigarette. Move in, in case he runs."

"And if *we* see him first?" Harry asked.

"Signal me and get out of there fast, before you spook him. I'll be watching."

There was no sign of their fugitive as they slowly made their way through the park. Williams entered the playground and looked around, seeing about a dozen young children playing. The four-seat swing set was filled, with parents standing behind, pushing. But as the FBI agent sat down, the other bench was still empty.

He could see Harry leaning casually against a tree trunk. On the other side, Fred was pretending to be admiring blossoms in some rose bushes. Not bad, he thought. As surveillance partners go, he could have done worse.

An hour or so passed. Then Williams noticed a man in a tan raincoat standing by one of the food trucks. He made his purchase and slowly walked over to the bench closest to the swings.

The man was wearing sunglasses and a hat. It was an effective disguise. There was no way to tell if he was Esposito.

But he is watching the children closely.

Williams saw Harry, on his feet, moving behind the man, trying to get a closer look.

A few minutes later, Harry shrugged.

The agent cursed under his breath. He'd have to take things up a notch. He walked over to the man on the bench and pulled out a cigarette. He stood out as a Black man, but at least Esposito wouldn't recognize him.

Williams could only speak a few words of German, but he gave it his best shot.

"*Bitte?*" he asked, motioning for help lighting his smoke.

"I don't have a lighter," the man said in English. "Sorry."

"*Danke,*" Williams said, smiling. He slowly walked away, heading for the street.

By the time he reached the car, Fred and Harry were right behind.

"I think it's him, but we won't know for sure until he returns to the safe house. We'll have to stake it out."

"The last time Harry and I did that, he spotted us," Fred said, remembering their ill-fated spy op outside the blue house. "And we were arrested."

"Right," Williams said. "We can't take that risk. I'll tail him from the park. You two take the car back to the building. Don't park too close."

———

Fred was sitting in the driver's seat with his eyes closed when he heard the passenger door open.

He turned and caught a glimpse of Harry, on the sidewalk, doing some kind of strange pantomime.

Looking closer, he could see Harry was holding an imaginary rifle.

Alarmed, he scrambled out of the car and ran to his friend. They were several blocks from the safe house but drawing attention to themselves was definitely not a good idea.

"Harry, what's the matter?"

"They're coming," he whispered. His forehead was damp with sweat, his breathing labored. "We need to get away."

"Who's coming? Where are they?"

"The assassins! *Can't you see them?* We need to run!"

Fred looked up the block and saw nothing at all menacing. The street was deserted except for a white-haired woman inching along with a cane.

Harry's body began convulsing and Fred grabbed him in his arms, guiding him back to the car. They sat together in the back seat.

"It's okay," Fred said, mopping Harry's face with a handkerchief.

"They're out there. They have guns. *They're coming for us.*"

"We're safe now," Fred whispered. "We're safe. They're all gone. Now close your eyes."

Despite his terror, Harry obeyed.

"Now open them," Fred said in a soothing tone a couple of minutes later. "What do you see?"

Harry leaned forward and looked out the windshield, expecting the worst. Then he sighed and fell back against the seat.

"I'm seeing things," he muttered. "I'm going crazy."

"No, my friend, it's your medicine. What you warned me about. And now it's over."

———

Williams returned to the playground in time to see the man in sunglasses tossing the trash from his meal into a waste bin.

The agent followed as the man made his way through the park. The key corner was fast approaching. If he turned left, he'd be heading to the brownstone. If he went right, he could be just another American tourist.

He turned to the left.

Here we go.

Williams waited as the man entered a small neighborhood market. Minutes later, he emerged with groceries in a sack. Then he resumed his stroll, moving straight toward the brownstone.

About 50 yards from the building, the man suddenly stopped. He turned and looked around, prompting Williams to duck into a narrow alley.

Despite all his training and experience, the agent's pulse was racing.

After one more furtive glance around, the man went down the steps to the basement apartment, disappearing from view.

Bingo.

Williams continued walking as calmly as he could until he reached the Audi. He leaned into the open passenger window.

"It's him."

———

The trio waited outside until the lights went out in Esposito's apartment. Then they drove to their ultra-modern hotel, about 10 minutes away.

The eight-story hotel had a rooftop lounge and the night was cool but not cold, so Williams went up there to pace and think.

After a while, Harry joined him, bringing a couple of Spatens. He handed a bottle to Williams, who examined the label before taking a gulp.

"It's a German beer that Fred likes," Harry said. "Don't tell him, but I've developed a taste for it. Are you really doing all this on your own time?"

"Afraid so. The Bureau wouldn't be happy if they knew I was here, but they can't stop me. It *is* my case, after all."

The men leaned over a railing and looked at the twinkling lights of the city, dotted with red and green neon.

"Well, this isn't exactly my dream vacation," Harry groused, prompting Williams to laugh. "By the way, what's your plan tomorrow?"

"Not much of a plan. We wait. When he leaves the building, we follow, get him alone and then make the arrest."

"And then what?"

"Then you and Fred go home. I'll notify the Bureau and then we squeeze this bastard hard, try to get him to roll over on The Organization, give up his contacts, maybe agree to wear a wire. That's my hope. My *hunch* is that he'll refuse out of fear and ignorance."

"And then they win."

"But at least *he* doesn't. We extradite him back to Oregon, throw the book at him, put him away for life. Two Rivers can close the book on its horror story."

Harry slapped the FBI agent on the back like an old friend. "I'm glad you showed up. You restored my hope in justice."

Williams smiled, feeling the same about the man standing next to him.

"Let's get some sleep. It's going to be a long day."

CHAPTER
FORTY

T he fugitive didn't leave the safe house until evening.

The sun was setting, coloring the sky a vibrant cantaloupe color, when he suddenly appeared, stepping up from his apartment onto the sidewalk. He had traded the hat and sunglasses for a black knit cap and blue track suit with white stripes.

Williams nudged Harry, who was dozing in the passenger seat. "He's on the move," the agent said.

Fred, rubbing sleep from his eyes, leaned forward from the back seat. "What do we do?"

Williams had pulled his government-issue Glock and was checking the clip. Sliding the weapon back into its holster, he answered, "We follow – from a safe distance."

He looked at Harry closely, saw that the entire right side of the older man was trembling.

"Are you okay?"

"Yeah, yeah. Slept past my medicine. Looks worse than it is." Harry, reaching for his pills, was grateful that he hadn't dissolved again into hallucinations.

"You can sit this one out if you want. You, too, Fred."

"Hell no," Harry said.

"Same goes for me," Fred added. "We've come this far."

Williams offered his usual tight-lipped smile. "I'll lead. He could be armed, so I'm going to try to get him away from people. You're my back-up if anything goes sideways, understand?"

The other men nodded solemnly. Moments later, they were all out of the car. Harry and Fred waited until Williams was a block ahead before they followed.

"Think our fugitive is going back to the playground?" Fred asked.

Harry shook his head. "Too dark, no kids."

They walked for six blocks until they reached a concrete path that hugged the riverbank. Surprising them, Williams suddenly appeared from behind a tree.

"He's jogging," he said, exasperated. "I was about 200 feet from him, and he just started running. I thought at first he was fleeing. Almost drilled him."

Harry groaned. "Damn, what do we do now?"

"We wait some more."

Fred watched a young woman run past, then his eyes widened. "I remember now. This trail goes about two miles that way, then over a pedestrian bridge and down the other side to another bridge. It's a loop, four miles or so."

"Good. If he runs that far he'll be too tired to resist," Williams said, thinking out loud. "Let's split up, cover this side of the river. I'll go further down, grab him if he makes the loop. You two head up there in case he doubles back. I know this sounds like a broken record, but stay out of sight."

"How do we signal you?" Fred asked.

"Wave. I'll be watching."

Williams walked away, staying by the trees, out of the glow of the street lamps that had just turned on. Harry and Fred went the other direction a few hundred yards.

One of the food trucks that served the park was nearby, shuttered for the night. "Let's get behind that," Harry said.

They leaned against the side of the truck, under a giant picture of a strawberry ice cream cone, and listened for approaching footsteps.

"Harry, you think this will be a story you can tell your grandson?"

"Depends on how it turns out."

"Yes, we must both live to tell the tale."

"Hey, I forgot to tell you earlier. I'm proud of what you're doing, you know, with the whole Holocaust thing."

"I'm sorry I didn't say something, my friend. I was afraid you'd want to get involved, and it's something I have to do on my own. My atonement, if you will."

"I get it."

"My father, I now know, wasn't merely a wartime opportunist. He was even more of a monster than our mailman. His ledger is swimming in blood money."

Harry was about to say something when the patter of running shoes slapping pavement started getting louder. He peeked around the corner.

"It's him. Signal Williams."

Fred began waving from behind the truck, but there was no sign of movement from the trees down the path.

Then the sound stopped. Esposito was leaning over a steel bench by the river, panting. He sat down heavily and leaned back. He was alone.

"This is our chance. Where's Williams?" Harry whispered.

"I don't know. Maybe we're too hidden."

"We have to get this bastard, hold him for Williams. I'm not going to risk this guy getting away again."

Fred responded with a frightened look. "What if he's armed?"

Harry risked taking another peek.

"Look, his back is to us," he said. "We have the element of surprise."

The German nodded, summoning his courage. "Let's do it."

The septuagenarians, the veterans of World War II who had taken down a deadly assassin, stepped out from behind the truck. As quietly as they could, they headed toward the bench.

Esposito was resting, facing the slow-moving water. They could hear his heavy breathing.

Harry and Fred were within a dozen feet of the bench when suddenly the fugitive's head snapped back, causing the men to pause. Had he heard them?

After a moment, they resumed their stealthy approach. At five feet, Harry signaled silently for Fred to go around the other side.

Then Harry jumped out to face Esposito, grabbing the fugitive's arm roughly.

"Got you!"

Fred dashed around the other side. And gasped.

There was a round hole in the center of the mailman's forehead and blood was starting to trickle down.

"He's been shot!" Fred exclaimed.

Williams came running over, half-crouching with his gun drawn. "Sniper! Both of you, get to the park, I'll cover you."

From his knees, the FBI man squeezed off a few rounds in the direction of the sniper as Harry and Fred scrambled over to a row of trees.

Across the river, a shadowy figure emerged from some bushes, a long rifle in his hands. Then he melted into the night.

Williams rose to his feet. He looked at the body and swore.

"Cockroaches," he said to himself. "Killing their own."

The sound of sirens in the distance caught Williams' attention. He walked up to Harry and Fred and shook his head. "There goes my informant."

"Will the sniper come after us now?" Fred asked in a squeaky voice.

"Nah," the man in the suit said. "His job is done. To him, the mailman was just another loose end. They probably brought him here to keep him from blabbing, maybe put him to use someplace else. And then we showed up."

Police cars, lights flashing, were drawing close.

"I've got this," Williams said. "You two get out of here."

CHAPTER
FORTY-ONE

A big blue kite with a long white tail was dancing on a breeze as the men studied the chess board.

Fred took Harry's bishop and replaced it with his own, drawing oohs from the youngsters watching intently.

"Nice," Harry said under his breath as he contemplated his next move.

The Bavarian turned and saw the kite he had made, watched it dip and take wing like a majestic bird.

"Buster is getting quite skilled," he said.

Harry couldn't quite hear. The squeals of the boys and girls running through the playground in endless pursuit were too loud.

A joyful clamor.

The swings were alive – kids in every saddle, feet pointed at the sky, moms and dads pushing from behind. A line of younger children eagerly awaited their turn on the twisty slide, where a knot of parents gathered at the bottom, armed with cameras. A kindergartener with pigtails rode the springy horse like a cowgirl, whooping in delight.

Over on the lawn, teenage sunbathers of both sexes sprawled on blankets, listening to music and pretending not to notice each other.

It was fall, but the leaves hadn't turned yet, and there was still warmth in the gentle wind caressing the heart of the community.

"Got a letter from our friend Williams," Harry said as he studied the board.

"How's Spencer doing?"

"He got them to reopen the investigation. It seems your ledger had a few coded contacts that he was able to decipher. The feds may be closing in after all."

Fred flashed a toothy smile.

"That is excellent news, my friend. He mailed the ledger back to me with a nice note, apologizing for delaying my givebacks. He hadn't, really."

"How's that going, by the way? Need any help?"

Harry slid his remaining rook the length of the board. "Check," he said casually.

He gave the blonde dog at his feet a pat and grinned at the spectators crunching their baby carrots. He was losing, but at least he was putting on a show.

"Is that what Americans call a Hell Mary?" Fred asked, momentarily distracted by the bold move.

"*Hail Mary*, but yeah. Desperate offense."

Fred countered deftly, then locked eyes with Harry. "I think I've returned everything I can. I was thinking of selling the rest and donating the proceeds to a worthy organization. Perhaps the national Holocaust museum. Any ideas?"

"I know a rabbi in Portland. I'll run it by him."

"*Danke.*"

"Did your brothers ever come around?"

Fred chuckled. "Perhaps. The Munich newspaper interviewed Hans. He made it sound like it was all his idea – so selfless and noble. He didn't mention the lawsuit, of course, but mother would have been pleased. Family honor and all that."

He pushed his queen forward and gave the children a slight bow, ending the show.

"Checkmate, my friend," he said.

The old veterans shook hands over the table. Harry's grip was a little firmer than usual.

He had visited Dr. Goldstein and received some unexpected good news. The progression of his disease had slowed. The ravages of Stage 4 were perhaps a few years away, not just around the corner as he had feared.

Goldstein had summed it up with two words: "Mazel tov."

Harry returned home vowing not to squander his new gift of time. Not after what his late wife had said.

Bonnie had appeared to him shortly after he returned from Germany, telling him he needed to enjoy life. When the time was right, she'd be waiting, but not before.

He felt her lips touch his somehow, and this time he didn't wake to find Honey beside him with her tongue out.

"Thank you, my love," he said to the ghost, who was slowly fading away.

And then she was gone.

AUTHOR'S NOTE

The heroes of this novel, Harry and Fred, were drawn from people I knew well.

The inspiration sprang from my father, who flew dangerous missions over Japan in a B-29, and his close friend, a German immigrant who reluctantly fought the Allies during the war.

My father suffered from Parkinson's later in life and his refined Bavarian friend of about the same age served as both a companion and caregiver. They would often share a bench at a park in their retirement community, watching grandchildren learn how to fish in a small pond.

I marveled at the bonds they forged, despite their many differences. In a way, they are role models for the rest of us in these deeply polarized times.

There are many people to thank for helping me bring *The Ghosts We Know* to life.

My love, Ann Butler, always tops the list. Her unwavering support is the rocket fuel that fires my engines.

I am also deeply appreciative of my journalist pal Bridget Murphy for her consultations and keen insight on matters of plotting and character development. Amy Kivel's thorough reads and fact checks saved me from embarrassment more times than I care to admit.

Jesse Miller and Jim Floyd offered valuable feedback after reading early drafts and too many others to name provided the kind of encouragement that keeps emerging novelists such as myself going. Kimi Miller, Jacob Miller and John Brush gave sage advice on how to spread the word about this book after publication.

I also want to thank the kind people of Astoria, Oregon, for embracing me as an East Coast transplant and supporting my work.

To learn more about my future endeavors, visit williamdeanbooks. com. Honest reviews of my books are always welcome, on Amazon, Goodreads and elsewhere. Thanks for reading!

———

While the exploitation of children depicted in *Ghosts* is fictional, the problem is very real.

The National Center for Missing & Exploited Children is a powerful nonprofit dedicated to reducing child sexual exploitation and helping find missing children. To report information, use the center's 24-hour hotline – (800)-843-5678 – or visit CyberTipline.org.

This book also contains scenes depicting suicide and suicidal thoughts. The National Suicide Prevention Lifeline offers free, confidential support. If you need help or just someone to talk to, call (800) 273-8255.

ALSO BY WILLIAM DEAN

DANGEROUS FREEDOM

"I'm free and I don't know how to act," Bud Baker says after he's rousted from his prison cell and seated on a bus in the middle of the night. He aims to make his way to Alaska, where he has a cabin and childhood memories, but he lingers in a sleepy Oregon town after falling for the beautiful Jo Jo Summers. She tells him the tragic story of an addict whose baby was stolen at birth. When she asks Bud to return the boy to his birth mother, he refuses – until she reveals that the woman is her sister. Bud risks his newfound freedom by reverting to his criminal ways, expecting a manhunt. But he's already being hunted – by demons from his past.

———

"*Dangerous Freedom* mixes armed robbery with kidnapping with a heart of tarnished gold. Astoria makes a great setting, of course, and Bud Baker is a strong central character."

"The book … will keep readers on the edge of their seats."

THE BOOKMONGER

———

"A page-turning suspenseful read that will keep you thinking about the story well after you've finished reading."

"Readers will find themselves devouring the pages to find out what will happen next in this story, as the tension builds around the characters and the plot quickly unfolds."

FEATHERED QUILL BOOK REVIEWS

ABOUT THE AUTHOR

WILLIAM DEAN is an award-winning writer and editor who had a lengthy career as an investigative journalist before becoming a novelist. He is the author of two suspense novels, *The Ghosts We Know* and *Dangerous Freedom*. He lives in Astoria, Oregon, where he enjoys locally brewed beer and can hear sea lions barking at night. They always make him smile.

FIND HIM ONLINE AT:

WILLIAMDEANBOOKS.COM